MW01032001

Cajun Kiss
of Death

Also available by Ellen Byron

CAJUN COUNTRY MYSTERIES

Murder in the Bayou Boneyard

Fatal Cajun Festival

Mardi Gras Murder

A Cajun Christmas Killing

Body on the Bayou

Plantation Shudders

CATERING HALL MYSTERIES
(writing as Maria DiRico)

Long Island Ice Tina

Here Comes the Body

Cajun Kiss of Death

A CAJUN COUNTRY MYSTERY

Ellen Byron

CROOKED
LANE

NEW YORK

Published in the United States by Crooked Lane Books, an imprint of The Quick Brown Fox & Company LLC.

Crooked Lane Books and its logo are trademarks of The Quick Brown Fox & Company LLC.

Library of Congress Catalog-in-Publication data available upon request.

ISBN (hardcover): 978-1-64385-738-1
ISBN (ePub): 978-1-64385-739-8

Cover design by Stephen Gardner

Printed in the United States.

www.crookedlanebooks.com

Crooked Lane Books
34 West 27th St., 10th Floor
New York, NY 10001

First Edition: August 2021

10 9 8 7 6 5 4 3 2 1

Dedicated to Ramona DeFelice Long.
You have no idea how much your stamp
of approval has meant to me.
To Jer and Eliza. You are my world.
To Mom, David, Tony, and my late father
Richard.
To everyone who has encouraged me on
this incredible journey: Friends. Readers.
Readers who became friends. Likewise,
blogger-reviewers like Dru, Mark,
Kristopher, Sandra, Lesa, Lisa, Debra Jo,
and so many others.
To the Malice Domestic and Left Coast
Crime conventions and attendees for their
incalculable support and inspiration.
Thank you all from the bottom of my
heart.
Laissez les bon temps rouler!
Let the good times roll.

The People of Cajun Kiss of Death

The Family

Magnolia Marie "Maggie" Crozat-Duran—our heroine

Bo Durand—detective and Maggie's new husband

Xander Durand—Bo's eight-year-old son and Maggie's new stepson

Tug Crozat—Maggie's father

Ninette Crozat—Maggie's mother

Grand-mère—Maggie's grandmother on her dad's side

Lee Bertrand—Maggie's new step-grandfather

Friends, Frenemies, and Locals

JJ—proprietor of Junie's Oyster Bar and Dance Hall

Ione Savreau—friend and coworker

Vanessa Fleer MacIlhoney—frenemy turned friend . . . adjacent

Quentin MacIlhoney—defense attorney, Vanessa's husband

Little Earlie Waddell—publisher, editor, and reporter for the *Pelican Penny Clipper*

Clinton Poche—local teen and occasional Crozat B and B employee

Brianna Poche—Clinton's two-years-younger sister
Abel Garavant—proprietor of Abel's Home Cookin'
Ash Garavant—Abel's son and Maggie's old flame
Vi De Lavallade—renowned painter currently in residence at Tulane University
Esme—Xander's young friend
Sandy Sechrest—fitness studio owner and Rufus Durand's wife
Lulu Colombe—Maggie's friend from high school
Ginny Parvenue—part-time Doucet Plantation tour guide
Lia Tienne Bruner—Maggie's cousin
Kyle Bruner—Lia's husband
Robert "Bob" Monnin—local bank president
Father Prit—the town priest

Pelican PD Law Enforcement
Rufus Durand—Pelican PD police chief
Cal Vichet—officer
Artie Belloise—officer

Chanson Restaurant Staff & Crozat B and B Guests
Phillippe Chanson—celebrity chef and owner of the Chanson Restaurant group
Kate Chanson—brand manager for the Chanson Group and Phillippe's ex-wife
Becca Wittenberg—*sous-chef* and Phillippe's current girlfriend
Patrick "Trick" Costello—mixologist

Scooter Pitot—oyster shucker
Luis Alvaro—young garde-manger for Chanson's new
  restaurant
Dyer Gossmer—former journalist turned Phillippe's
  ghostwriter

Chapter 1

Eight-year-old Xander, dressed in a suit for the first time in his life, slowly walked down the aisle of St. Theresa, the quaint church that had provided spiritual guidance to the Catholic citizens of Pelican, Louisiana, for over a century. The young boy used one hand to carry a small satin pillow holding a wedding band. In his other hand he held a blue leash attached to Gopher, the Crozat family's beloved basset hound. Esme, a platinum-haired sprite and Xander's best friend, followed him down the aisle. She tossed rose petals in a deep shade of peach with her left hand. The other held tight to a pink leash attached to Jolie, a stray Chihuahua mix who had found a happy home with the Crozats.

Gopher braked to inhale a couple of Goldfish crackers dropped by one of the toddlers attending the wedding with their parents, causing a minor scuffle as Jolie tried to get in on the snack action. The ring bearer and flower girl quickly untangled the dog's leashes and proceeded to the altar, where they made a left and took seats in the first pew. Cherie Claire, a violinist better known as the fiddler in the popular Cajun band Gaynell and the Gator Girls, segued into a slow, dreamy version of the Cajun classic "Jolie Blon," and the guests rose to their feet. Magnolia Marie "Maggie" Crozat, clad in an exquisite wedding gown worn by the generations of her mother's family that preceded her, appeared in the church doorway, a beaming parent on each arm. Tug and Ninette Crozat proudly led their daughter down the aisle to her waiting groom, Bo Durand, who managed to control the emotions threatening to overwhelm him at the sight of his beautiful bride.

Father Prit, Pelican's popular priest, motioned for everyone to sit, then began leading the wedding mass in an accent that would be incomprehensible to a new attendee but was easily understood by his congregation. "By the power vested in me," he concluded, "I now pronounce you husband and wife." Father Prit then focused on the couple next to Maggie and Bo—Maggie's grand-mère Charlotte Bringier Crozat and her new husband, Lee Bertrand. "I now pronounce you husband and wife." The priest finally turned his attention to a third couple, Pelican police chief and Bo's first cousin, Rufus Durand, and his lovely bride, Sandy Sechrest, an exotic dancer turned fitness studio owner. "I now pronounce *you* husband and wife." Father Prit favored all three couples with a warm, happy smile. "You may now share a kiss. Make sure it's with the right spouse."

The couples kissed. "It's almost time!" someone yelled, and the crowd began counting down. "Ten, nine, eight, seven, six, five, four, three, two, one . . . *Happy New Year!*"

Church bells pealed as the guests whooped and applauded. "Let's eat!" another guest yelled.

This engendered an even louder round of cheers and applause. A guest pulled out a trumpet and began playing "When the Saints Go Marchin' In" as the brides held up the umbrellas they carried instead of bouquets and danced down the aisle out of the church and toward the parking lot, followed by their guests in a boisterous second line.

People piled in their cars to make the short drive to Crozat Plantation B and B, where a special Réveillon dinner awaited them under a party tent on the expansive front lawn. Eager to protect the heirloom gown that would be handed down to future generations—perhaps even her own daughter someday—Maggie disappeared into the manor house, where she traded the gown for a simple white cocktail dress. She returned to the festivities and admired the scene with Gran. Thousands of fairy lights looped around the inside and outside of the tent and twinkled from the lawn's ancient oak trees. Every table sported a centerpiece of white roses, dahlias, snowberries, peonies, camellias, and magnolias, perfuming the air with a rich floral scent. "It looks gorgeous," Maggie said. "And those flowers . . ." She closed her eyes briefly and inhaled the fragrance.

Grand-mère gave her granddaughter the side eye and fluffed her own silver hair, which sparkled thanks to a last-minute shake of glitter. "If I had a dollar for every time you said, 'Gran, isn't that a little over the top?' . . ."

"I've never been so happy to be wrong." Maggie hugged her grandmother and kissed her on both cheeks. "Let's go find our husbands. Oooh, it feels so weird saying that."

"You get used to it," Gran said. "Of course, I am on my second."

The women went off to locate their newly minted spouses. Moments later, a chime announced that dinner was being served. "Newlyweds first," Rufus declared, leading his wife Sandy to the front of a buffet line. He waved to Bo and Maggie, who were surrounded by well-wishers.

"I thought the Creole tradition was to enjoy a Réveillon dinner on Christmas Eve." This came from DruCilla, a past guest who had returned to the B and B to celebrate the marriage. Lovie, her pet parrot, perched on her shoulder.

"In the nineteenth century, they celebrated Christmas *and* New Year's Eve with Réveillon dinners," Maggie explained. Bo clasped his bride's hand in his as they walked toward the nearest buffet line. "We cheated a little, since it's technically New Year's Day now. And we also mixed in some Cajun dishes with the Creole. But I don't think anyone's going to complain."

DruCilla surveyed the repast in front of them, spread out on tables decorated with tablecloths in two shades of peach and trimmed with ivory lace. One table groaned under the weight of an array of appetizers. The next featured chafing dishes loaded with gumbo, jambalaya, crawfish étouffée, shrimp Creole, seafood-stuffed pastries, and more. DruCilla emitted a low whistle, which Lovie the parrot parroted. "I think I'm looking at the best meal of my life."

"The best meal," Lovie said, copying the note of awe in her pet mom's voice.

Bo and Maggie exchanged an amused look, then piled their own plates with a selection of dishes provided by their close friend JJ, owner of Pelican's most popular eatery, Junie's Oyster Bar and Dance Hall.

The couple's trek to join friends and family who had staked out a large table was delayed by congratulations from yet more well-wishers. By the time they sat down, their food was lukewarm to cold. "The fact that this still tastes so good is a tribute to JJ," Bo said, devouring his bowl of jambalaya.

"Oh, yeah," agreed Gaynell Bourgeois, Maggie's close friend and founder of the eponymously named Cajun band garnering national attention. "I missed this when we were on tour." She speared a shrimp and popped it in her mouth, then speared a second one and dropped it with a giggle into the open mouth of her boyfriend, Chret Bertrand. Chret was the nephew of Maggie's new step-grandfather, which meant they were now related by marriage, although exactly how neither had figured out yet. Among the friends at the table were Maggie's cousin Lia and her husband Kyle as well as Rufus's former fiancée, Vanessa Fleer MacIlhoney. Vanessa had dumped Rufus at the altar, despite being pregnant with their daughter Charli, instead plighting her troth to Quentin MacIlhoney, the defense attorney who'd helped her dodge a murder charge and currently sat next to her enjoying a healthy portion of étouffée. Maggie had found that life in a small Louisiana village often proved way more complicated—and intriguing—than life in the New York City borough of Brooklyn that she had once called home.

"Hey there, muh friends. Y'all passing a good time?"

JJ, taking a break from his kitchen duties, appeared in front of them. He wore an apron over a sequined navy-blue caftan, one of many he'd inherited from his late mother along with the family restaurant. The chef bowed in mock humility as everyone at the table rose to their feet to give him a standing ovation. "I can't begin to tell you how fantastic everything is," Maggie said. Her friends seconded the compliment.

Bo pulled a spare chair away from the table next to them. "Here. Can you sit a while?"

"I'd say I earned a rest before dessert." JJ parked himself in the chair, his large body splayed out over its small seat. He picked up a printed menu and fanned himself with it. "It's so warm in the kitchen tent I sweated off my temporary beauty mark. I had to spoon it out of the whipped cream I made to go with the bread pudding that's gonna be coming out after the wedding cake."

"I think I put on weight just listening to that sentence," Maggie said.

"Good luck to Phillippe Chanson, opening a place that'll compete with Junie's," Vanessa said, or at least that's what Maggie thought she said. It was hard to make out, given that Vanessa was chomping on a big hunk of JJ's homemade French bread when she said it.

Phillippe Chanson, one of the most famous chefs in the country, had recently taken over LeBlanc's, Pelican's one "fancy" restaurant. He was in the process of a remodel that would transform the eatery into Chanson's Cajun Kitchen, the newest addition to his famed Chanson Restaurant Group. Chanson had explained why he'd anointed Pelican as the recipient of his culinary magic in an interview with Little Earlie Waddell, jack-of-all-publishing-and-editing-trades for the *Pelican Penny Clipper*, a local freebie Little E had transformed from a coupon tabloid to a genuine tabloid—with coupons.

Chanson claimed his goal was to position the new eatery as a "destination restaurant," along the lines of legendary European establishments found in tiny, off-the-beaten-path villages. "What better location for my take on Cajun cuisine," he'd opined, "than a picture-perfect postcard of a Cajun town?"

The locals were divided into two groups: those who were excited about a star chef descending upon their "picture-perfect postcard" and those who felt apprehensive. Maggie fell into the latter camp. National attention could be a good thing. Crozat Plantation B and B, her family's business, had seen a marked uptick in reservations after a recent profile on a TV travel show. But the increase in business had only put it on a par with nearby B and Bs. When a Phillippe Chanson outpost came to town, it could endanger humbler local restaurants, the drop-off in patrons sometimes dooming them.

Maggie forced her attention back to the conversation. "I'm looking forward to the new place," JJ was saying. "Chanson is a legend. His place is gonna be packed, and I'll be happy to take the overflow of people who don't feel like waiting hours to get in."

Gaynell, who'd left the table to join her band, struck a chord on her accordion. "*Allons à Pelican!*" she hollered. The young woman's mass of blonde curls bobbed as she launched into a catchy up-tempo Cajun tune. The dance floor quickly filled with revelers.

Bo held out a hand to Maggie. "May I have this dance, Mrs. Crozat-Durand?"

Maggie grinned and took his hand. "It would be my pleasure, Mr. Crozat-Durand."

Vanessa rolled her eyes. "Ain't that just so modern of ya. I couldn't wait to unload Fleer and take MacIlhoney as my last name."

"And I couldn't wait for you to do it as well, my dear," said her husband. Quentin patted his trim white beard with a napkin and offered a hand to his wife. Vanessa polished off her last bite of French bread and allowed him to lead her onto the dance floor.

After a lively two-step, the band segued into a Cajun waltz. Bo held Maggie close as she rested her head against his chest. The past months of danger and drama, of murders and accusations, faded away. There was only this moment and the promise of their future. "Did you ever think we'd get here?" she asked Bo as they danced.

"Always. I swear, sometimes it was the only thing that kept me going."

"Amen to that."

The song ended. Gaynell played a flourish on her accordion, and JJ wheeled out a spectacular wedding cake created by Lia at Fais Dough Dough, the bakery she and her husband Kyle ran along with its companion candy shop, Bon Bon Sweets. The cake, covered with peach fondant frosting and tiny candy pearls, stood five tiers high. A garland of white flowers made from sugar cascaded down one side of it. "Yikes," Bo said, a little overwhelmed. "Your grandmother?"

Maggie nodded. "Yup. Designed it herself."

Gran clapped her hands together joyfully. "Lia, it's perfect. Brides, grooms—let's do this."

"If you smush cake in my face, I'm filing for divorce first thing in the morning," Maggie murmured to Bo as they made their way to the cake.

"Noted, but don't stand too close to Rufus," Bo warned. "I'm sure he's got something planned."

The couples took turns cutting the cake and serving it to each other. Maggie held her breath as Rufus headed a fork toward Sandy. He fed his wife with decorum, and then the jokester took the cake plate and slapped it against his own face to roars of laughter. He fist-pumped the air in a gesture of triumph, then took a number of bows. "Thank you, thank you."

Maggie couldn't help herself. She joined the laughter, as did Bo. She saw JJ howling so hard he had to bend over and gasp for air.

It would be a long time before Maggie saw JJ laugh again.

Chapter 2

A few weeks later . . .

Maggie cast a discerning eye at the canvas on her easel. Then she glanced at her subject. Xander sat curled up with a book in the living room's club chair, which was upholstered in a soft, pale-green velvet. His pet cat, Maggie—named after his now-stepmom, who was deeply touched by the honor—slept in his lap while pups Gopher and Jolie snoozed at his feet.

Evening had come and the moon was behind a cloud. Maggie missed the lovely natural light it cast through the room's expansive picture window, but now was the best time to capture her stepson—how Maggie loved thinking and saying that—in repose. She used a fine paintbrush to feather a few strokes of light brown into Xander's sandy hair and added a touch of black to the view outside the window. Her phone pinged a text. Maggie checked it. "Your mom's here, Xander, *cher.*"

Xander closed his book. " 'Kay."

Maggie parked her paintbrushes in turpentine and took Xander's book so he could rise from the chair with the sleeping kitty in his arms. "You hold on to Maggie. I'll carry your backpack."

" 'Kay."

The two headed downstairs from Maggie and Bo's apartment, which took up the entire second floor of the B and B's expanded former garage. The building's downstairs contained Mo' Better Beauty and Day Spa. Maggie had originally envisioned her family running the spa, but when circumstances precluded this, friend and beauty expert Mo Heedles had stepped in to take over the facility, and the Crozats couldn't have been happier with the arrangement.

Maggie shivered as she and Xander stepped outside. Her thin T-shirt, stained with a rainbow of paint colors, was no match for the cold late-January night air. Whitney, Xander's mother and Bo's ex-wife, waved to them from the driver's side window of her SUV. "Hey, baby boy. You got everything?" Xander nodded. "Okay then, hop in."

Maggie kissed her stepson on top of his head and helped him into the vehicle. Her namesake gave a fretful meow but stayed in Xander's arms. "See you in a couple of days, buddy. Love you."

She waved them off, then scurried inside and upstairs, where she changed into fleece leggings and an olive-green sweater that matched the color of her hazel eyes. She pulled her thick chestnut hair into a high ponytail, then dabbed on a light touch of makeup. The heat kicked on, the breeze from the HVAC unit triggering ceramic chimes that Maggie had bought on her honeymoon in Mexico. She and Bo had toyed with the possibility of a European honeymoon but opted for a more frugal trip closer to home. While she'd been the recipient of an inheritance from a neighbor, most of the money was earmarked for turning the old man's dilapidated plantation manor house into a co-living space that would help ease Pelican's housing shortage.

Maggie slipped on a warm jacket, then removed the painting of Xander from its resting place on the easel, careful not to get wet paint on her clothes. She headed downstairs again, making the short trek to her former home, the cottage she'd once shared with her grandmother. It was Grand-mère and Lee's home now, and Gran was making the most of the change, redecorating with a vengeance. Maggie negotiated her way around a collection of antique furniture sitting on the front porch, which ran the length of the old house. She found Gran inside the empty living room. "What exactly is"—Maggie gestured to the bare room—"this?"

"I've asked Vanessa to help me redecorate."

"Wha . . . wha . . ." Maggie sputtered. "Vanessa? As in 'I hate all that old, gross stuff and only want new stuff that looks like old stuff' Vanessa?"

"That's the one. I've decided it's time for a whole new look, even if it's a new look that looks like an old look. I'd like to live out my final years not worrying about leaving a coffee stain on a two-hundred-year-old sideboard."

"Okay, let's skip the 'final years' talk. It's your and Lee's home now. Have at it."

Gran pointed to a couple of packed suitcases. "We'll be moving into the manor house for the duration. It was either that or move into Lee's old apartment above the service station, so the choice was obvious. While new-car smell has its merits, 'old car that needs *beaucoup* servicing' smell does not.

Once Valentine's Day is over, B and B bookings will slow down until the music festivals begin, and by then we'll be back in our newly appointed digs."

"Sounds like a plan. Speaking of Valentine's Day, is it okay if I keep this here?" Maggie held up the painting. "It's Bo's Valentine's Day present, and I can only work on it when he's not around."

"What a lovely gift. Yes. Put it in the closet for safekeeping." Maggie did so. Gran rubbed her hands together. "Now, let's get to our—what do you call it?"

"A GNO. Girls' night out."

"Yes. That. I am ready for a cocktail."

"You're always ready for a cocktail," Maggie said, teasing her grandmother.

Gran lifted her chin, affecting a dignified air. "But I am particularly ready when the cocktail is attached to an event and not merely free-floating. *Allons-y*. Let's go."

Maggie and Gran headed to the graveled parking lot. Two rental cars pulled in past them and parked next to each other. An attractive woman got out of each car, one in her early thirties, the other ten or more years older. The younger woman wore a hoodie over a chef's jacket. They made a point of ignoring each other as they went their separate ways. The older woman strode toward the carriage house, the younger to the overseer's cottage, recently renovated to serve as guest rooms. "How can two people who obviously can't stand each other work together so closely?" Gran wondered.

"I guess when the whole is bigger than the sum of its parts. And in this case, the whole is Chanson's new restaurant."

Famed chef Phillippe Chanson was wasting no time getting his new location up and running. While he chose to commute by motorcycle from New Orleans, home to his flagship restaurant, Chanson's in the Quarter, he'd parked most of the staff for Chanson's Cajun Kitchen in the Pelican area. Crozat B and B was home to three of them. The women in question were Kate Chanson, his ex-wife, and Becca Wittenberg, his young, attractive *sous-chef* and rumored current girlfriend. The third guest was Dyer Gossmer, the beleaguered coauthor aka ghostwriter of Chanson's "autobiography." The air quotes were courtesy of Gossmer, who never talked about the book without using them.

Becca, who'd raced to her lodgings in the overseer's cottage, darted out and ran past them. "Everything okay?" Maggie called to her.

"The handle on my offset serrated knife broke, but luckily I have a spare." Becca held up an odd-looking knife. She jumped into her car and kicked up dust as she sped out of the small lot.

"Do you have any idea what she's talking about?" Gran asked.

"Not a clue."

Maggie and Gran got into the vintage 1964 Falcon convertible Maggie inherited from her late grandfather on her mother's side, Papa Doucet. "I know it's early, but I'm surprised Becca was able to run home from the restaurant," Gran said. "You'd think she'd be indispensable."

Maggie started the car and backed out of her parking spot. "I'm sure she usually is. But according to Kate, they're in the middle of what she called a 'soft opening.' Meaning that the restaurant isn't officially open yet. They're still missing some tables and chairs and artwork, but the kitchen is up and running, and they're testing recipes on Chanson foodie superfans. I guess Phillippe figured he was better off with a happy *sous-chef* than one who was freaking out about a broken knife."

"They are a rather dramatic lot, aren't they? Much like those theatre people we had staying here in October. And from what I pick up, none of them like each other very much."

Maggie made a right turn onto the old road that ran alongside Crozat, then another right onto the Great River Road toward Pelican's historic district, the centerpiece of the quaint Cajun village. The levee, swathed in green grass even in winter, blocked a view of the mighty Mississippi, but the road followed its undulating curves. "I can see why Kate and Becca have problems getting along," Maggie said. "They resent each other's relationship with Phillippe. Whitney and I were like that in the beginning, but we came to an understanding. Having Xander in the mix helped. We both put him first."

"I wonder why Phillippe and Kate never had children."

"I got a little insight into that from Dyer, who's desperate to talk to someone who isn't one of Chanson's toadies. He said they both considered the restaurants their 'children,' which is why Kate's still in the mix post-divorce. She's the designer and brand manager of the whole Chanson group. She got him the book deals, the TV shows, the line of cookware. Kate is Phillippe's good-luck charm. He'll never let her go, which drives all his girlfriends—like Becca—insane."

"Now that," Gran said, "is some excellent gossip."

Maggie made another right turn into the heart of Pelican. Centuries-old brick buildings with lacy iron galleries lined three sides of the town square. The straight line of Bayou Beurre completed the square. Maggie drove past Junie's in search of a parking spot. Usually plentiful, they'd become scarce since Chanson's soft opening. "If this is what it's like before that place officially opens," Maggie grumbled, "I hate to think what it's gonna be like once it gets going." After her third run up and down the main street, she gave up. "I'll drop you off and find a spot on a side street," she told her grandmother.

"Normally I'd say, 'I'm not an invalid; I can walk, thank you very much.' But I'm wearing these high-heeled booties Vanessa helped me pick out. We wandered into a fancy shoe store on one of our furniture excursions."

Gran held up her foot, clad in a black, spike-heeled suede ankle boot sporting a large silver buckle on the side. Maggie frowned. "I'm not sure Vanessa's the best influence on you."

"You're just jealous because I saw them first."

"No, but let me know when you get sick of the pain from them pressing on your bunions and I'll buy them from you."

Maggie stopped in front of Junie's. Gran got out and made a show of sashaying into the local hangout. "See?" she called back to her granddaughter. "No pain."

Maggie, amused, shook her head. She left her grandmother and drove around until she finally found a spot several blocks away. She parked and started toward JJ's, walking past the village's tidy cottages and bungalows. She passed the parking lot for the Pelican Police Department. Pelican's five-car fleet of patrol cars, lined up against the lot's farthest wall, looked destined for a junkyard. Three were, two weren't, despite their battered appearance. A recent storm had flooded the lot and pounded the cars with hail and heavy tree branches. Much to the department's aggravation, their insurance company refused to total the whole fleet. Maggie's step-grandfather, Lee Bertrand, owner of the town service station, had done his best to breathe life into the two vehicles the insurance company declared salvageable, but even his wizardry didn't instill much confidence in the officers stuck behind the wheels of the beaters.

By the time Maggie entered Junie's cheerfully shabby portal, she'd worked up a sweat and a thirst. "I'm gonna go with an Abita Light," she told Old Shari, the restaurant's nonagenarian bartender.

Shari pulled a tap and filled a mug. She handed it to Maggie. "Wisht you asked for somethin' a little more fancy. I'm bored as anything."

Maggie scoped out the room, which was decorated for Valentine's Day with JJ's usual over-the-top, tongue-in-cheek flair. Glittery hearts hung from the embossed tin ceiling. Every table featured a centerpiece of a baby doll dressed as Cupid sitting on a bed of fabric red roses. The stuffed alligator, who'd been the odd pet of JJ's late mother and now stood guard over the establishment from a perch above the bar, was clad in a T-shirt covered with candy-heart images and sayings. But while parking might be scarce, seats at Junie's usually packed tables weren't. There were only a smattering of patrons, all regulars Maggie recognized. As she headed to her friends' table, Eula Banks, Pelican's mayor, waved to her. "Hey, chère. Welcome home from that honeymoon of yours."

"Thanks, ma'am," Maggie said with a smile.

"When y'all gonna have a baby?"

"When we're ready," Maggie said, the smile now forced.

"You're not getting any younger."

"Yes. You keep telling me that. Bo and I want to take a little time to enjoy married life. Especially since our dating life kept being interrupted by murders. Here's hoping that's over."

Eula used her cane to make the sign of the cross in the air, narrowly missing a customer heading to the bathroom. "Amen, *amen*."

Maggie reached her friends and took a seat between Gaynell and Sandy across from Gran, Vanessa, Lia, and Ione, Maggie's friend and boss at Doucet Plantation, where the position of exhibit coordinator had recently been added to Maggie's résumé along with her current title as art restoration specialist. "We went ahead and ordered, family-style," Gaynell said.

"We ordered way too much food, but we wanted to give JJ the business." Ione delivered this under her breath.

"Where is everybody?" Maggie said, in a voice equally low.

"JJ can't serve up Gulf oysters on account of the shortage, but Phillippe Chanson being who he is, managed to score some, and he's selling them for fifty cents each."

The price was so low it elicited a gasp from Maggie. Fresh-water from recent storms had inundated local oyster beds, killing off the crops and forcing restaurants to either import oysters or take them off the menu until the situation righted itself. Only a few high-end restaurants were offering Gulf oysters, and at exorbitant prices. "Fifty cents? How can he do that? He has to be losing a fortune on them."

Ione shrugged. "I guess what he loses on the cheap price, he makes up for by attracting new customers."

Maggie made a face. "Not me. Aside from the fact I'm Team JJ, I'm that rare breed of Louisianan who doesn't find oysters appealing."

Gaynell put a hand on her heart and mock-gasped. "*Whaaa?* Say it ain't so."

The others laughed, and a conversation about the merits and demerits of oysters ensued. "Hey, y'all, how about we put a pin in talking about slimy seafood and switch to something more fun, like, oh, I don't know . . . Valentine's Day?" Vanessa rubbed her hands together with unashamed avarice. "It's my first as Mrs. MacIlhoney, and I'm looking for Quenty to pony up big-time. Maggie, you should do the same. Sandy, you got the bad luck to be Mrs. Rufus Durand. That is one cheap man. He squeezes a nickel tight enough to make the president on it cry from the pain. He still owes me a push present for baby Charli."

"You did give birth right after dumping Rufus at the altar, so there's that," Maggie pointed out.

"Whatevs." Vanessa patted her burgeoning belly. She'd recently shared with her friends that she was expecting a second child, this one fathered by overjoyed husband Quentin, who'd taken to adding *#vasectomyfail* to his online signature.

"I can tell you that Quenty ain't getting off that easy when I pop out this little one. Lia, you must've cleaned up, what with popping out three kids all at the same time."

"Kyle and I kind of assumed the triplets were our present," Lia said.

Vanessa groaned. "Honestly, y'all are hopeless."

"Not me," Gran declared. "I'm with you, Vanessa. What is it they say now? Go big or go home."

"Preach, sistah!"

Vanessa held up a hand, and she and Gran high-fived. Maggie wrinkled her brow. "Should I be worried about this relationship?"

"Yes!" chorused Lia, Gaynell, Sandy, and Ione.

"Dinner's here, ladies."

JJ approached them carrying a tray laden with various dishes, his red chiffon caftan floating as he walked. He put the tray on a stand and transferred platters of food to the table. Maggie inhaled the rich scents emanating from the selection of Cajun and Creole dishes. "Phillippe Chanson may be pulling in customers off his name, but no way can he compete with you when it comes to cooking, JJ."

"I'm not worried," JJ said, although Maggie thought the dark circles under his eyes belied this. "There's room for both of us. I know it's quiet now, but people'll be back. Me and Abel's Home Cookin' are the only places around here with five-star reviews on that Tasteful app." JJ pointed north toward Abel's shack of a restaurant, a local haunt on the River Road that had been serving delicious po' boys and fried-fish plates for decades. "Eat up, *mes amis*."

The women passed the platters, spooning servings onto their plates. Gaynell took out her phone and snapped several photos of her meal. "I feel bad. I never reviewed Junie's on Tasteful, so I'm gonna do it now." She tapped on her phone screen and then stopped. "Huh. JJ doesn't have five stars."

"How many does he have?" Maggie asked. "Four?"

"No." Gaynell frowned. "Two."

"*What?*" Maggie took Gaynell's phone and stared at it.

"He probably got one bad review from some disgruntled customer that briefly knocked down his rating," Gran said.

Sandy nodded in agreement. "Like with a credit score. It dips and then comes back up again. I'm sure it'll be the same here."

"Except that Junie's didn't get one bad review," Maggie said. She held up Gaynell's phone to the others. "It got six."

Chapter 3

Gran took the phone from Maggie and read the reviews. She handed the phone back to Gaynell and gave her granddaughter a knowing look. "Trolls."

Maggie gave a grim nod. She and her family had experienced a similar situation when a rival hotelier posted a barrage of negative reviews about their B and B on a travel website called trippee.com. The trolling triggered a spate of guest cancellations, made even more frustrating by the herculean efforts it took to have the fake reviews removed. She hated to think what kind of damage the Tasteful slams might do to Junie's.

The faces of all the women were etched with concern. "Should we tell him?" Sandy wondered.

"Yes, so he can fight back," Vanessa declared.

"But first we flood the site with positive reviews," Gran said.

The women voiced agreement and pulled out their phones. "I'll talk to him," Lia said. "We both run food-oriented businesses. I can brainstorm with him about how to counteract something like this."

The women finished dinner and their reviews, showered JJ with compliments, and headed out. Maggie and Gran drove home in silence, a pall cast over the evening. Bo greeted his wife at the door with a kiss that raised her spirits a bit. "How was your GNO?"

"It started out good but took a turn." Maggie shared the news about Junie's rating drop. "Lia's gonna work with JJ on how to come back from this, and we all wrote raves on that dumb Tasteful website. Can you write one too? The more, the better."

"Of course. But I've got some news of my own. Good news. How would you like to go to the Vi De Lavallade gallery opening tomorrow night?"

Maggie gasped. "Seriously? Bo, she's my favorite artist."

Her husband grinned. "I know. Why do you think I called the gallery and got us on the list? We can head down to New Orleans soon as we get off work. I also made a reservation at Chanson's in the Quarter. I don't feel right giving him any business here in Pelican, but I wouldn't mind seeing if he's earned all the fuss about his food."

"Oooh, great art and a spy mission." Maggie wrapped her arms around Bo's waist. "Have I told you how much I love you?"

Bo quirked his lip. "Not in the last five minutes."

* * *

Maggie woke up early the following morning to a phone call from her mother. "Chère, can you handle serving breakfast this morning for me?"

"Sure." Maggie yawned and rubbed her sleepy eyes. "What's up? You sound excited."

"I am," Ninette said. "Guess what? Phillippe Chanson heard from some of our guests that I'm a good cook—"

"You're more than that; you're a *great* cook."

"Anyway, he asked if I'd mind making a meal for him." Ninette's voice rose to a squeak. "Can you imagine? *Me* cooking for *him*? What an amazing opportunity. It's not till tomorrow afternoon, but I need all the time I can get to prepare."

"Take whatever time you need, Mom. I'm happy for you."

Maggie showered and dressed for the day. She smiled when she found Gran's new ankle boots on her doorstep and brought them inside. They'd be the perfect footwear for her artsy evening outfit.

A few B and B couples enjoying an early Valentine's Day retreat had requested that breakfast be left at their door, which was fortunate, since Kate Chanson had commandeered the dining room for a meeting. While the restaurateur hailed from nearby Lafayette, she reminded Maggie of driven female executives she'd known in New York. Kate had the hard, determined look of someone who'd fought for a seat at the table in male-dominated businesses, and her painfully thin frame made Maggie wonder if she ever partook of Phillippe Chanson's cooking. "The real chairs and tables will be delivered to the restaurant this afternoon between lunch and dinner, and the rental company will pick up the temporaries," Kate told her sleepy coworkers as Maggie distributed plates loaded with crawfish boudin and her mother's popular Muffuletta Frittata. "For the final few meals before the official opening, I've slotted in some influencers who'll create a buzz on social media."

"So be nice to everyone who looks vapid and Botoxed. They could be important." Patrick "Trick" Costello's dry wit elicited a snort from the others. Costello was the Chanson Group's mixologist but seemed to play a vague yet more important role in the organization. He stood around five foot eight and boasted a trim physique for a man in his midforties. Costello had mentioned to Maggie that his last name was Irish, not Italian, and he had the classic Black Irish coloring of dark hair, blue eyes, and pale skin to back up the claim.

Scooter Pitot, a slight, pierced thirtysomething hellion from nearby Ville Platte who Maggie had learned would be manning the oyster bar, rubbed his hands together. "Vapid and Botoxed. Throw in built and you got my swipe-left."

Kate held up a hand. "Walk the line, Scooter. Eighty-six the sexism."

"Are we done? Because I have actual work to do." Becca, the *sous-chef*, sniped. "I have to meet Phillippe at the restaurant to go over some changes to today's menu."

"He didn't run them by you in bed last night?" Kate delivered this with a sweet smile.

Trick theatrically inhaled a breath and winked at Luis Alvaro, the group's youngest employee. Luis, a shy young man not long out of his teens, was staying with family friends in the area. He was in charge of the garde-manger, which he had defined to Maggie as meaning he focused on cold dishes. Luis, who seemed discomfited by the tension between the two women, ignored Trick.

The sound of a motorcycle roaring into the parking lot distracted the group. Becca jumped up. "My ride's here. Which would be your ex-husband. We didn't spend the night together, but not because we didn't want to. But hey, there's still a few hours before we open the restaurant. You might want to knock before you come into Chanson's Cajun Kitchen this morning."

Having shot this at Kate, Becca bounded out of the room. Scooter hooted and whistled. "She got you there, Katey Kay."

Kate glared at him. "Don't."

Scooter faked a contrite expression. "Yes, ma'am." He jumped up. "I got my truck for any that needs a ride. Thisaway."

He strode out the door, followed by Trick and Luis. Kate pulled a file folder out of her briefcase and slapped it in front of writer Dyer Gossmer, who was still eating. "I edited your chapters. This is Phillippe's autobiography. It needs to be more in his voice."

"It would be if he was actually writing it," Dyer muttered into his frittata.

Kate narrowed her eyes. "I heard that. I also saw you recording that little exchange between Becca and me. Delete it."

"Okay."

"*Now.*"

Dyer released an aggravated sigh. He put down his fork, picked up his phone, pulled up the Voice Memo app, and pressed delete. "With the amount of stuff you won't let me include, this 'autobiography' is gonna be about the length of a photo caption."

Kate cocked her head to one side. "How's the newspaper business these days, Dyer? Not too great, is it? You might want to think about that before you mouth off to me again."

She tossed her napkin on the table and walked out of the room, leaving behind an untouched plate of food. Dyer traded it for his own empty plate. "I don't care if you saw that," he said to Maggie.

"Saw what?" Maggie said, feigning innocence.

The writer responded with a weak smile. To Maggie, he looked like a man who'd given up on life and was merely going through the motions. His thin, graying hair was ragged around the collar of his worn button-down shirt, which was only half tucked into his old, belted chinos, as if he hadn't had the energy or motivation to tuck in the whole shirt. Dyer helped himself to Kate's still-pristine cappuccino. "I was an investigative reporter for the *New York Times*. I quit to write a book about the BP oil spill, which sold around five copies. When I tried to get back in the newspaper game, there was no game to get back into. Now I scrape by writing vanity BS like this project." He opened the file Kate had left for him and gave it a halfhearted once-over. "Of course she cut all the good stuff. Did you know that Phillippe Chanson is a totally made-up name? Well, not totally. Chanson is Kate's last name. Phillippe—or rather, Phil, as he was called before becoming who he is now—took Kate's surname because Singer, his real name, wasn't exactly prime for a guy painting himself as America's premier Cajun chef. Whenever this fact pops up, Kate bats it down like it's Whack-A-Mole. Drives other chefs crazy. You know what his nickname is in the business? Nonstick. Because nothing sticks to him. Negative stuff just slides right off."

Maggie studied Dyer. "I'll be right back." She left for the kitchen and returned carrying a bowl filled with a healthy serving of her mother's Brandy Pain Perdue. "My mom's famous version of French toast. Cajun comfort food."

Dyer flashed a genuine smile. "Thanks. You made my morning."

After the writer finished eating, Maggie bused the table, loaded the dishwasher, and set off for Doucet, where she spent the day restoring a painting that would hang in a new exhibit at the historic site. *Say Yes to This Dress: The Long Life of One Wedding Gown* was a Valentine's Day–themed exhibit showcasing generations of Doucet brides wearing the same wedding gown Maggie had been married in. The final piece of the exhibit was the dress itself, displayed on a mannequin. Eager to get to the evening's adventure, Maggie cut her workday short and raced home to meet Bo.

* * *

Maggie and Bo found New Orleans to be its usual vibrant self. Since Valentine's Day often landed in the middle of Carnival season, the party-happy city celebrated both with equal abandon. The romantic holiday was almost two weeks away, but that didn't deter the decorating. Red hearts duked it out with purple, green, and gold decorations in the store windows. A second line of people danced past Maggie and Bo on Canal Street, some participants wearing Mardi Gras masks, others carrying umbrellas festooned with red hearts. Bo held Maggie's hand as they weaved through the boisterous crowds toward the art gallery on Chartres Street. The sidewalk in front of the gallery was filled with the opening's overflow, well-dressed patrons of the arts holding plastic wineglasses and chatting with each other. The crowd parted to make way for the newcomers.

The couple stepped into the small space and looked around. Each wall of the gallery featured two large paintings. Maggie paused in front of the first piece of artwork and drank it in. A young African American mother sat on the stoop of a crumbling row house. She held a baby in her lap. A little girl had her arms wrapped around the woman's neck while a boy leaned against her, a serious expression on his face. Maggie pointed to a building in the background. "You see how that looks like collage? It's not. Vi painted it to look that way. And you see how there's a beautiful flower arrangement in every window, contrasting with the building's disintegration? It's a brilliant juxtaposition of hope and despair."

"Uh-huh." Bo stared at the painting. "Pretty."

Maggie chuckled. "An art critic you are not." Maggie walked Bo through the exhibit, explaining each piece to him. She stopped short and clutched Bo's arm. "That's her. Vi De Lavallade." Maggie pointed to an elegant, older Black woman wearing a nubby silk shawl and an off-white jersey dress that came to her ankles. Her hair was full and natural. She was tall—very tall. Maggie thought she might be eye level with Bo, who stood an inch over six feet.

"Why don't you introduce yourself and tell her how much you like her work?"

"I can't," Maggie said, suddenly overcome with shyness. She watched with envy as the artist engaged in an animated conversation with two young women Maggie guessed were college students. "I read she's doing a six-week residency at Tulane. Lucky Tulane students."

Bo checked his watch. "We're due at Chanson's in five minutes. I can push back the reservation if you want."

"No." Maggie took one last long look around the gallery. "I'm good. We can go." She squeezed Bo's hand. "Thank you for this. It's inspiring."

They left the gallery for the restaurant, located in the heart of the Vieux Carré. A line of people without reservations hoping to get into Chanson's in the Quarter stretched halfway down the block. As Maggie and Bo walked past the line to the front door, a would-be patron called to them, "I'll pay you fifty bucks for your reservation."

"Tempted?" Maggie teased Bo.

"Considering my detective's salary, yes. But with the Saints in town, finding an opening at another decent restaurant is a no-go."

Bo held the door open, then followed Maggie into Phillippe Chanson's flagship eatery. The restaurant was housed in a former stable with a covered courtyard in the center. Patrons' conversation bounced off the old stone floor, creating a wall of sound within the eatery. A maître d' led them to a small café table in a dark corner of the place. "Do you want to share an appetizer?" Bo shouted over the din.

"Sure," Maggie shouted back.

She opened the menu and did a double take. "Whoa. I think that appetizer might have to be our entire meal. This place is steep."

Bo took a gulp of water, opened his menu, and choked on the water. "Mercy. Well . . ." he added weakly. "How often do we do something like this?"

Maggie heard a blast of laughter coming from a six-top a few tables away from them. She glanced over and saw the group in conversation with Phillippe Chanson. She'd met him only briefly in passing, but between his rangy good looks, charisma, and neck tattoos, he was hard to forget. He caught her eye. Chanson excused himself from the other diners and segued to their table, greeting Maggie and Bo each with a clap on the shoulder. "I saw your name on the reservation list. Welcome."

"Thank you," Maggie said. "We're looking forward to it."

"Just an FYI that we don't have oysters tonight. This place is already gold, so we moved the action to the new place by you. Nothing like the press you get from being one of the only joints with genuine Louisiana oysters these days. And at bargain prices."

Not like on this menu, Maggie thought to herself. "That's okay. I'm not an oyster fan."

"I am," Bo said, disappointed.

Chanson's craggy face creased in a grin, accentuating a map of small scars that Maggie had read were the result of oil spatters from his frenetic cooking style. "Sorry, man. I'll make it up to you in Pelican." He turned his high-wattage smile to

Maggie. "Hey, your mama's making me a meal tomorrow. I hear she's some cook."

"She is," Maggie said proudly. "The best."

"We'll see." The chef's smile didn't dim, but Maggie picked up a hint of aggression in his tone. He clapped Bo's shoulder again. "I gotta get back in the kitchen. Go with the Louisiana Seafood Trio. You won't be sorry."

Chanson departed, waving and nodding to customers, who fawned over him as if he were a rock star. Which, it seemed to Maggie, was a reputation he fully embraced. "I didn't like the way he dismissed my mother. She's so excited about cooking for him. I hope her feelings don't get hurt."

Bo studied the menu as he spoke. "You can't get to where he's gotten without being competitive. I'm sure he'll be respectful. I don't see anything that beats the Seafood Trio, although I may have to take a chunk outta my pension to pay for it."

Maggie leaned in toward Bo. "If you can hold out for about an hour, I have an idea." She dropped her voice and spoke in a conspiratorial tone. "Let's ditch this place and head home to Junie's. We could use the savings, and JJ could use the business."

Bo chuckled and slapped his menu shut. "I like the way you think." He stood up and made a sweeping motion. "After you, Mrs. Crozat-Durand."

"Why, thank you, Mr. Crozat-Durand," Maggie said in her best imitation of a southern belle. She stood up, Bo clasped her hand in his, and they made their escape from the expensive, trendy eatery.

* * *

Maggie was relieved to find her fears about Chanson's attitude toward Ninette's cooking unfounded. He zipped over
between the lunch and dinner soft-opening seatings at the
new location and presented Ninette with a lovely bouquet
he pulled out of his backpack. Rather than treating the
famed chef to Cajun dishes he knew and served himself,
Ninette had excavated rare recipes that danced with extinc-
tion. She began the meal with an appetizer of mirlitons
stuffed with crawfish. The main course was a Cajun classic,
Butter Beans and Shrimp, followed by a dessert of calas—
fried-rice fritters. Despite the liberal dusting of powdered
sugar, Ninette liked to serve her calas with a side of pure
cane syrup for dipping. "Calas have made a comeback on
some menus," she told Maggie and Tug as she fried up the
sweet treat. "But nobody's doing my recipe for them. I got
a secret ingredient."

She said this with a smug attitude that amused Maggie.
"Whatever it is, don't waste sharing it on me."

"I wasn't planning to, chère. I know you can't cook worth
a lick."

"Hey, no fair," Maggie jokingly protested. "I can make
beer bread."

Ninette responded with a disdainful sniff. "I don't call
throwing a can of beer into a bowl of flour making bread."

Maggie followed her mother out of the kitchen into the
dining room. Ninette placed the steaming bowl of calas in
front of Chanson and hovered over him. She nervously tapped
her foot. Chanson closed his eyes and inhaled the fragrance,
then waited a minute for the steam to settle before tucking

into one of the rice balls. He took a bite and groaned with pleasure. "Best. Calas. Ever."

Ninette almost collapsed with relief, and Maggie released the breath she'd been holding on her mother's part. Doggies Gopher and Jolie, who had wandered into the dining, wagged their tails simultaneously like two furry metronomes. Ninette beamed with pride. "Oh my, thank you."

"The whole meal was outstanding." The chef stood up, clasped his hands together as if praying, and bowed to Maggie's mother. "Whatever you do, don't open a stand-alone restaurant. I'll never be able to compete." He grabbed Ninette by the shoulders and kissed her on both cheeks. "I've got to get back to the restaurant and start dinner prep. But thanks for this. I'll never forget it."

Ninette blushed and giggled. She waved a hand at him. "Stop now. Y'all want me to pack up some leftovers?"

"I would love that."

Ninette made for the kitchen. Maggie's father Tug, who'd watched from the sidelines, was on her heels. "Don't give him everything," Maggie heard Tug say under his breath. "I'd kill for a bowl of that shrimp."

Maggie left her parents to their kitchen tasks and returned to her apartment, where she worked on the painting of Xander. After a few hours, she realized she was running out of white paint, so she made a trip into Pelican to pick up a tube at the mom-and-pop hardware store that graciously stocked her art supplies. An affable Black teenager wearing a butcher's apron called hello to Maggie from outside Chanson's restaurant across the street. Maggie darted over to give him a hug. "Hey, Clinton. How's it going?" Clinton Poche and his younger sister Brianna were trusted occasional employees of the B and B.

"Awesome. I got a part-time job as a waiter at the new restaurant."

Clinton modeled his apron, then struck a lightning pose like Olympic gold medalist Usain Bolt. Maggie laughed. "That's great. Congratulations."

"Yeah. My mom's not too happy cuz I'm behind on my college applications. But I don't wanna go to college. I wanna be a chef like JJ and Mr. Chanson."

"Sorry, I'm with your mom on this. Get an education while you can. I'm sure JJ and even Mr. Chanson would tell you the same thing. If you're really committed to being a chef, maybe add a culinary school application into the mix."

Clinton didn't look convinced. "Maybe. Hey, I heard about your mom making a meal for Chef Phillippe. He was going on and on about how good it was."

"That's nice. I'll tell my mother. She'll be thrilled."

"I gotta go. I don't wanna miss dinner." His face lit up. "They give you a free dinner, a restaurant does. Did you know that? Tonight it's gonna be fried fillet-of-catfish po' boys. Talk about good, huh?"

Clinton grinned and patted his stomach, then dashed inside the restaurant. Maggie ducked into Fais Dough Dough to pick up a check for the commission she'd earned from the souvenir line she'd created depicting local historical sites with her fluid brushstrokes. Vanessa was behind the counter, pulling an espresso for a customer. She'd convinced Lia and Kyle to buy a fancy coffee machine and turn the no-man's-land between the bakery and candy shop into a small café area— sheer genius from a woman once anointed the laziest employee in Doucet Plantation history, her prior place of employment. "You sure you don't want to add my wedding dress to that exhibit of yours at Doucet?" Vanessa asked after finishing up with her customer.

Maggie gave her a look. They'd already been over this. "As I've told you a bazillion times, the exhibit traces the history of one particular dress that's been handed down in the Doucet family for generations."

Vanessa sighed. "I would so love to get a tax deduction for that thing. Sure, I'll get some use out of it as a Halloween costume, but I can't do that every year. I don't like repeating myself."

"Why don't you donate it to—"

The sound of a commotion outside distracted Maggie. She glanced out the glass door and saw Pelican PD officers Artie Belloise and Cal Vichet escorting Abel Garavant of Abel's Home Cookin' out of Chanson's Cajun Kitchen in handcuffs. Kate and Trick followed behind them. Vanessa craned her neck to look outside. "What all's happening out there?"

"No idea," Maggie said. "I'll take a look." She pushed the door open and stepped outside.

"Thieves!" Abel yelled at the Chanson restaurant employees as the officers pulled him toward their patrol car. "Robbers!"

A compact sedan screeched up the street, coming to a halt behind the police vehicle. Ash Garavant, Abel's son and an ex-boyfriend from Maggie's high school days, extracted himself from the sedan, which was too small for his tall, spindly body. He hurried to his father with long, loping strides. "Dad, I got your message. Who robbed you? What's going on?" Maggie saw Ash register the handcuffs containing his father's wrists. "What the hell? Why are you in handcuffs?"

"Good question. Ask Cal and Artie here." Abel cocked his head toward the restaurant entrance, where Phillippe, clad in a chef's jacket, watched the fracas with an amused expression. "You're the one they should be arresting," Abel, apoplectic, yelled at the celebrity chef. "You stole my recipe, you dang SOB. You know you did. You stole the recipe for my fried catfish fillet!"

Chapter 4

Cal and Artie led Abel to the patrol car, his son on their heels. "We'll get all this straightened out, Abel," Cal said. "But right now, we gotta take you in for disturbing the peace."

Cal reached for the rear patrol car door, but an angry Ash blocked him. "You're not taking him anywhere."

"Ash—"

"You're not arresting my father."

Maggie could see Ash was fighting the urge to explode. Vanessa, who'd come up behind Maggie, peered over her shoulder. "Should we do something?"

Maggie shook her head. "I wish we could, but I know Cal and Artie. They wouldn't want us getting in the way and possibly escalating instead of deescalating the situation."

"Ooh, listen to you sounding so police-y. From all those murders at the B and B, I guess."

"More from being married to a law enforcement official," said Maggie with asperity. Nothing aggravated her more than being reminded of the killings that had bedeviled her family's home and business. She turned her attention back to the unfolding drama on the street.

"Ash," Cal said. He kept his tone even but firm. "You need to move. *Now.*"

"No!" yelled Ash, unable to control himself anymore. "Release my father! Release him, or I'll—"

Artie shoved himself between the two men. "Hey! That's enough, Garavant." Artie got in Ash's face. "I'm gonna give you two choices. You can get in *your* car and follow us to the station, or you can get in *this* car"—he gestured to the patrol car—"and we can take you there in cuffs, like your dad. Your call. But make it quick. It's fifteen minutes past my lunch break, and the hungrier I get, the meaner I get."

"Son," Abel said, his voice quiet and tinged with defeat, "Don't fight them no more. Just get to the station. We'll hash it out there."

Ash paused, then backed away from the patrol car. He threw a furious look at the restaurant employees, then stormed back to his own vehicle. Artie and Cal maneuvered Abel into the back seat of the patrol car and got in the car themselves, Artie at the helm. He turned on the battered vehicle's engine, which sputtered and died. Onlookers could hear a stream of invectives through the closed window. Artie started the car again. This time the engine kept running. The officers took off, followed by Ash, and Phillippe disappeared back into the restaurant. Kate and Trick lingered, talking to each other in hushed tones. Maggie left Fais Dough Dough and walked over to them. "Is it true? Did Phillippe steal one of Abel's recipes?"

Kate waved a dismissive hand. "Of course he didn't. You can't steal a recipe because you can't copyright them."

"You can copyright the exact way a recipe is written," Trick clarified. "The wording of it. But you can't copyright the ingredients."

"But," Maggie said, getting a sinking feeling as she thought of her mother, "what if someone has a secret ingredient?"

"No such thing, really," Trick said. "Take Coca-Cola, maybe the most famous 'secret' recipe in the world. They can protect their production process, their 'trade secret,' but that's with their own employees, who could be sued for violating company policy for revealing anything about the recipe. If someone figures it out on their own, there's nothing they can do about it."

Maggie's sinking feeling sunk further as she recalled Chanson's raves about her mother's cooking. "Still, it seems like stealing a recipe—"

"Trick just told you," Kate snapped. "You can't steal a recipe."

"All right," Maggie said in an even tone. "*Borrowing* another cook's recipe would be bad form."

"Happens all the time," Trick said. "When you think about it, it's flattering."

Maggie pursed her lips. "I wouldn't call Abel's reaction flattered."

Kate huffed annoyance. "Typical reaction of an amateur. Come on, Trick."

"Abel's been running his place since he was out of high school," Maggie said to Kate's and Trick's retreating backs.

"Abel's Home Cookin' has been in the Garavant family for generations." Kate yanked the restaurant front door shut. "Amateur, my . . ." Maggie muttered the end of the sentence to herself. She turned to go but caught a glimpse of Clinton Poche through the restaurant window. Their eyes locked, but the teen quickly looked away, an unhappy expression on his face.

It occurred to Maggie that JJ had never come out of Junie's to see what all the noise was about. She walked over and stepped into the restaurant, which was empty except for Old Shari, who was wiping down the bar. "Hey, Shari. Where's JJ?"

Shari gestured to a side door with her bar rag. "The alley. Cleaning up."

Maggie left the restaurant for the alley through the side door. She found JJ knee-deep in rotting garbage. He wore plastic gloves, and a mask covered his nose and mouth. "Lord, what happened out here?" Recoiling from the smell, she put a hand over her nose.

"Racoons got into the trash. Good thing the health inspector didn't show up today."

JJ hoisted a shovelful of garbage into a heavy plastic bag. Maggie eyed it. "Since when do you serve crab legs?"

"I don't. I'd go broke if I had to charge my customers what it'd cost for me to make a profit on them. Someone else's garbage accidentally got mixed up with mine."

"Maybe it wasn't an accident."

JJ cast a melancholy look at Maggie. "It makes me sad that you've come to have such a suspicious nature."

"When you find yourself facing about a dozen murders in under two years, it's kind of bound to happen. Need help?"

"Sure. Grab a mask and a shovel."

Maggie did. She hefted a load into JJ's almost-full bag. "I've got a question for you. Is it true you can't copyright a recipe?"

"Not the ingredients, only the way it's written. You can trademark the name of a recipe if it's super unique, but that's it. Why do you ask?" Maggie filled JJ in on the Abel imbroglio. "Huh. Well, that's too bad for Abel, but nothing he can do about it." JJ tied off his trash bag and slung it into the restaurant dumpster. "People's been telling me Chanson's jambalaya tastes exactly like mine. Chanson stopped in here when he first took over LeBlanc's lease and had a bowl of it. Gave me lots of compliments. I'm guessing he figured out my way of making it and duplicated the recipe. He must've thought if people like it here, they'll like it there."

Maggie, infuriated, shoved a shovelful of trash into a bag with such force that the bag ripped. She grabbed a new one. "That's terrible. I hate him for that."

"Don't. I'm not worried. Junie's has got something he don't."

"What's that?"

JJ whipped off his mask, threw his hands in the air, and struck a pose. "Me!"

Maggie laughed. "Yes, sir. And that's something no one can compete with."

She helped JJ scoop up the rest of the garbage, then hied it home. Hungry, she stopped in the manor house and scouted the kitchen refrigerator for leftovers. The shrimp and calas were gone, but she dug up some shrimp remoulade, which she ate straight from the container. Gran and Ninette came in with a tray of dirty wineglasses and snack plates, having just finished serving the B and B's wine-and-cheese hour. Gran wrinkled her nose. "What's that awful smell?"

"Me," Maggie said. "Raccoons, who I cynically think may not have been raccoons, scattered JJ's garbage, and I helped him clean up."

"It sounds like you're implying someone from Chanson's might be messing with Junie's," Ninette said with a frown. She filled the sink with hot, soapy water and began handwashing the crystal goblets. "That's a bit extreme and not very nice, Magnolia Marie."

Maggie debated telling Ninette about the dustup with Abel, then decided not to. *I need more verification about this recipe thing*, she thought. *In the meantime, let Mom enjoy the accolades from Chanson.* "Sorry, Mama. I'm still recovering from an hour of dumpster filling."

"I highly advise a shower, chère." Gran's recommendation came out muffled, since she'd covered her nose and mouth with her hand.

"Talk about extreme," Maggie said.

She started for the kitchen door, stopping to tease her grandmother with a hug. Gran affectionately pushed her off. "Go. And take that ghastly scent with you."

Maggie left for her apartment. She noticed Dyer Gossmer sitting on a wrought-iron bench, puffing on a vaping pen. He nodded a greeting. "I'm taking a break. I needed a smoke, but I didn't want to burn the place down."

"That's very thoughtful of you, especially considering vaping could kill you faster than cigarettes."

"Here's hoping," the glum writer said.

"Can I ask you something about the restaurant business? I think I already know the answer but wouldn't mind a second or third opinion."

"Shoot. And I mean that literally. I just read Kate's notes on the chapters I gave her. I'm gonna have to type with one hand and hit the bottle with the other."

"Can chefs really steal each other's recipes?"

"Sure. It's common practice. They try to pass it off as inspiration or an homage. But . . ." Dyer stopped to inhale, then released a cloud of smoke. "It's a little different with Chanson. Chefs generally tinker with a recipe. Make it their own. Change the name. Not Chanson, at least not once he got famous. Too busy promoting himself to do the hard work of coming up with interesting new dishes. So, he began borrowing. He made a bad name for himself in New York, which is why he moved his operations here to Louisiana. Much easier when the recipes are generic like jambalaya or grits and grillades."

"Unless there's a secret ingredient," Maggie said, thinking of Ninette's calas.

"Oh, there are no secret ingredients with this guy. He's a genius at sniffing them out. More than that, he's got a way of knowing the exact amount to use, which is the real secret. Interesting stuff, huh?"

"Very."

"Too bad I can't use one word of it in his 'autobiography.' Or the fact that his last restaurant, Chanson's LA in LA, bombed. The reviews were vicious. LA is all about hype. The minute there's a stink on a place, it might as well have a communicable disease. Chanson couldn't even get a real housewife or bachelorette to show up and take a selfie."

Dyer took a big suck on his vape pen, held it in as long as he could, and then let the smoke burst out of him. Maggie coughed and batted it away. Her eyes watered. "I'm guessing you've got a personal interest in this question," he said. "My advice is, forget it. There's no going up against Nonstick."

* * *

Following Dyer's advice, Maggie dropped her concern about Ninette's recipe and spent the next few days focusing on prepping the Doucet exhibit. She brought her portrait of Xander with her to work, where she could paint in secret. She was working on it when Ione came into her studio carrying a large arrangement of roses. "What are those?" she asked.

"They came for you. I guess Bo's getting an early start on Valentine's Day." Ione raised her eyebrows suggestively, much to Maggie's embarrassment.

She took the arrangement from her friend and placed it on a table in front of the large window that flooded the space with light. Maggie pulled a small card off a stanchion tucked among the roses and opened it. *"Roses are red, violets are blue,"* Maggie read. *"This is the first of many gifts for you."*

Ione crossed her arms in front of her chest and made a face. "A poet he ain't."

"It's not from him." Maggie turned the card around to show Ione. "It's signed, 'From Your Secret Admirer.' "

"Huh." Ione took the card and examined it. "Well . . . maybe it's from him pretending not to be him. It's your first Valentine's Day as a married couple. Maybe he wants to make a big deal out of it and build to some kind of surprise."

"That could be," Maggie acknowledged. "I won't say anything to him, at least not yet."

Her cell pinged. Ione gave a sly grin and wiggled her eyebrows again. "Maybe that's your man seeing if you got any surprises today."

Maggie rolled her eyes as she checked her phone. "That's strange," she said. "It's an alert from my bank. My overdraft protection kicked in. It shouldn't have. I deposited my paycheck a few days ago."

"I hope it's not a problem from our end."

Maggie opened her bank app and scrolled through her most recent transactions. "It is. My paycheck didn't clear."

"What?" Ione said, incredulous. Her face darkened and she planted her fists on her hips, which where clothed in the gray silk antebellum gown she wore as her work costume. "That's ridiculous. I'm calling the bank to find out what on earth happened. Don't worry, we'll straighten this out."

Ione stalked off. Maggie, trusting she was in her boss and friend's capable hands, swished her paintbrush in turpentine, then wiped it clean with a rag. She checked the water in the vase of roses and added the packet of flower food she found attached to another stanchion in the display. She was about to return to work cleaning one of the wedding portraits destined for the upcoming exhibit when her phone rang. Maggie checked and saw that the caller was her father. "Hey, Dad. What's up? Everything okay?"

"Pretty much the opposite of that." Tug's voice was heavy with distress, sending a frisson of fear through Maggie. "We got a problem."

"What?" she responded, alarmed.

"Your mother is in jail."

Chapter 5

Maggie grabbed her purse. "I'm on my way."

"I haven't told you what happened."

"Let me guess. It has something to do with calas."

"Yes, how did you—"

"Leaving now."

Maggie ran down the hall and into the gift shop, which also housed Ione's office. "I've got to run into town. I'll explain later."

Ione nodded. "I'm on hold with the bank."

Maggie sprinted to her car and shot out of the parking lot. She drove east over Veteran's Memorial Bridge. Ten minutes later she pulled into a parking spot in front of the nondescript midcentury building that housed the Pelican Police Department. She threw open the double glass doors and rushed inside.

Tug was deep in conversation with Cal Vichet, who was manning the station's front desk. Artie had a gentle hold on one of Ninette's arms, which were clasped behind her back in handcuffs. Maggie approached her mother, who, next to the rotund police officer, looked even smaller than her just-shy-of-five feet. She wore an apron over her jeans, and her mess of graying light-brown curls were held in check by a bandanna. "Can I talk to her?" Maggie asked Artie.

" 'Course you can—if she's okay with talking to you without a lawyer present." He motioned to a worn wooden bench. "Have a sit. I'll stand right here."

Maggie helped her mother sit down and then joined her. "This is about your calas recipe, isn't it?"

Ninette pursed her lips. "I thought I'd make the calas as a breakfast treat for that cute millennial couple from Monroe staying with us. After one bite, the girl said, 'Hon, don't these taste just like the ones we had at the new place?' And he said, 'They sure do. Exactly like them.' It's all over town about Abel accusing Phillippe of stealing his catfish recipe, and I got a bad feeling about my calas, so I took myself over to Chanson's place and ordered a plate of them."

"You recognized your recipe."

"That so-and-so stole it," Ninette said, outraged. "I marched into the restaurant kitchen, grabbed the bowl of batter out of our guest Becca's hands, and dumped it right on the floor. One of them, I don't know who, called the police, and here I am."

"I'm sorry, Mom. I was afraid this might happen. I didn't want to say anything in case it didn't, because you were so excited about Chanson liking your meal."

Ninette looked down at the ground. When she spoke, her voice quavered. "I'm a simple person. And I've never minded that. A loving husband and daughter . . . a respectable home and business. . . . that's all I've ever needed. And my recipes. They've been handed down from one generation to the next, like your wedding dress. We each make our little changes to get with the times, then pass them on down. They're living history. There's great comfort to be had in knowing that when we've moved on from the physical world, a part of us lives on, maybe forever." Maggie pulled a tissue from her purse and wiped away a few tears that had rolled down her mother's cheeks. "Thank you, chère. When I went into the Chanson kitchen, that sweet Clinton Poche tried to defend me. I hope he didn't get in trouble for it. That's the only thing I feel bad about. Otherwise . . ." Ninette rose to her feet and stuck out her chin, defiant. "I'm ready to do my time. I plead guilty to defending my calas recipe from that terrible man. Send me up the river. Throw me in the hoosegow. Where did that word come from, I wonder? Someone look it up on their phone. I believe I'll have to surrender mine when they throw me in the slammer."

"Nobody's locking you up, Ninette," said Bo, who had emerged from his office in time to hear his mother-in-law's declaration. "I just got off the phone with Phillippe Chanson, who agreed to drop the charges against you as long as you promise never to set foot in his restaurant again."

"I have no intention of doing that anyway. But what about my recipe?"

Bo gave a helpless shrug. "I can't do anything about that."

Artie removed the handcuffs from Ninette's wrists. "I wouldn't worry about it, ma'am. Everybody around here knows who the real star chefs in town are—you and JJ. The only thing that shady Chanson's got going for him are Gulf oysters. I cannot lie, I am a big fan of those bivalve babies."

Ninette grimaced as she rubbed her wrists. "I appreciate the support, Artie. I'm gonna make a nice meal tonight to celebrate my freedom. You're welcome to join us."

The officer's face lit up. "It'd be an honor, ma'am."

Tug took his wife's hand. "Let's get you home. It's been one tough day and it's barely half over."

Tug led Ninette out of the station, almost colliding with Ione, who burst into the reception area. The woman, who was in a panic, still wore the top half of her costume but had thrown on pants instead of her hoopskirt. "It's gone," she gasped. "All gone." She dropped her head in her hands and rocked back and forth. "Oh my lord, oh my lord," she repeated over and over again.

Maggie grabbed her friend's hands. "Ione. Calm down and talk to me."

Ione raised her head. Maggie felt sick. She'd never seen such a look of despair. "Steve Collins, the executive board treasurer . . ."

"Yes?" Maggie prompted. "What about him?" While Ione had been promoted to executive director of Doucet, a non-profit historical site, she reported to a board of directors. Steve Collins served as the board's treasurer.

"He emptied the account. We've been wiped out. That's why your paycheck bounced. Mine too. Everyone's."

Maggie closed her eyes. Her head swam. Bo quickly left his post and went to the women. "Artie, cover for me. Ladies, this way."

Maggie, dazed, followed Ione and Bo down a hallway. Bo rapped on the captain's door, then opened it. Rufus sat behind his desk. He was doing paperwork while eating a po' boy. "Hey all." He referenced the meal in front of him. "Picked this up from that new place, Chanson's Cajun Kitchen. They were having a special. Tastes exactly like Abel Garavant's catfish po' boy."

"We have a situation," Bo said, sounding grim.

"Do we now? You got my attention. Pop a squat, ladies, and fill me in."

Bo helped Ione, who was unsteady on her feet, into one of the two cold metal chairs facing Rufus. Maggie took the other seat, and Bo rested a comforting hand on her shoulder.

Rufus eyed the distraught Ione with compassion. "It's okay, ma'am. You're with friends. Relax and tell us what happened."

Ione sucked in a shaky breath and released it. "I wish I knew. Doucet operates on a shoestring budget, mainly funded by attendance fees. We have enough to meet payroll every month, plus a small reserve for emergencies, like repairs. Maggie's paycheck bouncing was the first red flag. Then mine did, and everyone else's. I called Monnin National Bank to find out if it was a problem on their end. It's not. The money is gone. I straightaway called all the board members and talked to everyone but Steve. He's the only board member with access to our account, so no one else had any idea something was wrong. Steve never called me back. I have a number for his wife, Georgia, so I called her, and Lord have mercy, the poor woman was in a state. He'd wiped out *their* bank account too and disappeared."

Bo shot a look at Rufus, who responded with a nod. "Yeah. If he hasn't left the state, he's on his way out. I'll put in a call to the FBI."

"And I'll start digging into any bank or credit card activity on Collins' part," Bo said.

Rufus addressed the women. "We got this. Y'all go do whatever you can to stop the bleeding. We'll keep you posted on everything we find out."

Ione wrung her hands. Apprehension etched deep lines in her dark skin. "What are we gonna do? I don't know if Doucet can survive this."

"Oh, it will," Rufus said. "Nobody bilks a historic site and gets away with it on my watch."

Once out of Rufus's office, Bo pulled Maggie aside. "I'm gonna work until I trace this guy; I don't care if it takes all night. I'll be home when I'm home."

"I love you so much."

The couple stole a quick kiss; then Bo retreated to his office and Maggie exited the station for the parking lot. Ione was getting into her car. "I'm going home to call the staff and explain what happened." Ione choked back tears. "I can't bear to think about them going without money. A lot of the guides live paycheck to paycheck."

"I know." Maggie thought of the stress this put on her coworkers. "I'm going to call my accountant. I'll see if he can free up any funds from the Dupois inheritance for immediate use."

"We'll pay you back as soon as Doucet rights itself."

"No way," Maggie said, adamant. "It'll be a donation."

Ione drove off. Maggie got in her car. She called her accountant, Craig L'Etoile, who'd been designated the co-executor of the Dupois estate, along with a probate lawyer. Maggie explained the situation to L'Etoile. "You took a hit with capital gains taxes," the accountant said, "and you want to make sure you put aside an extra twenty percent for over-ages on the co-living space remodel. But let me take a look and see if I can work some money magic."

"If anyone can, it's you, Craig. Thanks."

Maggie ended the call. She evaluated her next step, then got out of the car and headed over to Monnin National Bank. Robert Monnin, the bank president, greeted her warmly. "We were honored to have you switch your account over," he said, leading her to his office.

"I decided I should be supporting a community bank, not a chain. Also, you got that app, which is helpful."

"Yes. When my granddaughter joined the bank staff, she announced she was moving us into the twenty-first century." Monnin didn't sound too happy about this. He bent down and retrieved a tote bag from under his desk. The logo on the front read *Bank Local: Make Money with Monnin*. "I wanted to thank you with a little bank swag." He pulled a pen out of the bag. "Look, it lights up."

The banker clicked the pen on and off with childlike glee, then dropped the pen back into the bag, which he handed to Maggie. "Thanks, Mr. Monnin," she said. "I wanted to talk to you about the Doucet situation."

That wiped the smile off Monnin's face. "Terrible," he said, his tone somber. He lowered himself into his heavy wooden office chair, which rolled back slightly. He pulled himself forward. "I'll help in any way I can."

It occurred to Maggie that she had no idea what to ask the banker. While the visual acuity born of being an artist had proved usual in solving murders, embezzlement was new territory for her. This was truly a case for law enforcement. But there was *something* she could do. "It's not confirmed, but it looks like the Doucet board treasurer absconded with the site's funds, which were supposed to cover payroll. This means all the employees' checks bounced. I know there's a fee for returned checks, but given the circumstances, I'm hoping you'll forgive them."

"Absolutely. I'm happy to do that for any employees who bank with us. I can't speak for the other banks, but I will get in touch with their branch managers, explain the situation, and ask them to join me in forgiving the charges. I am a bit of an elder statesmen in our little banking community." Monnin did his best to affect modesty.

"Thank you so much." Maggie rose and hoisted the tote over her shoulder. "And thanks for the swag. Love the pen."

"As my granddaughter would say, it's lit. Literally."

Monnin accompanied the pun with a wink, and Maggie responded with the requisite polite laugh. As she left the bank, her cell rang. She saw the caller was her accountant, Craig L'Etoile, and answered it. "I moved a few things around and freed up some funds," Craig explained.

The accountant named a figure. "That's good," Maggie said. "It will cover the last pay period. Luckily, it's a small staff."

"And you said it's a donation, not a loan, which will help taxwise. I'll release the money to your account, and you can write a check to Doucet."

Maggie thanked him and ended the call. The donation was a Band-Aid over a serious wound to Doucet. *A gala*, she thought. *And a silent auction.* She texted the financial news, along with the idea of a gala fund raiser, to Ione, who responded with a long string of exclamation marks, hearts, and flamenco dancers, followed by *GO FOR IT!*

Buoyed by the enthusiasm, Maggie put together a mental list of possible members for a gala committee. Her stomach growled. She decided to combine dinner with a chance to invite JJ onto the committee and headed to Junie's. She was stunned to find the front door locked. Then she saw a notice taped to the door at eye level, and her appetite disappeared. The sign read *Notice of Closure for Violation of the St. Pierre Parish Health and Safety Code.*

Her worst fears for JJ had come true.

Chapter 6

Maggie walked through the alley to the back of the building. She saw JJ's car in the parking lot. Hoping he might be in the restaurant, she rapped on the back door. "Come in," a beleaguered voice called from inside.

She found her friend in his tiny, cluttered office. He was stuffing paperwork into his briefcase. "I saw the sign," she said. "What happened?"

"You know that old saying *No good deed goes unpunished*? You're looking at living proof of that." JJ maneuvered his large body through the sliver of space between his workspace and a tall, beat-up metal filing cabinet. He motioned to Maggie to follow him out of the restaurant. "Someone put in a call to the health department that forced an inspection. They found evidence of vermin. Vermin!" he repeated, outraged. "In my restaurant. Practically all my profits go into making sure I run the cleanest establishment with the freshest, best food around. Vermin, my keister."

Maggie squinted as they exited the parking lot and faced the flare from the setting sun. "So you think someone did this on purpose? Like, planted . . . vermin feces?"

JJ gave a vehement nod. "I'm sure of it. I did the friendly thing and invited the Chanson folks over for a drink after they closed up. I keep bar hours and they keep restaurant hours, so I'm open later. It's what us restaurant people like to do—visit each other, share intel on customers and meals. At least that's what friendly ones do. I bet you every dime of my late papa's loose change that fell out of his pockets and wound up stuck in Mama's couch cushions that one of those Chanson people planted droppings in my kitchen when I was busy getting their drinks."

Maggie hated to think that what JJ said was true, but knowing her friend as well as she did and his almost fanatical dedication to running a clean, healthy establishment, she had a terrible feeling he was right. "Did you tell the health inspector?"

JJ gave a derisive snort. "Yeah, and got a 'That's what they all say' reaction. He also found a problem with one of the bathroom toilets. It backed up when he went to flush it."

"Do you think someone messed with it?"

"No idea. It's an old toilet anyway. Wouldn't be a bad idea to replace it." JJ looked exhausted. Something else was different about him, but Maggie couldn't put her finger on what. "But it's gonna mean days of being closed for business. That includes tomorrow when Chanson's Cajun Kitchen officially opens. I was counting on the overflow crowd from the event to make my nut for the week."

Maggie impulsively hugged JJ. He had a good six inches on her five feet four and his girth made encircling his waist impossible, but the message came through. He responded to her affectionate support by returning the hug. "Thanks. If it weren't for friends like you, I might just float out to sea on one of those Viking rafts they put bodies on and let 'em light me on fire."

"No funeral pyre for you, my friend." Maggie released him. "This is just a blip in the history of Junie's. You will come back, and be careful what you wish for, because I predict crowds like you've never seen before once word gets out that there's one true Cajun kitchen in town and it's yours."

"Don't forget your mama. And Abel."

"Well, Mama's not running an actual restaurant, and Abel's on the outskirts of town."

JJ slapped his forehead. "Listen to me, niggling like this. Instead I should be sending a prayer up to heaven that you're right."

"I will be. And when you've got things under control here, I want to talk to you about a gala we're going to throw for Doucet."

"Happy to do whatever I can, once I settle this mess." He planted a kiss on top of Maggie's head. "Love ya."

"Right back at ya."

JJ hauled himself into his decade-old pickup truck and took off. Maggie wended her way through the alley back to the street. She was almost at her car when she realized what was different about JJ. He was wearing jeans. Maggie thought back to high school and all her visits home during her years in New York. She'd never seen him wear anything but caftans

---

or tongue-in-cheek dramatic outfits. The jeans were a sartorial symbol of her friend's worry and possible depression.

Someone called to her. She turned and saw Clinton. He jogged down the block to her. "Hey, I'm glad I saw you. I wanted to say how sorry I am about your mama being arrested and all."

"She told me you stood up for her," Maggie said.

"Yes, ma'am," the teen said, puffing out his chest. "That Becca was making the batter for calas, and she kept getting on me to see if I knew the recipe cuz she knew I worked for y'all sometimes. Phillippe said it didn't matter, he'd figured it out, like always. After they called the police on Mrs. Crozat, I got real mad and said some things I probably shouldn't have, especially after Mister Famous Chef told me to leave and take my attitude with me. I was giving his kitchen 'bad vibes.' " Clinton pulled a face. "I threw down my apron and walked out of there." He held up his apron, a little sheepish. "But I picked it up, because it's a good apron and my grand-mère would like it."

Maggie knew Ninette would be devastated to learn that her impulsive act of anger had cost the teen his job. "Clinton, I'm so sorry about this. We'll find you work at Crozat to make up for it."

"Don't worry about it. My mama would call this a learning experience. Cuz I learned that I do *not* want to be a chef, no I do not. Those people are *crazy*."

*   *   *

Between the drama of her mother's arrest, JJ's restaurant woes, and Doucet's financial debacle, Maggie found it impossible to fall asleep. Bo crawled into bed around two in the morning. "I'm awake," she told him.

"That's too bad. After today, you could use a good night's sleep." He slipped an arm under her back, and she snuggled close to his side. "But I have some news for you. The FBI came through for us. They caught Steve Collins at the Houston airport. He was about to board a flight to Mexico. They also made quick work of his financials. He wasn't exactly a criminal mastermind. Turns out the guy had a second family in Houston. He's been banking part of his paycheck in a separate account for years to pay for them. I don't have all the details, but the feds got hold of the second wife, and she talked enough to fill a book. When she found out about the first wife thanks to a receipt for blond highlights she doesn't get because she wears her hair dark, she was not happy, to put it mildly. She threatened to tell wife number one about family number two, and Collins panicked. He stole the money from Doucet, hoping to buy her off. She took it, spent it as fast as she could—and told wife number one anyway. He was trying to beat town to get away from both of them."

"My takeaway from this story," Maggie said, gloomy, "is that the Doucet money is gone."

"The feds will try to claw back some of it from the guy's assets, but I wouldn't count on more than pennies on the dollar."

Maggie released an exasperated sigh. "I kind of wish one of the wives had gotten to him."

"He's lucky they didn't. They both know how to shoot and are licensed to carry." Bo caressed Maggie's arm. "Not a very sexy bedtime story, is it?"

"Oh, *so* not."

Bo tapped an index finger against his lip. "Hmm. Well . . . maybe I can seduce you with an early Valentine's Day present."

Maggie affected a pout. "You can't. My gift for you isn't ready yet."

"I hear it's a painting."

Maggie, miffed, sat up. "Who told you?"

"Chère, you're painting a kid . . . who's very good at keeping secrets. Charlotte let it slip."

"My grandmother?" Maggie crossed her arms in front of her chest and harrumphed. "Figures that the eighty-three-year-old would have less self-control then the eight-year-old."

"Don't be mad at her, because my gift works with yours." Bo pulled up to sitting. "I got you private lessons with Vi De Lavallade." He beamed.

Maggie gasped. "*No.* You did? Oh Bo, that's the best gift ever."

She threw her arms around her husband, then kissed him. "I did good?" he asked, a little insecure.

"Good? You did great. Beyond great. Lessons with Vi De Lavallade." Maggie bounced up and down on the bed. She shot a come-hither look at Bo. "Seduction accomplished, handsome."

She wrapped her arms around him, and the couple melted into the sheets.

* * *

When Maggie showed up to the manor house kitchen early in the morning, she found Gran there, already plating breakfast for their guests. "Our regular guests are still sleeping, but the Chanson group is up, having some sort of meeting before their official opening tonight."

"I'm surprised they're still here. I figured they wouldn't want to stay in a place where they had the owner arrested for disturbing the peace and vandalism."

"They were perfectly civil when I brought them their coffee. Like it never happened. According to our friend Dyer, who's desperate for an ear, blow-ups are the norm in Phillippe Chanson kitchens." Gran pulled bowls and a large baking pan out of a cabinet. "The hot plates are already on in the dining room. Help me fill these."

Maggie spooned scrambled eggs and bacon into separate bowls and loaded the baking pan with French toast. She speared a forkful of eggs. "This has to be the most boring meal Mom ever made. These eggs are blander than bland, and the French toast is made with white bread, not brioche. It's like what they'd serve for breakfast at a nursing home."

"I've breakfasted with friends at the Camellia Park Senior Village and it was far more interesting than this. Your mother made sure there was nothing here that might induce recipe thievery."

"Mission accomplished."

Gran wiped her hands on a dish towel. Maggie noticed a hint of sparkle on her grandmother's ear. She moved closer to her. Gran instinctively pulled away. "What?"

Maggie gaped at her. "You got your ears pierced."

Gran affected nonchalance. "So?"

"So," Maggie said, "I've been trying to get you to do that for years. Nobody wears clip-ons, I'd say. Ladies my age don't put holes in their ears, you'd say. Do we owe this to Vanessa too?"

"Sometimes outsiders get us to do what family members can't," Gran said. "How many times did I tell you to pay off your credit cards every month to avoid the interest charges? Did you listen to me? No. But you listened when Bo said it."

"Personal finances and jewelry bling are two separate issues."

Gran gestured to the food. "We need to put a pin in this conversation and serve our guests before the food gets irredeemably cold."

"Fine. But we also need to schedule some grandmother-granddaughter time. I'm starting to feel disposable."

Maggie took a bowl in each hand and hip-checked the swinging door that separated the kitchen from the dining room. She walked the bowls over to the centuries-old sideboard and placed them on top of the hot plates. Gran followed with the pan of French toast and placed it on top of a third hot plate. She disappeared back into the kitchen, but Maggie lingered, curious to hear the restaurant staff's plans. She made a show of checking the jam jars and other breakfast condiments as she took a read of the room. Becca buzzed with tension, but that was to be expected, given that she was directly under Phillippe—professionally and physically, considering their romance. Scooter was also jumpy, but Maggie pegged that as a general condition for him. On the other hand, Luis was alert to every detail Kate imparted about the day's schedule, making notes on his phone. Trick slouched in his chair, with one arm around the back of Kate's. On the surface he seemed relaxed, but the free hand relentlessly drumming on his thigh indicated underlying strain.

Ghostwriter Dyer, whom Maggie had mentally nicknamed Dour Dyer, got up from his place and shuffled to the sideboard. "We lost some of our waitstaff, thanks to them taking the side of that idiot Poche kid," Kate said. Maggie clenched her teeth, biting back an angry defense of Clinton. "Dyer, don't write that down."

The writer held up a bottle of ketchup and a plate of eggs. "There goes my plan of taking notes by squirting ketchup onto a plate."

Kate ignored him. "They're sending up fill-in waitstaff from the city, but that's only going to work for a few days. So, if you know anybody . . ." She turned to Luis. "You've got local connections. Use them. But no illegals. We don't need an ICE raid."

Maggie saw Luis work his jaw. "I'll see what I can do." His tone was polite, but Maggie easily filled in the rest of the sentence. *Which will be nothing.*

Scooter stood. He grabbed a slice of French toast with his hand and stuffed it in his mouth, digging a trench in the rug as he paced back and forth. Maggie was beginning to wonder if his antsy nature was intensified by a drug problem. "We done?" he asked, impatient. "I gotta get with my oyster guy."

"Almost," Kate said, skimming her notes.

A motorcycle roared up outside. Becca lit up and jumped to her feet. "Phillippe."

"He's gonna kill himself on that thing someday." Kate accompanied this pronouncement with an eye roll.

Maggie felt the tension in the room ratchet up a few degrees. Feeling a need to further justify her presence, she picked up a coffee carafe and circled the table to refresh everyone's cups, but no one paid attention to her. Phillippe's long, lean frame appeared in the archway separating the dining room from the manor home's wide entry gallery. He wore a black bomber jacket and had his helmet slung over his forearm. *He looks like the hot bad boy from a 1980s movie*, Maggie thought. The chef ran a hand over his tousled brown hair. "What'd I miss?"

"All the boring stuff," Becca said.

She planted a kiss on Phillippe that he acknowledged but didn't respond to in kind. Becca's lightly freckled face flushed, but she still threw a cocky glance Kate's way. Kate glowered at her. Maggie noticed Trick's arm drop onto Kate's shoulder in a territorial gesture. "Awesome timing on my part," Phillippe said, grinning. "We close at nine tonight. I want all customers gone by nine thirty. The fireworks start at ten."

"Fireworks?" Maggie blurted without thinking.

She inwardly cursed herself, but rather than bothering the chef, her response triggered an ebullient, "Yeah! Awesome ones. I hired the guys who do the show for the Christmas Eve bonfires on the levee. *And . . .*" He dragged out the word to create suspense. "I've got a big surprise." He slapped his hands together, startling Dyer, who dropped a forkful of eggs onto the floor. "To the levee, gang. Let's go. *Vamanos.* That one's for you, Luis."

"Ha. I do speak English, boss." Luis made a weak attempt to make this sound like a joke.

Maggie, overcome with curiosity, joined the restaurant employees as they filed out of the house and crossed the River Road. They climbed to the top of the levee and then down to the Crozats' dock, usually used for tourists from the riverboat excursions who booked a tour of the historic plantation as part of their itinerary. A speedboat wrapped in a garish ad for Chanson's Cajun Kitchen was tied to the dock. Phillippe raised his arms in a triumphant gesture, then ran to the boat and jumped in. "Anyone wanna join me?"

"I do!"

Maggie wasn't surprised to hear this from Becca. The *sous-chef* bounded over to the boat and joined the chef. He released the boat from the dock and started the engine. He shot up the river and arced back, earning a warning blast from a pusher boat guiding a barge. Maggie winced. "This isn't a great stretch of the river for pleasure boating," she said to Scooter, who happened to be standing next to her.

"Nope," the one other local in the group agreed. "But that's Phillippe for you. And he gets away with it. Good old Nonstick."

Scooter said this without a hint of affection. If anything, he sounded venomous.

"Playtime's over," Kate said. "We canceled lunch service today so you could get some rest, folks, so do it. We need everyone at the top of their game tonight."

The group trudged up the levee back to Crozat. Maggie stood watching the star chef steer figure eights on the river, earning a few more warning horn blasts. Then she headed home.

* * *

Rest seemed the last thing on any of the Chanson employees' agendas. Instead, the restaurant's official opening set off a tsunami of drama. Maggie, who was helping her mother harvest the B and B's organic garden, spent much of the day treading back and forth from the garden to the manor house. Every time she passed one of the guest quarters, she heard arguing. Kate and Phillippe; Phillippe and Trick; Kate and Becca; Becca and Phillippe. The last argument left the *sous-chef* in tears. She ran by Maggie, Phillippe in pursuit. He stopped to admire the greens in Maggie's basket. "Good stuff. I could use another produce supplier." Then he continued to chase down Becca.

A few hours later, Maggie was surprised to see the crew chatting and laughing together as they piled into Kate's black Cadillac Escalade and headed to the restaurant. *I do not get these people*, she thought.

Out of deference to Ninette, the Crozats boycotted the grand opening of Chanson's Cajun Kitchen. But Maggie and Bo succumbed to Xander's pleas to see the fireworks with his pal, Esme. "We get to stay up late, we get to stay up late," the little girl sang as they drove toward the Pelican town dock.

"And see fireworks," Xander added.

"If I can find parking," Bo muttered. Cars lined the road on both sides, while crowds gathered on top of the levee. A party energy filled the air. Music blared from speakers that a group of tailgaters had set up. They raised their bottles to Maggie and Bo and woo-hooed. "I'll be holding a Breathalyzer to that crew."

Maggie looked back at the group and noticed Rufus among them. "I think that last *woo-hoo* came from our esteemed police chief."

"I'm gonna let y'all out and find a space," Bo said. "Text me where you end up and I'll meet you there."

Bo pulled over. Maggie helped Xander and Esme hop down from the SUV, and then Bo drove off. She took each child by the hand and led them across the street. Esme literally bounced with excitement, hopping instead of walking to the levee side of the road. On top of the levee, Maggie recognized Vanessa's zaftig silhouette, made more so by her baby bump. Maggie led the kids to Vanessa's crew of Fais Dough Dough and Bon Bon employees, waving to Gaynell, who was leading the Gator Girls in an energic rendition of "Allons à Lafayette." "I didn't know the Gator Girls were performing tonight," Maggie said to Vanessa when they finally reached her group.

"Can you believe all this?" Vanessa gestured to the celebratory scene. "Chanson really cranked up the local-flavor theme."

"To an eleven," Maggie said with a grin. She glanced around, taking in the carnival atmosphere. Friends and neighbors packed the levee's crown. She couldn't miss Ash Garavant's lanky silhouette hovering over a small knot of people. Maggie remembered from their high school days that he was self-conscious about his height, which was north of six foot six, and hunched over in group gatherings to reduce himself by a few inches. She considered going over to him and commiserating about their parents' mutual arrests, but before she could make the move, the *Pelican Penny Clipper*'s Little Earlie Waddell sidled up to her.

"Ain't this awesome?" he said, elated. "We owe Phillippe Chanson for bringing some star power to this burg. We even got the lieutenant governor here." He gestured with the phone he was holding to an amiable, barrel-chested, middle-aged man chatting with a teen wearing a sash that read *Miss Pelican Penny Clipper*. Atop her head sat a large tiara decorated with a newspaper front page made of rhinestones.

"That's new," Maggie said, indicating the teen's outfit.

"Just growing my brand. And nothing grows a brand in Louisiana like a pageant queen with a kick-butt tiara." A firework shot into the air and exploded into a shower of gold. The crowd cheered. "Ooh, it's starting. I gotta record this for my YouTube channel."

More fireworks exploded, filling the air with noise and the sky with a rainbow of colors. Esme bounced up and down, crying out "Yay!" at each burst of color, while Xander split his attention between his friend and the fireworks.

There was a brief lull while the smoke from the pyro-technics cleared. Maggie heard a pop and looked toward the sound. A few feet away, the Chanson restaurant employees huddled around Kate as she filled plastic cups with champagne and distributed them.

Esme tugged on Maggie's hoodie sleeve. "What's the big boat doing?"

Maggie looked toward where Esme was pointing. A barge was making its slow way under the Sunshine Bridge, one of the iconic spans across the lower Mississippi. Painted in large letters on the barge's starboard side were the words *River Up*. "That's the river keeper's barge," Maggie told the kids. "They clean up the river by collecting trash that's gotten in it."

An engine's roar rose below, competing with another round of fireworks. Maggie looked down and saw Phillippe Chanson piloting his speedboat up the river. He waved to the crowd, which hooted its approval. He responded by steering a figure eight, to more cheers. Then he suddenly shot ahead at full speed. "He's going awful fast," Vanessa said.

"Too fast," Maggie said, concerned. "Give me your phone, Little E; I need to see something."

"No. I'm working here."

Maggie shot him a look, then pulled the phone from his hand, incurring an outraged squeak from the publisher. She peered at the phone's screen as it continued to record, then zoomed in and saw Phillippe struggling to control the speed-boat's throttle. Something else in the boat caught his attention, but Maggie couldn't make out what it was.

Little Earlie grabbed his phone back. "This is business. I gotta record this."

He aimed his phone at the river. The was the sound of a crash as Chanson's boat slammed into the fireworks barge. The horrified gasps and screams of onlookers were drowned out by another round of fireworks shrieking into the sky. A rocket went rogue, hurtling into the River Up trash barge and igniting its load.

"Is that part of the show?" Esme asked, confused.

"No, chère," Maggie said, fighting to keep her composure. "I'm afraid the show is over."

Chapter 7

A woman screamed. And kept screaming. Maggie looked over at the group representing Chanson's restaurant. The screams were coming from Becca.

"Help!" Trick yelled. Kate lay prostrate on the ground. "She fainted," Trick called to the crowd. "I need a doctor."

"I'm a nurse," a woman called back to him. She ran over and ministered to Kate while Luis clutched the hysterical Becca and tried to calm her down. Scooter stared straight ahead, muttering to himself, his body vibrating. Dyer scribbled on a notepad. The dock below filled with law enforcement officials shouting to each other. A plume of black smoke rose from Phillippe Chanson's speedboat, which smoldered under the spray of a fireboat. Fortuitously, two had been on hand to monitor the fireworks barge. One focused on the chef's boat while the other trained its efforts on the fiery trash barge. As if the scene weren't surreal enough, another round of rockets from the fireworks barge shot into the sky and exploded into a colorful display.

"Yay, more fireworks," Esme said, clapping her hands together.

"Cool," agreed Xander.

Maggie, anxious to get the children away from the traumatic scene as quickly as possible, marveled at their ability to compartmentalize. "Those were so big, I'm sure they're the finale. Right, Vanessa?"

"Oh, definitely," Vanessa agreed, instantly picking up the hint. "Time to go, everyone! Chop, chop."

She took Esme's hand and followed Maggie, who had Xander in tow, down the levee's slope. "Oh my lord," Vanessa said to Maggie under her breath. "This is terrible."

"I know."

"Do you think that chef is . . . ?"

She couldn't finish the question. Esme tugged on Vanessa's hand. "Can we get treats at your candy store?"

"I'm sorry, sweetie, it's closed for the night."

"We've got lots of treats at our house," Maggie said, grabbing on to the much-needed distraction. "Come on, let's get there before the ice cream melts."

"Ice cream's in the freezer," Xander said, perplexed. "Can't melt."

"It's just an expression, cher."

Maggie took Esme from Vanessa, mouthing *Thank you*. She pressed the alarm button on her set of Bo's car keys, then followed the sound until she found where he'd parked the SUV. She packed the children into the car, then checked her phone. There were texts and missed calls from Bo. Maggie called him. "Sorry I didn't get in touch sooner. I just saw your messages. It was too noisy to hear my phone on the levee and then . . . stuff happened."

"You've got the kids with you?" he asked.

"Yes."

"They okay?"

Maggie glanced at the back seat, where Esme and Xander were chatting and showing each other pictures on their phones. "Seem to be."

"Take my car home. I'll get a ride in one of the patrol cars. No idea when I'll be there."

"I figured." Maggie had a million questions for her husband, but they weren't the kind you asked in front of children and she knew he didn't have the time to answer them. "I love you."

"Love you too."

Maggie hurried the children home. While they were devouring Ninette's Sugar High Pie topped with ice cream, she called Esme's parents and Xander's mom Whitney. All were understanding and thanked her for looking after the kids, much to her relief. She shuttled the children to Xander's room, where they did "once, twice, three, shoot" to see who took the top bunk. "Yay me!" Esme crowed when she won.

Maggie tucked in Xander and Esme and retreated, closing the door behind her. Gopher lumbered down the hall with Jolie scampering behind him. The dogs assumed a prone position in front of the bedroom door as if to guard the children.

Maggie collapsed on the living room couch, unable to move. She hadn't liked Phillippe Chanson. It was obvious to her that under the veneer of casual charm lay a ruthless shark, a man who had no compunction about poaching recipes and patrons. But that didn't make his probable demise any less awful—especially for those he'd left behind. *I better let Mom and Dad know,* she thought. She checked the time: midnight. Her parents had turned in hours ago. Still, it wouldn't be the first time they got a middle-of-the-night call about a guest emergency.

She pulled her cell phone from her jeans back pocket and speed-dialed her father. He picked up on the last ring. "What's wrong?" he asked in a groggy voice.

"There was an accident." Maggie recounted the boat disaster. "Kate, Becca, Dyer, and Trick will be coming back here and in a state. Becca was hysterical. Kate fainted."

"I'll rouse your mama. We'll get coffee and snacks going. And booze."

"That'll probably go first."

Tug signed off. Maggie forced herself off the couch and into the kitchen, where she reheated a half cup of leftover coffee in the microwave. She took a sip, made a face, and downed the rest. She needed fortification.

Xander's bedroom door opened. He stuck his head out, then padded from the room in his bare feet. Without his wire-rim eyeglasses and clothed in Star Wars pajamas, he looked small and vulnerable. "Can't sleep?" Maggie asked. He shook his head. "Want some warm milk?" He nodded.

Maggie pulled a container of milk from the refrigerator and heated up a cup of it. She brought it to the couch, where Xander joined her. He took the cup and sipped. "The man," he said. "On the boat. Is he okay?"

"I don't know. I hope so."

Xander took another sip of milk. "I think he died. Do you?"

Maggie replayed the scene post-accident in her head. The boat had caught fire. While she knew first responders would have done everything in their power to save the victim, the atmosphere had quickly given the impression that it was more of a recovery than a rescue effort. She thought about how to answer her stepson's loaded question.

Xander had Asperger's syndrome. Ever since meeting him, she'd navigated their relationship with care, respectful of his boundaries. Like so many with the condition, he was extraordinarily bright. He had finally come out on the other side of a long struggle with social interaction, but Maggie was careful not to push him past his comfort zone. She debated whether to dodge the question or be honest with him.

"Tell me the truth," the boy said, as if reading her mind.

"I think," Maggie said, "he died." She saw his cup was empty and took it from him, placing it on the coffee table. "Would you like a hug?"

Xander nodded, and she wrapped her arms around him. He put his head on her chest. "Can we have cake and ice cream for breakfast?"

Maggie couldn't help a small laugh. "Yes," she said with affection. "But just this once."

After Maggie returned Xander to his room, she called on Grand-mère to babysit so she could help her parents handle the Chanson guests in the aftermath of the tragedy. "It's a good thing my A-G-E syndrome precludes a full night's sleep," Gran said as she settled into the room's comfortable club chair. She rested her slippered feet on the chair's matching leather ottoman.

Maggie covered her grandmother's lap with an afghan crocheted in Mardi Gras colors of purple, green, and gold. "If you need anything, text me."

"I'm sure I'll be fine." She held up a stack of decorating magazines, then brought them down. Her tone was serious. "Unlike those poor restaurant people."

Maggie threw on a hoodie and left her home for the manor house, using her phone as a flashlight to guide her in the darkness. The only sound in the still night came from the crunch of crushed oyster shells and decomposed granite under her feet as she trod the path linking the two locations. She found her parents in the dining room, where they'd already laid out a spread of comfort food and beverages. They heard a car drive into the B and B parking area, followed by a second car. "I'll check on them," Maggie said.

She pushed open the back door and left for the parking area, where she saw Trick helping a distraught Becca out of his BMW sedan. Dyer had already exited his economy rental car. He stood next to it, a lost look on his face. Maggie went to Trick. "Can I do anything? We set up food and coffee in the dining room for you. And drinks."

"Thanks," Trick said, "but I'm going to get Becca inside and then go to the hospital."

"Phillippe?" Maggie asked, hoping against hope.

"No. Kate's there. She's in shock. They took her to be checked out." Trick cleared his throat, but when he spoke, his voice was husky. "Phillippe's gone."

Trick helped Becca, who seemed almost catatonic, toward her room in the overseer's cottage. "I'll take a drink," Dyer said.

"Great," Maggie said, feeling guilty. She'd forgotten he was there.

She led the writer into the house, where Tug poured a healthy measure of bourbon for each of them.

"I needed this." Dyer knocked back his drink and held out his glass. Tug poured him a second round.

"Trick said Phillippe is gone." Maggie drained her own glass. "Was that a guess or fact?"

"Fact. We didn't leave until the Coast Guard showed up and verified it. It was a piece of luck those fireboats were there. They extinguished Chanson's boat as quickly as they could. But when we left, that trash barge was still burning big-time." Dyer finished his second drink and looked longingly at the bottle of bourbon. "Any chance I can buy that bottle from you?"

Tug handed it to him. "It's yours. On the house."

"Thanks." Dyer took the bottle and held it up, a rueful expression on his face. "The stereotypical image of a washed-up alcoholic writer is complete." He lowered the bottle. "I'm actually not an alcoholic. At least I wasn't until tonight." He shuffled off to the garçonnière. Ninette glanced at the late-night repast she'd laid out. "I guess I'll put all this away."

Maggie heard another car pull into the parking area. "Don't yet. That might be Bo."

A car door slammed. There was a murmur of male voices, and then the car drove off. A few moments later the back door opened and slammed shut. Bo came into the dining room. He went to his wife, kissed her, then said to his father-in-law, "Drink, please."

Tug left for a minute, then returned from the parlor bar with a fresh bottle of bourbon. "Good thing I buy these by the case."

"Are you hungry?" Maggie asked.

"Oh yeah. Disasters tend to work me up an appetite."

Maggie fixed him a plate of food, Tug poured him a drink, and the four sat down at the dining room table. Maggie was dying to ask Bo a million questions, but she made herself wait until he'd taken at least a few bites of food.

"Thanks for letting me eat a little something before hitting me with the questions, chère," he said to her with a slight grin.

"You know me too well."

Ninette passed Bo a breadbasket. He pulled out a thick hunk of baguette and used it to wipe his plate clean of remoulade sauce. "They were getting the barge fire under control when I left, but it may have created a problem for the parish. There's concern it affected the structural integrity of the bridge. We closed it off, and the state's department of engineers will inspect it first thing in the morning."

Maggie grimaced. "Oh boy. If they close that bridge, anyone who's got to commute west from here is in big trouble. Which would be me."

"The good news, if I can call it that, is that Chanson's boat didn't sink. The Coast Guard took possession of it. They'll be taking the lead on figuring out what caused the accident."

Once again, the word *accident* triggered a frisson of doubt in Maggie. *Stop it*, she scolded herself. *JJ's right, I'm becoming way too suspicious.* "Did you see any of what happened?"

"Unfortunately, no. By the time I got to the levee, the crash had happened."

"Little Earlie may have recorded it on his phone. A lot of people probably did, but he's all about getting stuff he can share on social media, so he may have zoomed in on the action."

"Thanks, cher. I'll look into it." He held up his plate to Ninette. "Ma'am, may I trouble you for seconds?"

Ninette favored her son-in-law with a warm smile. "The only trouble would be if you didn't want seconds. That would surely pain me."

While her mother filled Bo's plate, Maggie filled him in on Xander's reaction to the accident. "He asked me to be honest with him, so I was. I hope that's okay."

"Absolutely," Bo said. "If he asked for honesty, that's what he needed. I know you handled it in the best possible way."

"I told Esme's parents and Whitney to watch out for any delayed reaction from the kids, like nightmares."

Bo nodded. "Good idea. We'll do the same. The thing about kids their age is that they're resilient. Still, we'll keep a close eye on Xander."

Maggie mulled over what she'd witnessed from the levee. "When I borrowed Little E's phone to see what was going on, it looked to me like Phillippe was having some trouble with the boat. I thought the throttle might be stuck. But he seemed to get that under control. Then something else distracted him. Right before he crashed."

"Huh." Bo took this in. "I'll alert the Coast Guard. If they can identify what distracted Chanson, we might be able to figure out what caused this disaster."

Chapter 8

The next day, there was a collective heart sinking on both sides of the river when the engineers confirmed that the bridge had sustained structural damage from the fire and would be closed until further notice—*further notice* being ominous words in Louisiana. They could mean two days, two weeks—or two months. In any scenario, the bridge being out of commission meant hours-long commutes for locals. But there was cause for cheer on day two. A state senator who lived west of Baton Rouge and hated his new commute called in the favors he needed to bring a ferry back to the parish. Ferry service had once been the main form of transportation across the Mississippi. New bridges and a fatal ferry accident in the mid-1970s had doomed it to only a few locations. Longtime residents welcomed the ferry's return with nostalgia, and it offered the younger generation a chance to see for themselves what all the fuss was about.

In a less positive development, the death of celebrity chef Phillippe Chanson brought unwanted national attention to

Pelican. After Little Earlie shared his zoomed-in video of the accident with the police, he made good money selling it to multiple outlets and positioning himself as the local journalist of note. Maggie was amused when an annoyed *Penny Clipper* reader interrupted the publisher while he was pontificating for yet another news station to complain that Little E had printed the wrong date on a Laundromat coupon.

Reporters descending on Pelican to cover the story hit up Crozat for lodging, but out of deference to their guests, the B and B hung up a NO VACANCY sign. "Thank you for that," Kate Chanson said to Maggie, who was helping the restaurateur wheel a suitcase to her car for a trip to New Orleans, where the funeral and second line honoring Phillippe Chanson would be held. "I confirmed with your father to hold our rooms. We'll all be back in a couple of days."

"Are you planning to reopen the restaurant?" Thinking of JJ, Maggie selfishly hoped the answer was no.

"Oh, of course. But with Phillippe . . . gone . . . we have to recalibrate."

They reached the parking area. "I thought we'd take my car and leave yours here," Trick said.

"I'm happy not to drive," Kate said.

Trick took Kate's suitcase and hefted it into the trunk of his car, then put a proprietary hand around her waist and led her to the passenger side of the car. He and Kate had been inseparable since the accident, with Trick officially moving into Kate's suite. Dyer, who was desperate for an outlet to share all the gossip he'd collected but couldn't use about his subject, told Maggie that Trick and Phillippe's friendship went back to the low-rent Manhattan restaurant where they'd both first worked. Phillippe met Kate through Trick, who dated her until he was sidelined by Chanson's charisma and sex appeal. After the Chansons divorced, Trick wasted no time making a move on Phillippe's ex-wife. "How did Phillippe feel about that?" Maggie asked.

"Chanson didn't care. His first love was his restaurants. Many have tried, but no woman has ever successfully competed with them. If anything, I think he was relieved Trick and Kate hooked up. He needed them both to maintain his success. They each bring something different to the table. Kate has mad design and marketing skills. And Trick is way more than a mixologist. His instincts on what to say yes or no to—location, theme, menu choices—balanced Phillippe's more off-the-wall ideas."

Trick and Kate drove off, and Maggie returned to her apartment to work from home. Detouring around the closed Sunshine Bridge added an exhausting two hours to her back-and-forth from Doucet. She planned on giving the ferry a try but assumed there would be a logjam of commuters the first few days it was operational. Today, she chose to take advantage of an online archive of Doucette's historical items that local high school students had built as a computer science project. Maggie scrolled through the archive, creating a list of what she needed for a couple of future exhibits. She planned to retrieve the items from storage, evaluate their condition, and outsource restoration to the appropriate specialists. But for this, Doucet needed money, which was why seven PM found her in the Crozat parlor for the first official meeting of the Doucet Plantation gala committee.

The committee comprised Maggie's friends and family. She and Ione were the committee cochairs; Vanessa would oversee invitations and party decor; Lia and Ninette took on food and beverages; Gaynell and Sandy, entertainment. Gran had volunteered to helm the event's silent auction, which was a coup, because it was impossible to imagine anyone saying no to the Pelican doyenne when she dunned them for donations.

"How was the ferry ride over?" Maggie asked Ione once they'd all settled down with their snacks and beverages.

"Waited over an hour for a ten-minute ride," Ione reported with an eye roll. "But the ride itself was fine. We were all greeted by the captain, this Italian guy I swear was a hundred."

"That would be Antonio DiVirgilio, and he's a few years younger than me," Gran said with a hint of annoyance.

"I'm sure it's working in the sun that aged him," Ione said in an attempt to placate the octogenarian.

"Probably," Gran said, graciously acknowledging the effort. "His family is from New Orleans, but he came up our way as a teen and has been working the river ever since. I heard they called him out of retirement to pilot the ship."

"I wanna take Charli for a ride on the boat, but it'll probably involve a lotta hurling." Vanessa patted her stomach. "On my part, not hers."

"Let's get started," Maggie said, eager to dispel images of throwing up, which were making her queasy. "I put together lists of duties for each category." She handed out sheets of paper to the women. "I'll email them too. I set up a groups. net page for us to communicate and plan through. We can store files there, databases, et cetera. Basically, everything we need."

The women examined the sheets, and Maggie and Ione answered all their questions until everyone felt clear on their specific assignment. "I'm so glad we're gonna be in town for this," said Gaynell, who'd been touring recently with her band. "I've gotten friendly with a lot of New Orleans and Lafayette musicians. I'm sure some of them would love to do a slot here."

"I've got a wonderful idea on how to fill a slot," Gran said. "A senior citizen talent show."

There was silence for a minute; then the group recovered. Maggie responded with diplomacy. "We'll see how the schedule lays out, but that's definitely a possibility."

"Definitely a possibility?" Gran folded her arms across her chest and shot a look of reproach at her granddaughter. "That's lip flap if I ever heard it. I don't appreciate being patronized, chère. Nor do I appreciate what I'm sensing here is a whopping case of ageism. Just because someone is of a certain age doesn't mean one should say RIP for their talent. Plus, the seniors in our small town far outnumber the youngsters. Those who aren't living on a fixed income have disposable income, which is less true of the younger citizens, especially those with families. Seniors also have a respect for our town's history which may not have trickled down to the next gen. All that adds up to a market waiting to be tapped. And in the case of Adelia Heloise, who was a Broadway chorus girl in the 1950s, some genuine tap-dancing."

Maggie looked to Ione, who responded with a slight nod. "Gran, I think I speak for everyone here when I say go for it. The gala's entertainment will feature Gaynell and the Gator Girls, some other musicians Gaynell rounds up, and the Pelican Performers' Senior Showcase."

"The Gator Girls better go first," Gaynell said with a grin, "because that showcase will be one tough act to follow."

The women settled on the date of their next meeting, then relaxed. They chatted as they helped themselves to Ninette's Gooey Pineapple Pecan Cake and handfuls of Lia's brown-sugared pecans. "How are the Chanson's people holding up?" Ione asked Maggie. "I hate to think what it must have felt like to see that accident."

"They all went to New Orleans for the funeral. I'm going there myself tomorrow, but not for that. Bo got me the most thoughtful Valentine's Day gift—art lessons with Vi De Lavallade. The first one's tomorrow morning."

"That is something," Ione said, "I think that man of yours is a keeper."

"I drew the long straw," Maggie agreed. Her face glowed with anticipation. "I can't wait until tomorrow. It's going to be a day I never forget."

*   *   *

"Have you bought one of my paintings yet?"

This constituted Vi De Lavallade's greeting when Maggie arrived in her studio. "No," Maggie said, trying not to sound as meek as she felt. "I want to more than anything. It's not in the budget right now, but it will be."

"Well, don't wait too long." Vi took a chocolate from a large box on her desk and popped it in her mouth. "I'm in terrible health. I don't take care of myself at all. You see this box of chocolates? I'd offer you one, but it's all I plan on eating today. A palm reader once told me I have a short lifeline, and I'm doing my best to live up to that. I'll be dead sooner rather than later, and the value of my paintings will go through the roof. I thought about faking my own death to take advantage of this and then moving to a Caribbean island under an assumed name, but it's too much work. Let's see what you've got."

Maggie unwrapped the plastic protecting her painting of Xander and placed it on an easel. Vi creased her brow as she studied it. The skies had opened right after Maggie parked in a lot on the far edge of the Tulane campus. She'd managed to protect the painting as she ran to the artist's studio in the university's Woldenberg Art Center on the Newcomb Quad, but at the expense of herself. By the time she reached the gracious brick building, she was drenched. A student working in the dean's office took pity on her and dug up a space heater. Maggie stood in front of the heater in the Advanced Painting Room, shivering from both the clammy cold of her wet clothes and anticipation of the renowned artist's reaction to her work. Finally, Vi spoke. "Is this one of those custom paint-by-numbers kits? I've heard about those but never seen one before."

"No." Maggie suddenly felt sicker than Vanessa on a ferryboat. "It's all me."

"Oh." The artist didn't bother to disguise her disappointment. "Hmm." Her cell rang. She answered the call. "Jermaine, hello." She held the phone away from her ear and addressed Maggie. "My contractor in New York. I need to take this."

"Yes, sure." Maggie took the hint and stepped out of the studio into the hallway. She couldn't make out words but heard the artist speaking in an authoritarian tone, punctuated with a raised voice.

After a minute or so, the door opened. Vi crooked a finger at her. "Come." Maggie followed her back inside the studio. "I'm in the middle of my fourth divorce. Neither of us will leave our loft, so we're building a wall down the middle of it."

Having spent twelve years living in uber-expensive New York City, Maggie didn't find this strange. "I know a couple who lived in a one-bedroom apartment on the High Line. They were getting divorced and their lawyers told each of them that if they moved out of their apartment, they'd lose all claim to it. The woman woke up one night because her husband was trying to smother her with a pillow. She took out a restraining order against him—but they both still lived in the apartment."

"Ah, restraining orders." Vi said this as if talking about an old, familiar friend. "Back to your work." Vi crossed to Maggie's painting. "Technically, it's perfectly serviceable. But where's the passion? The you-ness? By that I mean, what would make it something you and only you could paint? Where people would go, now *that* is a—what's your name again?"

"Magnolia Marie Crozat. Maggie."

Vi nodded with approval. "Wonderful name for an artist."

At least she likes something about me, Maggie thought glumly.

Vi pointed at Maggie's portfolio with her phone. "Let me see your other work."

Maggie, feeling the heavy pain of the condemned, unzipped her portfolio case. Vi thumbed through the enclosed artwork. "I wasn't intending to show you these," Maggie said, hating how apologetic she sounded. "I just used the case to transport the painting here."

"These would make a nice line of greeting cards."

"I do have a line of souvenirs with these images." *I hadn't thought about cards, though. Not a bad idea.*

Vi pulled a sketch pad out of the portfolio pocket and handed it to Maggie. "No painting yet. Only sketching. I want you to sketch until you find your it."

"Sure. Great." Maggie hesitated. "How will I know when I find it? Not *that* it, *the* it."

"You'll just know it. Not the general it." Vi made a fist and thumped her heart dramatically. "*The* it."

I hate this conversation, was Maggie's internal response.

She spent an hour sketching halfheartedly, hiding her work from Vi whenever she happened to pass, which wasn't often, fortunately. The artist seemed to forget Maggie was there as she ate chocolates and yelled over the phone at a litany of those in her service, from her divorce lawyer to her New York gallery representative. The session was finally, blessedly over. "I'll be in touch about scheduling our next lesson," Maggie lied to Vi as she headed out the door.

"Stop," Vi ordered. Maggie froze. The artist took her by the shoulders and stared down from her impressive height. "Do. Not. Give. *Up*. You will find it. *Your* it." Vi accompanied this with another dramatic heart thump.

"Oh . . . okay." Maggie's tone was weak. *Darn. Now I have to come back.*

Traffic on I-10 was light, and Maggie made it home by lunchtime. Gran and Vanessa corralled her the minute she stepped out of the car. "They finished painting the guest room," Gran said, excited. "Come. You must see it."

Maggie let the women lead her to the shotgun cottage she'd shared with her grandmother, where her former bedroom had been designated the guest room. The walls, once a soft white, where now a blinding yellow. Maggie searched for a response that wouldn't telegraph her dismay. "It's so . . . bright." She tried her best to put a cheerful spin on this.

"That was the plan," Vanessa said with pride. "No matter how crummy the weather is outside, it'll be a sunny day in here."

"It's the color of the year," Gran said. "Oh so trendy. Do you like it?"

Ugh, no! Maggie thought. But beset by the insecurity of her disastrous session with Vi De Lavallade, she didn't trust her instincts. So instead she responded, "Yes. I like it."

Maggie left the cottage and trudged home. She made herself a sandwich and pulled open a package of Zapp's potato chips. Her cell phone rang as she sat down to eat. She saw the caller was Bo and hesitated. *I need to spin my session with Vi,* she thought. *He can't know that it was a big disappointment.* She formulated a response to give him if he asked about the lesson. But he didn't.

"They completed the forensics on Chanson's boat," he said. "The report shows evidence indicating someone tampered with the thermostat. With deadly results."

"Meaning . . ." Maggie said.

"That the accident was no accident."

Chapter 9

"I know zero about boating," Maggie said. "What happened to the thermostat on Chanson's boat?"

"It was installed backward, which means the heat-sensing part was on the wrong side. This led to the engine overheating and then the fire. The boat was inspected recently, and everything was up to code. Someone switched the thermostat post-inspection."

"So, it has to be someone who knows boats."

"Not really. All it takes is someone searching 'How Fires Start on Boats' on the internet. Apparently, it's an easy mistake to make. Even the pros do it. Which is why whoever did this probably assumed it would be written off as maintenance failure."

"When I borrowed Little Earlie's phone, I could see Chanson was distracted by something. It must have been the thermostat." Maggie reached for a potato chip, then stopped as a thought occurred to her that put hunger on the back burner. "If that's all it takes . . . it doesn't rule out a lot of suspects."

"Nope."

"Which means the list of people with a grudge against Phillippe Chanson would have to include JJ. And my mother."

"Law enforcement will be looking at everyone who had any issue with him."

"Way to deflect, Detective Durand."

Bo sighed. "This is going to be a joint investigation with detectives from the parish sheriff's department, the state police, the levee district police, the Coast Guard, maybe even the FBI—and us. Little Pelican PD. If you think all this man and womanpower means a quick resolution, you'd be wrong. I was on a couple of cases like this when I worked in Shreveport. It's gonna take hella coordination on everyone's parts just to keep from tripping over each other. Hey"—Bo's tone lightened as he made a purposeful change of subject—"how did it go with Vi De Lavallade today?"

"Great!" Maggie answered, hoping she didn't put too much English on the spin of her response. "She's a fascinating woman."

"Glad it's working out." Bo sounded pleased with himself. "I wanted to make the first Valentine's Day present to my wife a winner."

"Oh, it's a winner all right."

Maggie, realizing this came out totally snarky, cringed. Luckily, Bo didn't pick up on the tone in her voice. "Not sure when I'll be home, so don't wait up for me," he said. "Love you more."

"Impossible."

The couple blew kisses to each other, then ended the call. Maggie, plagued by a sense of doom, toyed with her food.

Friends and loved ones had been murder suspects before. Maggie herself had been one. She knew the horror and anxiety of facing charges for a crime you didn't commit, and the pain of people you considered friends suddenly doubting you. It was impossible to imagine Ninette resorting to such vengeful behavior. But JJ . . . if Maggie was totally honest with herself, she had to admit she could envision anger driving him to desperate lengths.

The way friends once doubted her, she now doubted a friend.

* * *

In the morning, a blunt banner headline on the front page of the *Penny Clipper* delivered the latest development in Phillippe Chanson's death to locals. "You'd think Little Earlie would come up with something a little cleverer than 'Celeb Chef Death Ruled Murder,' " Gran said.

"He doesn't have time." Maggie pointed to the kitchen television, where the publisher was once again being interviewed by a reporter from a national news show.

"I hope all this attention generates enough money for him to hire a copy editor." Gran held up the paper. "Abel's restaurant has an ad for a Valentine's Day special and it's spelled Valen*time's*."

Ninette pulled a tray of biscuits out of the oven. "The Chanson guests returned from New Orleans last night. I didn't see Becca or Dyer, but Kate said she and Trick would take breakfast in her room. Would you mind bringing it to them? I don't think my delivering it would be appropriate."

Gran grunted and tossed the newspaper aside. "Ninette, chère, you can't possibly think they consider you a suspect in this case."

Ninette split open two biscuits, added tomato slices that she sprinkled with Cajun seasoning, topped each half with a fried egg, and smothered the dish in a creamy boudin gravy. "I *was* arrested for vandalizing their restaurant and disturbing the peace."

"So was Abel Garavant," Gran said.

"Then he's a suspect too."

"I'll bring them breakfast," Maggie said, eager to end the conversation. "I'll check on Dyer and Becca too."

"Dyer texted me that he'll come by for his breakfast," Ninette said. "But check on Becca. I worry for her. I can't imagine how devastating it is to lose someone who was your mentor *and* romantic partner."

Maggie added a carafe of coffee to the breakfast tray, then headed to the carriage house. The building's front door was open, so Maggie carried the tray inside. The carriage house had been divided into two suites. One was empty; the other housed Kate and now Trick. Hands full, Maggie used her head to tap lightly on the door to the suite. "Breakfast."

Trick opened the door. "Let me get that." He took a deep inhale. "Smells fantastic."

For a moment, Maggie feared another stolen Ninette recipe. Then she reminded herself the person who might pilfer was gone.

Trick set the tray down on the room's small, round antique dining table. He took a plate and began eating. Kate, immersed in paperwork, ignored the food. "Again, I'm so sorry about your loss," Maggie said.

"Thank you," Kate said without looking up. "I'm a little distracted. We're reopening the Cajun Kitchen tonight."

The news took Maggie aback. "Oh. Well . . . I'm glad to hear that. Will Becca take over?"

"Not yet," Trick said. "We're bringing up Jerome Gravois, our *sous-chef* from Chanson's in the Quarter. He's set to take over there as executive chef in a couple of weeks. This way he'll get some experience under his belt. Becca's having a tough time emotionally." This earned an eye roll and sound of annoyance from Kate. "She is, hon. Have a little pity on her. She was in love with Phillippe."

Kate threw down her papers. "What a waste of time on her part. He didn't love her back. He didn't love anyone but himself and his restaurants, and he probably got himself killed by one of his discarded exes."

The woman's voice crackled with emotion. A shadow crossed Trick's face. Maggie wondered if they were thinking the same thing—that Kate could count herself among those discarded exes.

Kate cleared her throat. When she spoke, her tone was cold and businesslike. "Now it's up to us to keep the Phillippe Chanson brand alive or go out of business. It can be done. Look at all the fashion houses that stay alive after their namesakes die. Chanel, Valentino, Dior, Saint Laurent . . ."

"A little harder with a restaurant," Trick said.

Kate gave her head a vigorous shake. Her brunette, shoulder-length pageboy whipped back and forth. "I made sure every restaurant we opened included his name for branding. Even if the menu changed, the name always stayed the same. And here's the good news. With Phillippe dea—gone, we can talk up your drink menu. Ooh, here's an idea going forward. We separate out the bar from the restaurant and brand it on its own. Instead of mixology, we call it 'Tricksology.' Make you the face of it. We lean into that direction and slowly shift the chain's focus."

The mixologist quirked his lip in a sly smile. "I like it. A lot. To be honest, I've thought about that myself. Not necessarily replacing Phillippe as the face of the brand—"

"Why not?" Kate gave him a sultry glance. "It's a very handsome face."

Trick returned her sexy expression, then said, "Maggie, my friend, someday you'll be able to tell your friends that you were at the birth of Chanson's brilliant reimagining."

"Exciting," Maggie said politely. Finding the couple's behavior bizarre, she excused herself as quickly as possible. Kate and Trick seemed more annoyed by the star chef's death than upset by it, any hint of sadness disappearing with their brainstorming of the restaurant group's new direction.

Becca, on the other hand, was a study in grief. Her eyes were red rimmed, her face wet with tears, her hair and clothes unkempt. Maggie held her hand as the two women sat on the couch in the *sous-chef*'s room. "He was a visionary," Becca wept. "Phillippe was ahead of the curve in every trend. Farm to table? Phillippe. Plant-based entrees? Phillippe. Sustainable and locally sourced? Phillippe. He's the only chef on earth who could bring Cajun cuisine back from the culinary cemetery."

"It's not like it totally died," Maggie said, feeling defensive.

"Yes, it did. Big in the eighties, then dead everywhere but here until Phillippe." Becca burst into a fresh round of tears. "Dead. Phillippe. Oh God. I can't believe those words are in the same sentence."

Maggie pulled a tissue out of a box on the coffee table and handed it to Becca. The young woman wiped her eyes and blew her nose. "I heard they're reopening the restaurant tonight. You're not going in, are you?"

Becca shook her head. "I'm not ready. I need at least another day or two. I can't stay away too long because I need the money. But I'll be looking for another job. I can't be in the kitchen where Phillippe and I worked together. It's too painful."

"I can imagine." Maggie stood up. "I have to get to work myself. But if you need anything, let my mom or dad know. They'll be here."

"Thanks so much. I really appreciate how nice you're all being." Becca hung her head. "I haven't even processed the fact they think Phillippe was murdered. I can't deal with that now. I can't."

"Then don't. Take the time you need to heal."

Becca looked up. "The police will want to interview us all, won't they?"

"Yes," Maggie had to admit. "But don't worry about that now."

Becca nodded, her face drawn and pale. "Except . . . what if someone I know did this? What if I'm working with a murderer?"

Or what if this is all an act and the murderer is you? Maggie, ever the skeptic these days, thought but didn't say.

* * *

Maggie counted the cars in front of her in line for the ferry and said a silent prayer that she'd make it on board. She'd already sat in the line for over half an hour and was beginning to wonder if her time might be better spent making the trek up or down the river to a functional bridge. The last car from the eastern-bound trip off-loaded, and a deckhand waved the waiting cars onto the ferry's deck. Maggie was second to last. She breathed a sigh of relief and turned off her engine. Rather than sit in her car, she decided to take advantage of the full ferry experience. She got out of the Falcon and went to the boat's railing, enjoying the day's cool breeze. The wind blew the scent of cigarette smoke her way. Maggie wrinkled her noise and turned toward the odor. A grizzled, elderly man wearing a cap and windbreaker, both decorated with the state seal, leaned against the railing, smoking a cigarette. He tossed the butt in the river and doffed his cap. "*Buongiorno, signorina.* Welcome to the *Baroness Pontalba.* A fancy name for an old rust bucket." He gave the ship's railing a fond pat.

"You must be Captain DiVirgilio."

"I am indeed, young lady." He extended his hand, and Maggie shook it. "And you are?"

"Maggie Crozat."

A wide smile decorated the ferry captain's weathered face. "Maggie Crozat. Granddaughter of that heartbreaker,

Charlotte Bringier Crozat. There wasn't a young man for miles who didn't long for her affections."

"I can see that," Maggie acknowledged with a laugh.

"Well, Miss Crozat—it is Miss Crozat?"

"Ms. Crozat-Durand. I got married recently."

"Miz Crozat-Durand, why don't you join me in the pilot house for the ride?"

DiVirgilio gestured for Maggie to follow him inside and up a flight of metal steps to the ferry's pilot house. He introduced her to his engineer, then the old man positioned himself at the helm and checked the array of instruments in front of him. There was a crackling of communication, to which he responded. A moment later the ferry began its journey across the Mississippi River. "Great view, ain't it?"

Maggie gazed through the wide expanse of glass. "I love it." She reached into the tote bag she'd carried with her and pulled out her sketch pad. A lackluster drawing later, she traded the sketchbook for her phone, taking photos she hoped might inspire her. She turned her attention back to the ferry captain. "Grand-mère said you're originally from New Orleans."

DiVirgilio nodded, never taking his eyes off the river. "My family's been in Louisiana since 1866, right after the Civil War. We came over from the Naples area. There's snobbery in every culture. Here in Louisiana, it's about genealogy. In Italy, it's geography. Northern Italians look down their noses at the rest of the country. They say, 'Everything below the Po river is southern Italy.' "

"I haven't been to Italy in years. I forget exactly where the Po is."

DiVirgilio held up an arm. "My hand is northern Italy," he said, pointing to his hand. "And all the rest"—he wiggled his arm—"is southern Italy, according to the snobs. I grew up in the French Quarter. There were so many of my people living there they almost called it the Italian Quarter, you know."

"I didn't," Maggie said, embarrassed by how little she knew about her home state's history. She vowed to take a refresher course sometime. *Maybe I can do that at Tulane instead of sessions with Vi.* She quickly abandoned the thought, knowing it would disappoint Bo.

"My friends would run around the Quarter making trouble. I spent my time at the river's edge, right by Café du Monde." The ferry slowed as they approached the landing. "I love this river with all my being. But I learned early on not to trust it. It may look calm, but its current is ruthless. And sometimes deadly."

Shouts rose from below as deckhands moored the boat. "I better get back to my car," Maggie said. "Thank you so much, Captain."

His face crinkled with another smile. "Antonio. *Ci vediamo al ritorno.* I'll see you on the return."

Maggie hurried back to her car. As she drove off the ferry, she pondered Antonio's description of the river. How the calm disguised a deadly undercurrent. The same could be said of people, she thought. Possibly Phillippe Chanson's murderer. But who might that be?

She got to Doucet as a busload of tourists from New Orleans was disgorging its passengers. All thoughts of murder were tabled when Ione drafted her as a tour guide. Two part-timers had quit for other jobs when their paychecks bounced, ignoring Ione's pleas to return after replacement checks were issued. "This was been a *day*," Ione said toward the end of it. She and Maggie were taking a break, recuperating with cups of tea in her office. "I'm sorry I had to drag you down to your old job."

"No worries. I'm happy to do it." Maggie took a sip of Earl Grey. "It's a welcome change of pace from comparing my painting to better artists."

Ione sat up in her chair. She wagged a finger at Maggie. "Stop it. You're an incredibly talented artist. Don't let anyone tell you otherwise."

"Someone already did." Maggie shared the story of her ill-fated session with Vi. "I hate that I don't want to see her again."

Ione blew a raspberry. "Don't let that woman get inside your head. I've read about the great Vi de Lavallade, and she's full of herself. She probably needs to put people down to build her own self up. I bet she's jealous of you."

Maggie tried to buy into this, then gave her head a rueful shake. "No. Her approach may be harsh, but I think she's right. Something's missing in my work. I've lost my artistic edge. I've become too . . . normal."

"There's nothing wrong with normal, Maggie. Whatever normal is. I don't think it's the same for everyone."

"True."

"We cling to what gives us comfort."

"Wow." Maggie shot her friend a grin. "Profound."

Ione kicked out her legs and threw her hands in the air. "That's me. I put the *found* in *profound*. Which makes no sense but sounds good." The women laughed; then Ione said, "Oh, I almost forgot." She rose and picked up a vase of roses sunning on the windowsill. "You got more flowers from your secret admirer. They must have been delivered last night after we closed. I found them on the steps to the front door. I put the first bouquet in your studio with plenty of water."

Maggie took the vase from Ione and eyed it. "These already look half-dead. I keep forgetting to ask Bo about them. I don't see a note."

"There wasn't one this time."

Maggie's eyes met Ione's. "I don't think they're from Bo. And that's weird."

"It very much is," Ione said with concern.

Maggie's cell rang. She handed the flowers back to Ione. "It's Brianna Poche."

"That sweet little teenager? See if she wants an after-school job as a tour guide."

"Hi, Brianna," Maggie said into the phone. "What's up?"

"It's Clinton," the teen sobbed. "The police wanted to talk to him about that chef's murder. He freaked out and ran away."

Chapter 10

"What's going on?" Ione whispered. "What happened? I can hear her crying."

Maggie put a finger to her lips, then said into the phone, "It's okay, Brianna, chère. We'll get Clinton home. Take a breath and then tell me everything."

She heard the girl inhale and exhale. When she spoke, her voice was shaky. "He got a message from someone at Pelican PD that they wanted to talk to him about his job at the restaurant. He guessed the police heard about how he got fired and think he may be the one who killed the guy. He said he had to leave town before he got arrested. I tried to talk him out of it, but he wouldn't listen."

"Do you know which direction he headed?"

"South. His old girlfriend, Alexia, is a year older than him. She's a freshman at Loyola University. My brother dated an older woman. That's how cool he is." This brought on a fresh bout of tears.

"Do you and Clinton follow each other on a 'find friends' app?"

"I think so." There was a beat while Brianna checked her phone. "Yes. I can see him. He's on I-10, going towards New Orleans."

Maggie grabbed her purse with one hand, holding on to her phone with the other. "Here's what we're going to do. I'm going to start for New Orleans. I assume he's on his way to Loyola, but you're going to keep following Clinton and call me with any changes to his route."

"Thank you, ma'am. Thank you, thank you."

"Don't worry, honey. Everything's gonna be fine." Maggie disconnected the call.

"I heard most of that," Ione said. "I can't believe the boy ran away. Oh, wait," she said, her tone tart, "he's a Black male teenager getting a call from the police. I *can* believe it."

"I have to go. I'm sorry."

"Don't be. We can finish the day without you. Bring the boy home before he gets himself into serious trouble."

Maggie hurried to her car. She called Bo and explained the situation as she drove down the West River Road. "I'm the one who called Clinton," he said with a groan. "I only wanted to talk to him to get a feel for the dynamics between the other employees at the restaurant. I love the kid. I'd never see him as a suspect."

"You might not, but like you said, there are a ton of other agencies involved in this investigation. And they might."

"I swear I'll do anything to protect him. The whole force will."

"Let me talk to him first. We'll take it from there."

Maggie continued the drive toward the Crescent City, crossing the river and following route 310 North until it deposited her onto I-10 East. Brianna called to confirm Clinton was on the Loyola campus. "Which dorm?" Maggie asked.

"Biever."

"Got it."

Maggie exited the interstate at Carrollton Avenue. She made a left turn onto South Claiborne Avenue, a right on Calhoun Street, another right on Freret Street, then a left onto the campus. She parked and asked a student for directions to the dorm housing Clinton's ex, Alexia. She reached Biever after a quick walk and tugged on the door. "You can't get in without a pass," a student walking by the dorm told her. Maggie called Clinton. Like a typical teen, he didn't answer the phone call, so she texted him: *I'm outside Biever. Just me. Need to talk.* There was no response. She texted *Please* and waited. A few minutes went by; then Maggie saw the doors on one of the dorm's elevators open and Clinton emerge from it, followed by a pretty African American girl.

Clinton pulled the door open. "Hey, Maggie. Brianna get to you?"

"Yes. You've got a wonderful sister."

Clinton gave a halfhearted shrug. "You didn't have to come."

"Oh yes I did. Can we talk?" Maggie noticed the curious expression on the face of the student manning the admittance desk. "Somewhere private?"

"We can go to my room," the girl said. "My roommate's at the library."

The three got into the elevator. "You must be Alexia," Maggie said to break the tension as they rode to the third floor.

The tactic didn't work. When Alexia spoke, her tone was ice-cold. "I am."

"It's cool, Lexi," Clinton said. "Maggie's good people."

Alexia's glare told Maggie she'd have to prove this. The teen led them to the end of the hall and unlocked her door. The room was decorated in typical dorm style, one side of the room a mirror image of the other except for the personal details the occupants had added. "That's my side," Alexia said, gesturing to the right. The bed offered the only seating besides the desk chair, which Alexia took. Maggie climbed onto the bed, positioning herself under a poster of a fist made up of the words *No Justice, No Peace*. Clinton took a seat next to her.

"Bo's the one who called you," Maggie began.

"I know," Clinton said.

"He needs to talk to you about the people you worked with at Chanson's. What you saw. What you might have heard. That's it."

"I don't think so." Clinton hung his head. "I was mad when I got fired. You know how I told you I said some things I shouldn't have when the chef guy fired me? One of them was really bad."

"Stop!" Alexia held up a hand. "Don't say anything without a lawyer. Or a law student, maybe. I can run and find one."

"Lex—"

"She's right," Maggie said.

Clinton expelled a profanity. "Alexia's studying criminal justice. Did you know Black people are imprisoned five times more than whites? In some states, it's ten times more. Here in Louisiana, it's probably a zillion."

"That's awful," Maggie said. "Despicable. But we've known you and Brianna your whole lives. We adore you. I know you're scared but running away is not a good move. It looks like there's something you're running from. You have to trust Bo on this. He'll do whatever it takes to make sure you're treated fairly." Maggie took out her phone and tapped in a message. "I just texted Quentin MacIlhoney."

"The lawyer guy? Married to the big blond lady?"

Maggie suppressed a laugh. "Vanessa would pass out if she heard that, but yes." Her phone chirped an incoming text. Maggie read it as she said, "I asked him if he'd do me a favor and represent you in your meeting with Bo. He just texted back one word: 'Absolutely.' "

Clinton looked to Alexia, who give a slight nod. "Fine. I'll go home. And I'll talk to Bo."

* * *

Maggie walked Clinton to his car to make sure he didn't have second thoughts. Rather than heading straight home, she detoured to the Tulane campus, located next door to Loyola. She made her way through the campus to the art department on the chance Vi might be leading a session with students. *I'll feel better if I see that she's rough on all her students*, Maggie thought to herself. *And boy am I insecure these days.*

Maggie entered the building. The lights were on in Vi's classroom, and she heard voices coming from inside. Maggie peeked through the glass of the old door and saw several students immersed in painting. Vi strolled by a young woman whose canvas was a riot of color and intricate design. "Shayna, this is fabulous. Your passion informs every tiny line and every bold explosion of shape."

That is a pretty impressive piece, Maggie had to admit.

Vi moved from one student to another, lavishing each with praise as Maggie's ego deflated to nonexistent. She was busy mentally flagellating herself when she realized Vi was staring at her. Caught, Maggie gave a weak wave and entered the room. "Hi, sorry, I didn't want to interrupt you. I'm in town on business for the exhibit I'm curating," she lied. "I'm the art restoration specialist and exhibit director at Doucet Plantation. Basically, their resident expert. And an artist myself." She added this for the benefit of the students, who responded with polite disinterest, exacerbating her humiliation. "Anyway . . ." She turned to Vi. "As long as I'm here, I thought I'd set up my next session."

"Let me check my schedule." Vi retrieved a tablet from her desk and scrolled through a calendar app. "How's Monday?"

"Perfect. That's my day off." *It's not, but it will be now.* "Thanks. I'll let you get back to work. Nice meeting y'all." The students, absorbed in painting, assumed Maggie was Vi's responsibility and didn't respond. She let herself out of the studio and scurried from the building. "I hate myself," she groaned as she trudged back to her car.

"We all do," responded a sour-looking student who overheard her as he walked by.

In an effort to emerge from her funk, Maggie spent the ride home reminding herself of the blessings she enjoyed. A wonderful family. A lovely home. A job that not only fulfilled her but preserved history for future generations. And the old Dupois manor house she had inherited that would eventually be home to economically challenged Pelican residents. *If I have to come to terms with being a hobbyist rather than a true artist, so be it. There are a lot of ways to make your mark on the world.* Comforted by the internal dialogue, Maggie answered her cell phone when it rang in a cheerful tone.

"You sound in a good mood," Ione said.

"I convinced Clinton to go home and Quentin to be with him when he meets with Bo about the murder."

"Good job." Ione paused. "You got more flowers."

Maggie's good mood evaporated, replaced by an ominous sensation. "I did?"

"Yes. When I was closing up tonight, I found them in the employee break room. No note. Only a piece of paper that said, 'For Maggie.' Typed, not handwritten. Still red roses, at least what's left of them. They're old and withered. A couple are full-on dead. And the bouquets seem to be shrinking. Maybe your secret admirer's running out of money. Wait, there's a note this time."

"What does it say?" Maggie heard Ione rip open an envelope, then suck in a breath. "Ione?"

"It says, 'Soon.' In black marker. That's it."

Maggie's heart began to thump. "Are you near a calendar?"

"I've got one on my phone. Just opened it."

"How many days until Valentine's Day?"

Ione counted. "Six."

"Now, can you count the roses? How many are there?"

Ione muttered as she counted, then stopped. "Six." The women were silent for a moment. Then Ione said, "These aren't just flowers."

"I know," Maggie said. "They're a countdown."

Chapter 11

"This whole thing is creepy," Ione finally said.

"Yup. I'd written the flowers off as either harmless or some kind of bad joke, but the note kicks this up a notch. With everything that's been happening, I haven't even mentioned the deliveries to Bo yet. I'll talk to him about them tonight when he gets home from work."

"Who do you think might be sending them?"

Maggie took the exit off I-10 for Route 22. She headed west through swamps, the only light coming from the other cars on the road. "I don't have a clue. I'm an old married lady now."

"You're not old, and you're beautiful. But if it's a local sending the flowers, you'd think they would've come out as an admirer a lot sooner. What about the restaurant people?"

"Maybe," Maggie said, sounding doubtful.

"Run down the list."

"There's Trick, the mixologist. He's one of those general flirts, but he's involved with Kate, and from what I picked up, he's more into her than she's into him. Scooter, the restaurant's oyster guy and the only local on staff, is a hot mess. He's got more baggage than a jumbo jet cargo hold. Someone put thought into organizing the flowers and deliveries, and I can't imagine him having the focus for it. I sense zero romantic interest in me coming from Dyer, the writer working on Chanson's 'autobiography'—his sarcasm, not mine. The poor man's just trying to survive. That leaves Luis, the garde-manger chef."

"The what-ma-what?"

"Guy in charge of salads and cold foods. He's quiet. A bit of a cipher. I get the impression he wants to maintain a low profile."

"Do you think he's illegal? I don't mean it as a put-down. I only bring it up because a lot of low-level kitchen workers are."

"He's not low-level. I think the garde-manger guy is, like, third in line to the chef. But he might be undocumented." Maggie made a right turn onto the River Road, following its curves as it hugged the levee. "What would you think about me telecommuting for a couple of days? I'm feeling like maybe I should stick closer to home. I can write up the exhibit descriptions and design the program, then email everything to the printer."

"I think that's a good idea," said Ione, who lived on the west side of the river. "I can pick up whatever you order. The printer is only a few blocks from me."

"That's perfect. Thank you." Maggie reached the side road next to Crozat and turned onto it. "I'm almost at my place."

"Good." There was relief in Ione's voice. "It's probably nothing. The flowers. Some high school kid with a crush on you."

"Probably," Maggie said, wishing she believed this.

Ione signed off. Maggie parked and stepped out of the car. A text from Brianna, accompanied by hearts and kisses, let her know that Clinton was currently meeting with Bo at Pelican PD. Maggie headed toward the manor house. She stopped when she heard live music coming from the B and B's party tent. Curious, she detoured to the tent. She found a group of senior citizen musicians playing "Boogie Woogie Bugle Boy" while a group of female contemporaries—Gran included—dressed in ersatz Rosie the Riveter costumes performed a synchronized dance routine to the song. The dancers and musicians finished with a flourish to applause from Maggie.

"Break time," Gran called to the performers as they exited the dance floor with much huffing and puffing. "Union five. Help yourself to treats and sweet tea."

Gran pulled a tissue from her sleeve and patted her brow. She sat down to rest. "Brava, Gran," Maggie said. "I'm assuming this is an act for the senior talent show."

"*Mais oui.* The Rosé the Riveter Senior Marching Club invited me to become a member. They were sucking up to me, of course, to try and get a slot performing at the gala. We'll also be doing various performances for charities and events like Mardi Gras. I don't know what took me so long to sign on. I'm already having buckets of fun. Sandy did a wonderful job choreographing the number."

CAJUN KISS OF DEATH

Maggie looked in the direction Gran pointed, where she saw a stressed-out Sandy taking a slug from a flask. "I don't think that's sweet tea in there."

"Probably not. Trying to keep all of us in line is like herding geriatric cats."

Maggie looked askance at her usually elegant grandmother, now clad in a blue jumpsuit with a red bandanna wrapped around her hair. "Your new look is going to take some getting used to."

"It's *très* patriotic. And I rather like the jumpsuit. It's comfy. Like Dr. Denton pj's."

Lee, a trumpet under his arm, delivered a cookie and a cup of tea to Gran. "Here you go, madame."

"Thank you, monsieur." Gran took a dainty bite. "Now go rest." Lee kissed his wife on both cheeks and did the same to his step-granddaughter. Then he went to join the other musicians. "Older musicians need a lot of downtime between numbers. Not enough breath control, especially with the smokers."

Maggie gave her grand-mère's hand an affectionate squeeze. "I think it's wonderful you're advocating for your fellow seniors."

"Someone has to keep us from being written off as doddering our way to the grave. We still have talents, which brings me to another idea. Many of my peers are wonderful crafters. Needle arts, woodworking, sewing. I propose that we display their work for sale at the gala, with a fifty-fifty split of the proceeds between Doucet and the creator."

"Done. I love it."

Gran checked her slim gold watch, a long-ago gift from her late first husband, Maggie's grandfather. She stood up and clapped her hands together. "Break's over. Everyone on stage for 'This Joint Is Jumpin'.'"

Maggie heard a groan from Sandy and saw her take another swig from her flask.

Hungry, Maggie headed to the manor house kitchen. She passed Dyer Gossmer, who was on the phone. He ended the call and fist-pumped the air. "*Yes.*"

This was not the Eeyore of an author Maggie was used to seeing. "It looks like somebody got good news."

"Fantastic news," Dyer enthused. He made a show of tiptoeing over to her and spoke in a stage whisper. "This is a secret, but I have to tell someone. I just sold the book I really want to write about Phillippe Chanson for buckets of money. I'm off the Chanson dole. It'll be the unauthorized but a hundred percent true story, as opposed to the fluff job they were paying me to write. I'll let you know as soon as the contract is signed, and I can go public with it. I'll be paying for my own stay here, so bill me directly."

"Until the news breaks about the new book deal?"

"I'll be sticking around after that for sure. I wanna see how this whole murder thing plays out. It's the theme of the book. Who hated Chanson enough to kill him? I get to use my investigative skills again. I'm back, baby!" Gossmer conga-danced away, an odd sight that Maggie found disconcerting. *There goes a man with a strong motivation for murder*, she thought as she watched him shake imaginary maracas.

Once in the kitchen, she joined her parents for dinner at the large trestle table. "The gumbo's delicious, Mom," Maggie said, polishing off her second serving and helping herself to a third.

"Thank you. I was interviewed by a homicide detective from the St. Pierre Parish sheriff's department today."

Maggie dropped the soup ladle into the pot, where it sank to the bottom. "*What?*"

"I wondered where you were this afternoon," Tug said to his wife. "You should have told me, chère." He exchanged a worried look with his daughter.

"It came up very quickly. I think they were hoping the element of surprise might throw me off. But the detective was quite respectful, I must say. When I told him how I calibrated the temperature of this oven and how I was a bit of a savant when it comes to climate control and our old thermostat, he was quite impressed."

"Mom," Maggie said, alarmed, "please tell me you didn't."

Ninette gave her daughter a look. "Of course I didn't. But I saw that look between the two of you. Like you don't trust me to take care of myself. I'm not proud of what I did at Chanson's Cajun Kitchen, but I know enough not to blather myself into a worse position."

"Sorry, Mom," Maggie said, sheepish.

Tug echoed her apology. "When you marry the smartest, most beautiful woman in the world, you should have more faith in her."

Ninette gave him the side eye. "You saw me put a Sugar High Pie in the oven, didn't you?"

"I sure did, and I'm ready with more apologies if that's what it takes for me to get a slice straight out of the oven."

"Me too, me too," Maggie said, waving a hand in the air.

Fortified by a hefty slice of pie, Maggie left the manor house for her apartment. She almost collided with Kate, who was leaving the spa below with a bag of products. "How are you doing?" Maggie asked the late Chanson's ex-wife.

"Great. I mean," she added, backtracking, "great because of my facial with that woman, Mo. She's a genius. And her masseur is a magician. He released every knot in my back and neck." Kate circled her head, and Maggie heard crackling sounds. "Those are the calcium deposits he loosened up. I'm telling you, the pressure of losing our brand ambassador and switching from the face of Phillippe to the face of Trick—just thinking about it makes me want to march back into the spa and get another hot stone massage. But challenge that it is, it's also, I don't know . . ." She searched for the right word. "Invigorating. Yes. In the long run, I think the change will invigorate the brand." Her voice softened. For a moment Kate looked like she might cry. "But it's awful it took poor Phillippe's death to make it happen."

"Not just death," Maggie said. "Murder."

Kate paled. "That word. It's hideous. I . . . I . . . I need to go."

She hurried toward the carriage house. Maggie watched her leave, then let herself in and hiked up the stairs to her home. Xander was with his mom and stepdad, so she had the place to herself. She wondered if law enforcement had interviewed JJ yet and made a note to check with him in the morning.

She heard the downstairs door open. "Honey, I'm home," Bo called, tongue-in-cheek.

Maggie had a kiss waiting for him when he came inside the apartment. He pulled off his sport coat and tossed it on the couch, then sat down next to it. He rubbed his face with his hands. "Long day."

"You and me both."

Maggie sat next to him. Bo put an arm around her, and she rested her head on his shoulder. "Clinton and I had a chat," he said. "With Quentin hovering over us."

"As he should be."

Bo pulled away and faked a frown. "Ouch. That was a little scold-y. But noted." He chuckled. "Both of them watch too many TV police shows. Quentin was doing his best 'I *am* a lawyer and should play one on TV' act, and then Clinton announced with a lot of drama that he had a confession to make. I half expected a director to yell, 'Cut!' "

"Hoo boy. Can you tell me what he confessed?"

"Yes. Apparently when he was fired, he told the staff they'd be sorry. He says he meant that he'd punish the restaurant by telling all his friends not to eat there. Which I believe."

"I'm glad. I love those Poche kids. They're like siblings to me."

Bo rested his feet on the coffee table. "We got some other news today. CGIS—that's the Coast Guard Investigative Service—established a timeline for when someone tampered with the power boat's thermostat. The boat passed inspection before it was delivered to Chanson at two in the afternoon. There was a window between two and five when no one was in the vicinity, but from five PM on, people were going back and forth from the dock to the fireworks barge. They've all been interviewed, and no one saw any activity on the power-boat. So, if a suspect has an alibi that checks out for the hours between two and five, they're off the hook."

"Here's hoping my mom does. And JJ." Maggie turned to face Bo. "Something else is going on that I haven't had a chance to talk to you about. You haven't been sending me flowers at work, have you? Red roses?"

"No," Bo said, his voice reflecting a sense of guilt. "Does that make me a bad husband?" He sat up and pulled his feet off the coffee table. "Wait—are you telling me someone's been sending you roses? Anonymously?"

Maggie nodded. "The first one came from with a note that said they were from a secret admirer. The others didn't. And the arrangements are getting smaller. The last one only had six blooms. Valentine's Day is six days away. It's like—"

"A countdown." Bo's expression darkened. "Chère, I don't think you have an admirer. I think you have a stalker."

Chapter 12

"Tell me everything you can about these deliveries," Bo said.

Maggie did so. "Ione knows more than me. They never seem to arrive when I'm there."

"Which I'm sure is intentional." Bo stood up. "But everything is still at Doucet? Untouched by anyone except you and Ione?"

"As far as I know."

Bo paced as he talked. "I'm getting Rogert on this," he said, referencing the young detective he shared duties with. "I want him at Doucet first thing in the morning with another officer to collect the evidence. I'll get on the horn to every florist in the region to track down where the flowers came from. I'm gonna put together a list."

He pulled out his cell phone and speed-dialed Detective Rogert. "I'm feeling kind of jittery now," Maggie said. "I'm going over to the big house for a bit."

Her husband, already in conversation with Rogert, nodded, and Maggie left. She found Gran, still wearing her Rosie the Riveter costume, fixing herself a Sazerac in the manor house front parlor. "Lee's sound asleep," she said. "Blowing on that horn of his for a couple of hours knocked him right out." Gran eyed Maggie. "Are you all right? You look perturbed."

"I'm perfectly fine except for one of our guests might be a killer, I may have a stalker, Doucet is in trouble, and I've lost whatever artistic talent I once had."

"Hmm . . ." Gran pulled a bottle of bourbon from behind the bar. She poured a shot into a whiskey tumbler, considered it for a minute, then poured another shot into the glass. "Come." She motioned for Maggie to follow her. The women took a seat on the room's antique sofa, upholstered in a rich burgundy velvet, stepping over Gopher, who was splayed out in front of it. "Talk to me."

Maggie poured out her fears and frustrations to her beloved grand-mère, touching on everything from her worry about loved ones being suspects in Phillippe Chanson's murder to the nerve-racking mystery of the red roses. "And there's Vi putting down my artwork. I know that's the least important thing going on right now. I'm trying not to let it bother me. But it does."

"I'm going to put a hard question to you." Gran looked her granddaughter in the eye. "Do you think this Vi person is right?"

Emotion welled up in Maggie. She closed her eyes and scrunched her face to keep from bursting into tears. Gopher, as if sensing his human's pain, released a sympathetic basset howl. Maggie inhaled a deep breath, exhaled it, then opened her eyes and met her grandmother's glance. "Yes. I do think she's right."

"Well, then. . ." Gran took a sip of her drink. ". . .Let's evaluate the situation. Or situations, as it were. When it comes to that poor chef's murder, there are a bajillion, as the kids say, law enforcement agencies tripping over each other to solve the case, so I believe it's best if you stay out of their way. As to Doucet, you're doing everything humanly possible to save it. Regarding your flower-delivering fan—or fanatic, more likely—we know that handsome husband of yours will do everything humanly possible to ferret him out. Or her. You never know these days, do you? And as to finding your 'it,' whatever *that* means—I have no patience with those kinds of pretentious statements. The expression *A watched pot never boils* comes to mind."

"That expression never made sense to me. Watching a pot doesn't stop it from boiling."

"Focus, please," Gran said in a stern tone. "What I mean is that obsessively thinking, 'I need to be better,' will not make you better. Let that go. Your 'it' will come to you, I promise. Instead of focusing on what you can't do, focus on what you *can* do. Which is . . ." she prompted.

"Support my friends," Maggie said with conviction. "I keep thinking I should check on JJ, but I haven't done it yet. That's going to the top of my agenda tomorrow."

"There you go." Gran raised her glass to her granddaughter.

Maggie rose from the sofa. "Bo's going to be busy the rest of the evening. I'm on my own schedule for a couple of days, so I'll spend tonight finishing work assignments and take tomorrow as a personal day." She bent down to hug her grandmother. "I love you so much."

"I love you more."

"Impossible," Maggie said with affection.

* * *

In the morning, Maggie was relieved to learn that Ninette's alibi had checked out. "Thank goodness I got into that long discussion at the grocery store with the seafood department manager about how imported oysters don't stack up to our local species," Ninette said, while the family had their breakfast after serving their guests. "The market even has me on the security tape. If I'd known law enforcement would be looking at the tape, I would have put on makeup."

After breakfast, Maggie texted JJ. Half an hour went by without a response. She followed up with a phone call. Still no response. Worried, Maggie decided a welfare check was in order.

The day was drizzly and overcast. Maggie put on fleece leggings, a mustard cable-knit tunic sweater, and a pair of purple fleece-lined boots and set out for her friend's house.

JJ still lived in the homey cottage where he'd grown up, next to a grassy field that abutted Bayou Beurre. Maggie parked on the road in front of the house. A couple of mutts who lived next door ran over to her, barking the whole way. They stopped and engaged in an active sniff of her leggings and boots. After a minute, they grew bored and sauntered away.

Maggie walked up the stone path that led to the house and knocked on the front door. A breeze set the porch swing swaying back and forth. "JJ?" she called. "It's me. Maggie."

She waited a few minutes, then knocked and called to him again. She was about to give up when she heard footsteps. The door opened.

"Hey," JJ said. His round face was devoid of makeup and his short, light-brown hair lacked the usual accessories. Instead of jeans, he now wore sweat pants, indicating a further decline into depression. *This is bad*, Maggie thought. But she forced a smile.

"Hey yourself. I tried calling and texting but didn't hear back, so I thought I'd take a chance and drive over."

"I was on the phone with the insurance company. Come on in."

Maggie stepped into JJ's living room, a small, tidy space decorated with furniture that, as in so many Pelican homes, had been in the family for generations. JJ's collection of Jazz Fest posters lined three walls, their bright graphics adding a contemporary touch to the room. A large flat-screen TV decorated the fourth wall. "Come in the kitchen. I'll fix us coffee."

JJ had recently remodeled the kitchen, updating the appliances to stainless steel while keeping the traditional white beadboard wainscoting. He poured himself and Maggie coffee. "I'm gonna get reimbursed by insurance for the bathroom repair at Junie's, so I should be able to reopen in a few days."

"JJ, that's great."

JJ gave a lackluster shrug. "Don't know who's gonna come back after what happened."

"You know all the locals will."

"I can't survive on just locals. I need tourists too. And they'll all be going to Chanson's, even with him gone. Maybe because of that. The nosy factor. They're adding music and a dance floor. Did you know that?"

"No," Maggie said. Kate and Trick were certainly doing an aggressive pivot from the star-chef emphasis.

"I can't compete with them."

"Yes you can, JJ." Maggie spoke with determination. "We'll make sure of it." She used her hands to paint a picture. "I see a grand reopening with special musical guests Gaynell and the Gator Girls. Your menu laid out buffet-style for the party. By invitation only, meaning anybody who didn't get one will be dying to get in. Word will get out that"—Maggie did jazz hands—"Junie's is back and better than ever!"

Maggie's attempt to cheer up JJ didn't work. He glanced down at his mug. "A detective from the sheriff's office interviewed me. I don't have an alibi for the time he was talking about. Sulking at home by myself don't count." He made a weak attempt to sound like he was joking.

"Lack of an alibi isn't evidence against you, JJ."

JJ put his untouched mug on the counter. "No, but this is. I got in a fight with Chanson in the alley. He was walking by when I was throwing out the rodent droppings. I called him over to look at them. I blamed him or his people; he laughed and said I must be high to think that. I got yelling, and he pulled out his phone to record me. I went for the phone. He pushed me off and stopped recording, but he got everything up until then. Including me saying if he ever came near Junie's again, I'd make sure he'd rue the day. I was proud of myself for that one because I used the word *rue*, like it was *roux*. A play on words I made sure he got. I'm in trouble, Maggie."

"You're assuming his phone survived the fire."

"The way the detective was talking to me, sure sounded like it did."

"Well . . ." Maggie digested this; then a thought occurred to her. "I bet it was password protected. And had two-factor authentication. Everything does now. A password and a fingerprint or facial recognition. I think there's a window that closes on being able to bypass those and get into a phone." Maggie did a quick search on her own phone. "I'm right. There's a seventy-two hour window. See? And Phillippe's been gone longer than that." She handed the phone to JJ.

"That would certainly ease my mind," he said, reading. "Hold on. This article's four years old. That's Jurassic when it comes to technology."

Maggie released a profanity. "Let me find a more recent article." She took back her phone and entered a search. She scrolled through it with increasing annoyance, then let loose another profanity and gave up. "Why is it you can never find the one thing you're looking for on the internet?"

"You tried. Thanks for that. It's truly appreciated."

Maggie pocketed her phone. "When I was going through a rough stretch in New York, I saw a therapist. I told her I was trying to do better, and you know what she said? 'Try is a fail word.' "

"How so?" JJ asked, confused.

"Because it gives you an out. It implies you may not succeed. I don't want to 'try' and help you, JJ. I want to do it. And succeed. Pelican needs Junie's. And we all need our friend." Maggie gently poked him in the chest. "Who is *you.*"

JJ managed a smile. "You're a blessing, that's for sure."

"We'll see about that. If nothing else, maybe I can suss out who tried to put you out of business."

"You said 'try' is a fail word," JJ said, showing a glimmer of usual sense of humor.

"And"—Maggie gave her friend another affectionate poke—"we'll show them they failed."

* * *

Now on a mission, Maggie headed into Pelican. Unable to find a parking spot in the village center, she parked blocks away and walked to Chanson's Cajun Kitchen. She got a pang of sadness as she passed the shuttered Junie's Oyster Bar and Dance Hall. The sight increased her determination, and her steps became more purposeful. She opened the door to Chanson's, and the white noise of a crowded restaurant greeted her. Every table was taken, mostly by people Maggie didn't recognize and assumed were tourists. She did see a few familiar faces, locals whose loyalty to their stomachs outweighed their support for JJ. She took in the restaurant's layout and saw he was right; Chanson's had carved out space for music and dancing.

"Need a table?"

Maggie turned in the direction of the question and saw Dyer seated at a two-top, a tablet with a keyboard and an empty plate in front of him. "Oh hi, Dyer. Thanks." She took the seat across from him. "I didn't expect the restaurant to be this crowded."

"Lunch special." The writer pointed to a postcard on a stanchion advertising a low-cost array of lunch choices. "Also, they're short-staffed, so food's coming out slower, meaning people are sitting longer."

Maggie saw a frazzled Kate, a black butcher's apron over her designer jumpsuit, deliver an order to a table, then move on to take an order. "Kate's waiting on tables, so they must be super short-staffed. I don't see her as someone who'd do that unless she was forced to."

"Nope. She hates it." Dyer leaned toward her and spoke in a whisper. "FYI, word's not out yet on my new contract. Kate and crew think I'm still on Operation Whitewash Phillippe Chanson. But"—he lowered his voice even more—"I've got a lead on some possible criminal activity that could have led to his death if he knew about it." He favored Maggie with a sly smile. "The money's on me being the one who breaks this case wide open."

The author's arrogance concerned Maggie. "Dyer, be careful. Unfortunately for my family, we've had some experience with murder."

"I know. I want your family's story—make that stories, plural times however many bodies—to be my follow-up true-crime book."

"Oh, a *hard* no on that. The thing is, trying to solve a murder is a dangerous business. Believe me, I speak from experience. Whatever you've uncovered, you should share with the police. Let them take it from here."

Dyer released an annoyed breath. "Do you have any idea who I am? Or was, before the internet scorched-earth annihilation of the printed word? I've been embedded with troops in Iraq. Gone undercover to expose political corruption in DC. Been nominated for the Pulitzer Prize—twice. I think I can handle a couple of inbred deplorables running a scam in backwoods Louisiana."

The writer rose, threw some money on the table, and exited the restaurant. *That was insulting on so many levels,* Maggie thought.

A very pregnant young woman came into the restaurant, accompanied by her attentive husband. Noticing an empty seat at the bar, Maggie gave them her table, which generated profuse thanks. She went to the bar and grabbed the one empty stool. Trick, who was pulling a draft beer, gave her a nod. "Hi. Didn't expect to see you here."

His tone was polite but with an edge that made Maggie nervous. Gran was right. She couldn't interfere with law enforcement's investigation into Phillippe Chanson's murder. The only way she could hunt for clues that might steer the murder investigation away from JJ was to employ talents not utilized by the professional agencies. Chanson's Cajun Kitchen was the most likely place to begin her search, but if she was going to spend time at the restaurant, she needed a good reason for doing so. She remembered the sketchbook in her purse and pulled it out. "I'm studying with the artist Vi De Lavallade. I'm supposed to be sketching, and I figured a restaurant's a good place for people watching. And doing some sketches."

To her relief, this explanation assuaged the mixologist. "Ah, got it," he said, the edge in his voice gone. He delivered the beer to a patron, then took a whiskey tumbler and began measuring liquors into it.

"Why didn't you expect to see me?" Maggie asked. "Because of my mom? She's sorry she blew up like that. She knows it wasn't appropriate."

Trick added a block of ice to the tumbler and gave the drink a gentle stir. "Truthfully, I can't say I blame her. Or the other guy who went postal on Phil. Stealing recipes was one of his less likable traits. Didn't make him too popular with his fellow chefs, that's for sure."

"But you guys were friends for years."

"Uh-huh," Trick said, his tone vague. He finished stirring and pushed the glass toward Maggie and gave her a sexy smile. "The Cajun Country Mystery. One of my own recipes. *Laissez les bon temps rouler.*"

Maggie took a sip and coughed. Her eyes watered. "It's good," she gasped. "But *strong.*"

Another customer hailed Trick. Maggie pondered what she'd just learned. The mixologist hardly seemed broken up about his supposed close friend's death. He'd highlighted the fact that Chanson's itchy recipe fingers had made him many enemies. Was he trying to deflect attention away from himself? He was possessive of Kate, yet he'd definitely been flirty with Maggie. Was he the kind of guy who flirted with everyone, or was he in a relationship of convenience with Kate and shopping around? Maggie took another sip of her Cajun Country Mystery, choked, and decided sketching was a better option than day drinking. She did a desultory rendition of Trick as he exchanged sultry glances with a pretty twentysomething who had bellied up to the bar. But Maggie noticed he turned off the charm as soon as his back was to the woman, making it obvious that flirtation was the mixologist's stock in trade. Judging by the tip the woman left behind after being served, the strategy worked.

There was a roar from the lunch crowd and then applause. Maggie adjusted her position and saw Scooter toss an oyster in the air, catch it behind his back, then open it with lightning speed. Maggie, fascinated, spent twenty minutes sketching the oyster shucker in action. Finally, Scooter threw his hands in the air like a triumphant prizefighter and took an exaggerated bow. "Thank you, thank you." He pulled off his bandanna and used it to wipe off the sweat that poured down his face, making his neck tattoos glisten. "I'll be back after a brief break. Rock on, peeps!"

Scooter disappeared into the kitchen. Kate approached Trick with a bar tray. "Two Pimm's Cups, a Gin Fizz, and a club soda. Hi." She directed the greeting toward Maggie.

"Hi. You look dead on your feet." Maggie winced. "Sorry. Poor word choice."

"Don't apologize; you're right. I am." Kate blew a stray hair off her face. "Half our waitstaff quit in solidarity with that Clinton kid."

Good for them, Maggie thought.

"I'm trying to hire replacements, but the local pool is small, as in nonexistent. I may have to bring a couple of waiters up from New Orleans, but that's expensive." Kate sounded near tears. "It's a big problem."

Maggie sat up straight on her barstool. The universe had dropped into her lap the perfect opportunity to ingratiate herself with the Chanson staff and do some high-level snooping. "I'll do it," she said. "I'll waitress for you."

Chapter 13

Kate eyed Maggie with skepticism. "I know I'm low on options, but I don't have time to train someone. I need experience."

"I wait on our guests at the B and B all the time." This didn't impress Kate. Seeing the opportunity slipping away, Maggie lied, "And I waitressed in college. In New York. Brooklyn. A tough crowd. Very tough."

Kate relaxed. "Oh. Yeah, the Brooklyn customers can be rough. But don't you have a full-time job?"

"I'm taking a couple of days off. If you need me after that, I can do the night shift here."

A patron called to Kate for his check. "You're hired," she said to Maggie. "Apron is in the kitchen. There's a tablet in the pocket."

"A . . . tablet?" Maggie paled. She'd seen the tech device at restaurants, and they looked intimidating.

"Ugh, right, you waitressed back in the last century. Yes, a tablet. Order goes to a monitor in the kitchen, bill goes to Trick here." Trick gave an amused salute. Kate craned her neck toward the door and uttered an epithet. "Party of six walked in. Go, go!"

Maggie scurried into the kitchen, where she donned her uniform of apron and tablet. She took a deep breath and marched onto the restaurant floor.

The next two hours were a blur of taking orders, delivering food, apologizing for delivering the wrong food, delivering drinks, and apologizing for delivering the wrong drinks. Watching the kitchen staff in action gave Maggie a new respect for all of them. They worked at their stations without a break and with laser focus, producing dish after perfect dish. Finally, blessedly, lunch service was over, heralding a welcome break before dinner service. Maggie bussed a four-top, clearing it of a mess left behind by a couple with two hyperactive children. She picked up some loose change and cursed. "Seventy-five cents on a sixty-dollar check? I know these people. They're getting a spitter on their next visit."

Becca, who'd come out of the kitchen with the rest of the kitchen staff and was nursing a drink at the bar, gave a weary smile. "Working for tips is the worst. One of the waiters at our New York place once got left a MetroCard on a two-hundred-dollar check. He went to use it and it was empty."

"Considering a new MetroCard costs a buck, he still did better than me." Maggie brought her bin of dirty dishes into the kitchen for the dishwasher, then went back to the dining room and collapsed into a chair.

"Get some rest before the dinner shift," Luis advised. He picked up an unused napkin. Pushing back his black hair, he swiped the napkin over his damp, dark skin. "I know that's what I'm gonna do."

Maggie, exhausted, drove home to follow Luis's advice. The hectic afternoon gave her no time to commingle with her Chanson coworkers. She knew from JJ that restaurant staff often caught a drink together at the end of the night to unwind. She'd take a nap, serve dinner, and suggest a nightcap if no one else offered the idea.

As soon as she reached the apartment, Maggie fell into bed. Agile little Chi mix Jolie jumped onto the bed, snuggled into the curve of Maggie's back, and passed out alongside her. Maggie woke up an hour later to the sound of a voice gently calling, "Chère? Chère?" She rubbed her eyes. Bo stood over here. "You all right? You're not a big napper. Are you coming down with something?"

"No." Maggie yawned and stretched. She planted her feet on the floor with a groan, feeling every minute of the lunch shift on her body. "It's a long story, but I waitressed at Chanson's this afternoon."

Bo raised an eyebrow. "Go on."

Maggie limped to the bathroom, where she splashed water on her face. "JJ's in a bad way. Kate needed an extra hand. A few of them, really. I thought if I spent time with the restaurant staff, I could at least pick up some intel about who sabotaged Junie's."

Bo assumed a thoughtful expression. "Hmm . . . I'm trying to remember when we hired you as an undercover agent."

Maggie gave her husband a playful swat. "I'll be careful. I might be able to dig up something you can use. People reveal stuff in a casual setting that they hold back during an interrogation."

"Oh, now you're a criminal behavior expert."

"You know I'm right."

The couple left the bedroom for the kitchen. Bo took a can of beer out of the refrigerator while Maggie reheated a cup of coffee in the microwave. "I've got a stalker update," Bo said, now serious.

This gave Maggie a jolt. "I was so busy today I forgot about that."

"You can bet I haven't—and won't, until I've locked up whoever it is. We traced the flowers to three different florists in the parish—not the shops. Their drivers. It's the same story with all three of them. The delivery guys admitted that they found the arrangements next to their trucks with fifty-dollar tips and delivery instructions."

"But the shops didn't sell the flowers?" Maggie asked, confused.

"No. We think the suspect bought them at different grocery stores in the area. A person is way less memorable going through a grocery line than buying one-on-one from a florist. We're checking with cashiers, but the fact it's so close to Valentine's Day makes it hard for someone buying a dozen roses, more or less, to stand out."

"Whoever's doing this put a lot of thought into it."

Maggie drained her cup. But the buzz she felt wasn't from the coffee. It was from fear. Her cell chimed with a text alert.

She checked and saw a message from Vi: *Need you to come tomorrow. 10 a.m. Bring bottle of single malt scotch. And talent.*

Maggie's face fell. Bo noticed. Concerned, he asked, "What's wrong?"

Caught, Maggie faked a smile. "Nothing. I mean, I thought it was bad news, but it's good news," she tap-danced. "That was from Vi. I was afraid she needed to cancel our next lesson, but she just wants to move it up to tomorrow morning."

Bo's expression cleared, happiness replacing worry. "I did good, huh?" he said, with a touch of self-satisfaction.

Maggie, amused by the rare sight of her husband puffed up, kissed him. "You did *great.*"

* * *

Bo had eagerly returned the kiss, but Maggie was forced to put the brakes on their romantic interlude when she remembered the Doucet gala committee was scheduled to meet at Crozat that evening. She texted the committee members a change of location to Chanson's, explaining that she would be waitressing. The question marks she got in response to the odd situation were answered with a simple text of *Helping JJ*.

The women met up at the restaurant at five, before the dinner rush began. "You didn't get any more flowers today," Ione whispered to Maggie as they settled in for the meeting.

"Maybe whoever's been sending them heard the police were looking into it," Maggie said. "Here's hoping that scared them off."

"I'm sure it did," Ione said with a conviction Maggie knew her friend didn't feel, because she didn't feel it either. Ione pulled a folder out of her tote bag. "All righty, let's get subcommittee updates. Refreshments?"

"We'll be supplying all the sweets," said Lia, Fais Dough Dough and Bon Bon proprietor.

"And I've got an army of food donations lined up," Ninette said. "Appetizers, casseroles, gumbos, jambalayas. It's gonna be a feast."

"Good to know," Vanessa said. She helped herself to a fistful of popcorn shrimp. "I'm eating for two now. 'Least that's the excuse I'm using until I pop out Quentin or Quentina Junior."

Ione shot her a look. "Tell me you're not really gonna name some poor child Quentina."

" 'Course not. If it's a girl, she's gonna be Tookie. After my mama." Vanessa pressed her lips together to keep from crying. Her mother, a tiny, peppery airboat operator rarely seen without a cigarette dangling from her leathery lips, had recently passed away from lung cancer. Maggie and the other women murmured condolences and support.

Ione gently pivoted focus back to the meeting. She went down her list, getting updates on invitations, decor, and entertainment. "Charlotte," she said to Grand-mère, "how's it going with procuring silent-auction items?"

"I have a big announcement on that score." Gran fluffed her silver hair. She couldn't have looked more pleased with herself. "Lee had some . . . plumbing issues . . . so we paid a visit to his urologist, Dr. Berg in Ville Platte. I'm pleased to share that the good doctor has kindly offered to donate an incredibly special procedure to our cause—a vasectomy."

There was a collective jaw-drop, and then the women burst into laughter. "Brilliant." Gaynell wiped tears from her eyes as she chortled. "I bet that raises a ton of money—from *wives*."

"Can we bid on it for someone else?" Ione said, laughing so hard she developed a case of hiccups. "Because I can think of a few people who'd be doing the world a service by undergoing the procedure."

"Stop," Vanessa begged. "I'm gonna laugh this baby out of me right here."

"You can't." Maggie gasped for air as she laughed uncontrollably. "I'll get stuck cleaning up after you."

"My goodness," Gran said. "If I had known the reaction this would generate, I'd have asked Dr. Berg to donate two vasectomies."

This engendered more peals. "We're only laughing because she said the word *vasectomy*," Lia snorted. "How old are we?"

There was a sudden wall of sound. Maggie glanced toward the front of the restaurant. A tour bus had disgorged its load of passengers. Kate and Lisa, the one waitress the restaurateur had managed to hold on to, frantically tried to seat them all. Kate caught Maggie's eye and mouthed, "Help!"

"Sorry, all," Maggie said to her friends. "I've been summoned."

Maggie spent almost two hours trying to prove to herself and her customers that she wasn't a terrible waitress. She failed. But the tourists were good-natured and big drinkers, which helped ease Maggie's embarrassment about her ineptitude. Unlike her, Scooter was in his element, putting on an oyster-shucking show he could have taken on the road. Orders delivered and a lull in new arrivals allowed Maggie a short break. She staggered over to her friends, picked up an almost-empty pitcher of Pimm's Cups, and gulped the dregs of it. "Y'all didn't have to stick around, but it was nice knowing I have friends here. Lord knows I wasn't making any from the customers, and I don't blame them."

"We're having a fun time watching the oyster guy," Gaynell said. "We got the table closest to him. I'm like to leave here covered in oyster juice."

Scooter juggled two oysters to roars of approval from the patrons.

Maggie took another gulp from the pitcher. "At least someone here knows what they're doing."

"You have many talents, chère," Gran said in a comforting voice. "But best to leave waitressing to the professionals."

"I think what Maggie's doing to help JJ is awesome," Vanessa said. "It's like that show where bosses go undercover, only it's Maggie." She spread her hands to mime a marquee. "*Undercover PI.* And this episode is called 'To Catch a Killer.' "

An oyster clattered to the floor. Scooter's work glove slipped off, following the oyster onto the floor. He clutched his left hand and yelled profanities. Diners watched horrified as blood shot out of a wound caused by the shucker missing the oyster and instead impaling his now-naked hand.

Chapter 14

Maggie grabbed a napkin and rushed it to Scooter. Groaning and cursing, he wrapped the napkin around his injured hand. Kate ran to him. "Scooter, what in the—" She finished the sentence with a string of epithets that brought a *whoa* from a patron wearing a United States Marines baseball cap. "This never would have happened if you weren't showing off."

Kate pulled another napkin off a table to replace the one Scooter's blood had already soaked through. He mumbled something Maggie couldn't make out.

"Great, you probably need stitches." Kate didn't bother masking her annoyance. "You better get to the hospital."

"I can't drive my truck." Scooter, wincing, held up his hand.

Kate released an aggravated grunt. "God forbid they should have something useful like a rideshare in the boonies here."

"Not quite the way to endear yourself to the community," Gran said, affronted.

Kate ushered Scooter to the door. "Trick, hold down the fort," she called. "And Maggie . . . try not to chase off too many customers with lousy service." She pushed Scooter out of the restaurant.

"Looks like the gala committee meeting's adjourned," Maggie said to her friends. "I'll see you all tomorrow. If I survive tonight."

Fortunately, the dinner crowd thinned after the shucking debacle. With some side coaching from Lisa, Maggie transformed into a passable waitress. She fell into a rhythm that even allowed for a bit of musing about the night's turn of events. Maggie replayed Scooter's accident in her mind. It had come right after Vanessa announced the joke title for an imaginary episode of an undercover PI show. Was that coincidence? Or had "To Catch a Killer" triggered Scooter's loss of control? He'd been nothing but confident—to the point of arrogance—until then. Why the sudden change?

"Closin' time," Trick announced after the last table of customers finished dessert and headed out. He locked the door behind them. The waitstaff bused and cleaned the dining room. Maggie transferred dirty dishes to the kitchen, where the chefs and assistants were busy cleaning their own areas and storing all foodstuff. She returned to the dining room and pulled all the linens, depositing them in a pile by the door for the linen service. Lisa departed amidst a shower of profuse thanks from Maggie. Becca and Luis straggled out of the kitchen and plopped down at a table. "I'm closing out the register," Trick said. "Anyone besides you two left in the back?"

"Jerome and the others are gone, so only Lawton's still here," Becca said, referencing the dishwasher. "As soon as he finishes running the last batch of dirties, he's taking off too." Trick tapped on a computer screen. "I'm going to the hospital to see how Scooter's doing. If you want a drink, fix yourselves something and then lock up for me."

Trick left for the hospital. Becca stood up and stretched. "Ugh, I so don't feel like hanging out here." She made a face. "This town is so boring. Usually when the dinner shift's over, we go to another restaurant to have a drink, do a tasting. Chefs like to show off. Sometimes it's the reverse—people come to us. But there's nowhere to go here."

"There would be if Junie's wasn't closed," Maggie pointed out, hoping for a reaction to the mention of Junie's. Neither Becca nor Luis bit. Her opportunity to hang out with Chanson employees and hopefully pick up some gossip was fading fast. "We can have a drink at our place. Crozat. We've got a full bar and a fridge full of my mother's fine leftovers."

Becca evaluated this option. "Sounds good to me. Added advantage of not having to get behind the wheel after a drink."

"Thanks, but I'll pass," Luis said. "Long day. I'm fried."

"Speaking of fried," Becca said, "if Scooter can't do his thing tomorrow, we should put a fried oyster po' boy on the menu. Put his stock to use so it doesn't go bad."

"Good idea. Run it by Kate."

"Why should I run it by her?" Becca snapped. "If I had to run it by anyone, it would be Chef Jerome, but he's cool with whatever I say. He knows I'm next in line."

"Sorry. Didn't mean to insult you."

While Luis's words were apologetic, Maggie picked up a definite undercurrent of hostility, with a hint of a sneer. But Becca didn't seem to notice. "I'll lock up here," she said to Maggie, "and meet you at your place."

Maggie left for the B and B. She stopped in the kitchen, where she warmed up two slices of Sugar High Pie. She added a dollop of fresh whipped cream to each plate and brought them into the front parlor to wait for Becca. The *sous-chef* arrived a few minutes later, still wearing her chef coat. Maggie welcomed her with the piece of pie. "This looks good," Becca said. She fell into one of the room's comfortable club chairs, upholstered in a dusty rose damask, and dug into the pie.

"What would you like to drink? FYI, there's a dash of bourbon in the pie," Maggie said.

"Then I'll have a bourbon, on the rocks."

"You got it."

Maggie fixed two bourbons on the rocks. She handed one to Becca, then, with her own drink and pie in hand, took a seat on the sofa opposite her guest. "How are you doing with everything? You seem like you're feeling a little better."

"A little. Not much. But I have to power through the grief." Becca washed down a forkful of pie with a slug of bourbon. "It's so strange being in the kitchen without Phillippe." She rested her fork on the plate and grew contemplative. "I've spent my whole career with the Chanson Group. He recruited me from the Culinary Institute and trained me. And then . . ."

She paused, overcome with a wave of emotion. "You fell in love," Maggie prompted.

Becca nodded. "He and Kate have been divorced, like, ten years or something, so I wasn't Phillippe's first 'kitchen wench.' " She said this with a sad half smile. "That's what he called me. His kitchen wench. He was a true genius, you know. I learned so much from him."

"Hopefully not how to steal recipes," Maggie felt compelled to say. "I should tell you that if my mother's Sugar High Pie ever ends up on a Chanson menu, the group will be out one *sous-chef.*"

Becca quirked her lip. "Noted."

"Now that I've worked at Chanson's, I have to say, I noticed some drama with y'all."

"No more than at any restaurant," the *sous-chef* said, sounding defensive. Maggie had a feeling this wasn't true but let Becca continue. "Trick and Kate are a couple, but even though he and Phillippe were besties, Trick's always been threatened by Kate and Philippe's connection. It kind of bugs me too. I don't understand how you can divorce someone and still need them so much. Kate says it's all about business. Trick calls it codependent." Becca was now all in on dishing about her coworkers. "Luis is basically ticked off twenty-four/seven because he was supposed to move up to *sous-chef* when I move up to executive chef, but Phillippe told him he's not ready to make the move. Between us, Phillippe wasn't sure he'd ever be. Luis would love to look for another job, but he's DACA. Phillippe kept promising to hire an immigration lawyer who'd help him with his case, but he never got around to it, which is another reason Luis has a serious attitude problem. And then there's Scooter." Becca punctuated this with an exaggerated eye roll. "He's the newest addition to the group. But what a head case."

Having failed to generate any useful tells by dropping Junie's name earlier, Maggie opted to take a blunt approach this time. "So which one of your group framed Junie's for health violations and got the competition shut down?"

Becca gaped at her. "Is that what you think? It was one of us? You think someone who works with one of the most successful restaurant groups in the country was threatened by a local dive restaurant?" Her tone was derisive.

"Junie's is not a dive," Maggie said, bristling. "It's world famous for being one of the best and most authentic Cajun restaurants in the state."

"Oh, please." Becca's tone was the vocal equivalent of an eye roll. "If it makes you feel better, it wasn't me who got Junie's in trouble. I can't see Luis ever doing anything like that because he lives in fear of being sent back to whatever you-know-what-hole country he comes from. I could maybe see Scooter doing it as a goof or a dare because he's such a nutjob, but even that is, like, a total reach."

"You didn't mention Kate or Trick."

"Because I don't have to." Becca hesitated. "I mean, yes, they need Chanson's Cajun Kitchen to work. Some of the other restaurants in the group are getting a little, I don't know . . . stale? They're hoping if this one is a hit, they can raise money to turn it into a national chain. But they'd never do something as desperate as setting up a competitor to fail an inspection."

Or would they? Maggie thought.

"Sorry, but you'll have to stick your nose into someone else's business to solve that little mystery." Becca scraped her plate and licked the fork, then finished her drink. "Thanks for the drink and snack. I'm whipped. I'm gonna crash. Should I put the dirties in the kitchen?"

"I'll take care of it."

Becca departed for her room. Maggie brought the plates and glasses into the kitchen, loading them into the dishwasher. Feeling "whipped" herself from the long, hard day, she set the dishwasher to run during the night and left the manor house for her and Bo's apartment.

Walking past the parking area, Maggie noticed the shadows of two figures. As she drew closer, she saw Trick and Kate, deep in conversation. "Hi," she called to them, and they instantly stopped talking. "How's Scooter?"

Kate affected a smile and gave a thumbs-up. "Fine. They stitched him up and told him to rest for a day. Then he'll be good to go. 'Night."

She took Trick's hand and pulled him with her toward the carriage house, leaving Maggie to wonder why they found it so important to end their conversation and get away from her.

* * *

Worn out by her adventures in waitressing, Maggie slept late—late for her being eight AM. She woke up to an empty home, Bo having already left for work. She checked her phone and saw a text from Kate: *Hired waitress. Thanks for helping.* Maggie viewed the text with relief and skepticism. While she was happy to avoid further upending her schedule, she had a sense that Kate had moved quickly to replace her for reasons other than Maggie's mediocre waitressing skills. *Or*, she had to admit, *it was exactly for that reason*. She showered and threw on black leggings and a stretchy teal-blue top, then ate a pear on the cusp of overripeness. *Someday I have to actually go shopping instead of helping myself to the B and B food.*

Maggie checked the weather through the apartment's large picture window and saw it was raining. She pulled an umbrella out of the stand in the entranceway and left for the main house to see if her parents needed her for any B and B duties. She detoured to the party tent and peeked in to see Gran in the middle of auditions. A handsome older gentleman in full Colonial regalia was in the middle of reciting Thomas Paine's famous pamphlet. "These are the times that try men's souls," he orated with genuine feeling. "The summer soldier and the sunshine patriot will, in this crisis, shrink from the service of their country; but he that stands by it now, deserves the love and thanks of man and woman."

Maggie listened, moved. He finished his abbreviated version of the pamphlet to applause from both her and Gran. "Bravo, Ian," Gran said. "You're in the show."

"Try men's souls," indeed. Maggie thought of the many things trying her soul at the moment, the most trying of which was her impending session with Vi De Lavallade. She found her parents in the kitchen having coffee with her step-grand-father, Lee. "There you are," Tug said. "Your order came. Lee found it under the back door overhang, so it didn't get wet."

"What order?" Maggie asked, confused. "I didn't order anything."

This confused the others. "I figured you ordered an early Valentine's treat from Fais Dough Dough," Ninette said. "Whatever's in there smells delicious."

She motioned to a flat white bakery box on the kitchen counter. Maggie examined the box. She pulled out a pair of the disposable gloves the family used when handling food and carefully opened it. Inside lay four heart-shaped doughnuts decorated with red frosting. Lee and her parents peered over her shoulder. "Four, huh." Lee rubbed his bearded chin. "Odd number for a doughnut order."

"It's not an order," Maggie said, heart racing. "It's a message."

Her stalker hadn't been scared off. He'd merely recalibrated.

Chapter 15

"Stalker?" Her father's voice was low, his tone dark. "Explanation," Tug demanded. "*Now.*"

"Someone's been sending me flowers at work," Maggie said, aiming for factual rather than fearful. "The number of blooms reflects a countdown to Valentine's Day. Bo jumped on the situation, and I thought it stopped. But whoever is doing it bailed on the flowers and appears to have switched to doughnuts."

"Four because it's four days to Valentine's Day." Lee stared daggers at the doughnuts.

"The solution's simple," said Ninette, on the verge of hysteria. "You don't leave the house between now and the day after Valentine's Day."

Tug put a hand on his wife's shoulder. "Chère, calm down. We need a sensible approach. Lee and I will take turns being Maggie's personal bodyguards for the next four or five days. We'll take shifts so's one of us is on duty all the time. Lee, get your shotgun."

"I'm on it," Lee said, and he started for the door.

"Whoa." Maggie made a time-out gesture. "Simmer down, everyone. No one said my life is in danger. It crossed my mind someone might be pranking me, and that could still be the case. And remember, my husband, highly regarded law enforcement official Bo Durand, is all over this. Now, can one of you take a picture of the box and send it to him?"

"I will." Tug took his phone off the counter and shot a series of pictures. "I'll text them to him and explain what's going on."

"Good. I'll put the box in a safe place to protect any clues that might be on it, although I doubt there'll be any. Whoever's doing this knows how to cover their tracks."

Ninette opened a cabinet door for Maggie. She placed the box on an empty shelf and closed the cabinet. Tug held up his phone. "Bo just got back to me. He's in a meeting of all the agencies investigating the chef's death, but he'll call you soon as he gets out."

"I hate feeling helpless," Ninette said, wringing her hands. "There has to be something we can do."

"We can ask the guests if they saw anything but in a way that doesn't make them suspicious and lie, in case it was one of them," Maggie said. "I know. We'll say a gift was delivered for me but the card got wet in the rain, so we don't know who it's from."

"Good plan. I'll make a list of our guests and divvy it up between us so we don't ask the same person twice," Ninette said. "That would be a red flag."

Ninette retrieved a pad and pencil from a drawer and began writing. Maggie saw an opening to wriggle out of her art session with Vi. "I was supposed to have an art class at Tulane today, but I better cancel and deal with all this."

This was met with a chorus of *Nos* and *Don't do that*s. "Bo told us about that gift before he told you," Ninette said. "He was so proud of himself for thinking it up. It was such a sweet gesture."

"Besides," Tug added, "you're better off in New Orleans than here right now. Benefit of being in a city. What do they call it? Hiding in plain sight."

"We'll take care of the guests," Lee said. "You take care of yourself. The lesson's exactly what you need. Something to feel good about instead of something to worry about."

Trapped, Maggie faked a positive attitude. "Right. Yes. I'm off to New Orleans and Vi De Lavallade." She held up a fist and added in a weaker voice than she would have liked, "Yay."

* * *

Maggie was exiting I-10 onto Carrollton Avenue when Bo called. "Your dad texted some kind of garbled message about stalkers and shotguns and sent a picture of doughnuts. Is this what I think it is?"

"Afraid so. My stalker's back." Maggie shared details of the morning's developments. "Mom, Dad, and Lee are gonna canvass our guests to see if anyone knows anything but do it in a way that doesn't tip the guests off."

"A trio of amateur sleuths," Bo said, not happy about it.

"I can't see any of those three being suspected of ulterior motives. And guests will probably be more relaxed and open with them than if someone from PPD was grilling them."

"True," Bo admitted. "But . . ."

"I know. It's like I told the others. Whoever's doing this is working overtime to make sure they can't be traced. I don't think the Crozat Amateur Detective Agency will be able to dig up anything useful, although I give them props for trying. Mom and Dad have resisted putting in security cameras. The whole 'violation of privacy' issue. But I think the time has come."

"Oh chère, I love your parents, but that time came a few bodies ago. I gotta run, but have a great session with Vi."

"I'm so looking forward to it." Maggie impressed herself with how sincere she managed to sound.

Seconds after Bo signed off, Maggie's Trombone Shorty ring tone alerted her to another caller. Maggie pressed the Bluetooth in her ear to answer. "Hey, Maggie, it's Little Earlie." She groaned. "I heard that," he said, insulted.

"Sorry, but there's a history of your calls not being good news. What's up?"

"I hear you have a stalker."

"And there you go, proving my point. I'm not confirming or denying. But wondering where you heard this."

"From the girl I'm dating."

"You're dating someone?" Maggie couldn't hide the incredulity in her voice.

"Yes," Little Earlie said, even more insulted. "I'm not a total toad."

"My bad," Maggie said, feeling guilty. "That came out wrong."

"No it didn't, it came out exactly how you meant it to. I may be vertically and hirsutely challenged, but like my mama always said, there's a lid for every pot. And I think I found my lid."

Hearing the emotion in Little Earlie's voice, Maggie softened. "I'm happy for you, Little E. Who are you dating?"

"Ginny Parvenue. She's a part-time tour guide at Doucet."

Maggie called up an image of Ginny, an amiable, slightly chubby, mid-twenty-something devoid of ambition. She could see the girl being a supportive match for Earlie. "I know Ginny. She's good people. But I wish she'd kept her mouth shut. How'd she hear I have a stalker? Which, again, I'm not confirming or denying."

"She was working the gift shop counter and overheard Ione talking to you from her office. You might want to put this story out there, Maggie. The attention could scare him or her off or make a person recall seeing something they didn't realize was suspicious at the time."

"Or," Maggie posited, "if attention is what they're looking for, the publicity is a gift."

"True, but—"

"Can you put a pin in this, Earlie? At least for a while? I promise you'll get the story when the story is ready to be told."

"All right. I'll sit on it, but only for a few days. I'll focus on the Chanson murder investigation. I got a great front-pager on that."

Maggie's nerves tingled. "There's a new development?"

"A big one. JJ got brought in for questioning again, and one of the detectives from the sheriff's department confirmed he's not *a* person of interest, he's *the* person of interest."

Maggie's stomach churned. *The authorities must have found a way to get into Phillippe's phone.* She made a mental note to check in with JJ after her session with Vi. "Do you know if any of Chanson's employees alibied out?" She recalled the restaurateur besides her mother who'd been dragged off by police after confronting the recipe-stealing chef. "And what about Abel Garavant?"

"Aside from your mama, I haven't heard about any alibis being established. Which doesn't mean they haven't been; it only means I haven't been able to dig up dirt on it. There's some tight-lipped folks at the Coast Guard and parish agencies. It's not like Pelican PD, where I can wheedle info out of an officer with a box of pralines from Bon Bon. I got one more question for you."

"Oh boy."

"Relax, this one's personal. Me and Ginny have only been going out about six weeks, but I wanna do something special for Valentine's Day. I've never had a girlfriend I could celebrate with before. I don't wanna do too little. Or too much."

Maggie heard the insecurity in the publisher's voice and felt for him. Little E managed to be annoying yet endearing, and dealing with him always engendered a seesaw of emotions. "Take her out for a nice dinner," she advised. "If you want to give her a gift, like jewelry, keep it simple." She flashed on the rows of earrings that marched up both of Ginny's earrings, ending in cartilage piercings. "Maybe earrings."

"Awesome. Thanks a ton, Mags."

And there was annoying Little Earlie. "Oh, no, no, no, no. Never 'Mags.' "

"Maggie. 'Bye. Keep me posted on the stalker sitch."

"Will *not* do," Maggie said, burying the *not* in a mutter.

Maggie pulled onto the Tulane campus. She shelved concerns about JJ and focused on parking, lucking out when she located a metered spot on Newcomb Place near the art department. She retrieved the portrait of Xander from her back seat, along with the bottle of Four Roses Single Barrel Bourbon she'd hijacked from Crozat's supply. She girded herself for her rendezvous with Vi and got out of the car.

To her relief, she found Vi in a particularly good mood, which Maggie hoped boded well for their session. Fresh paint stains coated the woman's artist's smock. Maggie noticed that she'd changed her hairstyle. Instead of wearing it natural, she now had a tall bun of microbraids atop her head. "Four Roses," Vi said, taking the bottle from Maggie and admiring it. "Excellent choice."

"I'm glad you like it. You changed your hair. I love it."

Vi patted the bun. "Thank you. I'm celebrating. I fired my divorce lawyer and used the money I'm saving on that shyster to buy my ex out of our loft. Start painting. I'll watch."

Vi's abrupt conversational shift threw Maggie, but she placed her painting on an easel, angling it to take advantage of the light pouring through the large, north-facing windows. As she painted, she thought about how Vi's hostile divorce contrasted with Phillippe and Kate's cozy relationship as exes. Or was it that cozy? Civil divorces did exist. Bo's relationship with his ex-wife Whitney offered an excellent example of one. But the Chanson team went into overdrive when it came to convincing people how well Kate and Phillippe got along post-breakup. *Maybe it's a facade*, Maggie mused. *A way to allay investors' fears that the business would take a hit from the dissolution of their marriage.*

"Stop," Vi ordered, startling Maggie, who'd forgotten she was there. "Sit." The artist patted the desk chair next to her. "Let's talk." Maggie took a minute to clean her paintbrush, then took the seat Vi offered. "I spent time studying you closely today. Your technique is excellent."

"Thank you," Maggie said, buoyed.

"But I can't reach inside of you and pull out an artist. I'm going to refund your money."

"*What? No.*" Overcome by humiliation and frustration, it came out of Maggie as a wail. "You can't. It'll break my husband's heart."

Vi shook her head. "I don't know what I was thinking when I agreed to do this. Yes I do—I was thinking, I have an expensive lawyer I need to pay. But it was a mistake. It's not in my nature to give painting lessons to privileged white housewives."

"*Housewives?*" Maggie, furious, jumped up from the chair, knocking over a jar of paintbrushes. "*Privileged?* Are you kidding me? My family has a business that could go under any minute. Between my husband and me, we barely make ends meet, and let me tell you, I do not make up for that with 'housewifely' duties." She grabbed a tube of paint and shook it in Vi's face. "I'd rather eat this paint than ever clean my house, and if it weren't for leftovers from the B and B, Bo and I would starve to death because I can't cook to save my life. Oh, and speaking of saving my life, I've found dead bodies and almost ended up one myself, one of my best friends might go to jail for a murder I know he didn't commit, *and* I have a stalker who's scaring the hell out of me. *You want passion? I'll give you passion.*"

Maggie, pulsing with anger, took a paintbrush coated in black paint and slathered Xander's portrait with violent, angry strokes. Then she froze. "Oh my God." She stared at the ruined painting. "What have I done?"

She dropped the paintbrush and, head in hands, began to sob. Vi put a hand around her waist and led her back to the chair. "It's okay, honey. You can do better than that painting."

"Argh!" Maggie screamed, shaking her fists and stamping her feet in frustration. "You've spent every second of our time together telling me I suck!"

Vi sat back and appraised Maggie. "Because you've been phoning it in. No connection to your work. No passion. Just . . . painting. That's why I decided to watch instead of teach. Your mind drifted, didn't it?"

"Yes," Maggie admitted through sniffles.

Vi leaned into Maggie. "Make yourself worth my time, Maggie. And yours. Leave whatever's going on in here"—she pointed to Maggie's head—"out there." She gestured to the window. "If you can do that, I won't refund your money. Can you?"

Maggie held Vi's glance. "Yes," she said with determination.

161

Vi picked up the bottle of bourbon. "Let's drink to that." She handed Maggie a tumbler.

"It's not even noon," Maggie said.

"Honey, it's New Orleans. We should be on our second drink by now."

*　*　*

The relationship tide turned for Maggie and Vi. Instead of painting, Maggie casually sketched while she and Vi chatted and drank—Vi bourbon, Maggie, cognizant of the drive home, water. Vi listened enraptured to Maggie's tales of life in Pelican, from its quirky citizens to its spate of bizarre murders. She roared when Maggie shared the story of her family holding a funeral for Tug's beloved cast-iron pot, handed down through generations of Crozat men. "That's it," she declared, slapping Maggie's knee. "*Your* it. Pelican, the place and especially the people. Get inside them. Find their purpose, and then find a special way to convey that." She gestured to Maggie's portrait of Xander. "If you want to paint this for your husband, start fresh. Or get him a wallet."

Maggie laughed. "He could use a new one. His is so beat-up it looks like it was in a wallet prizefight." She finished her water and brought the empty glass to the studio's sink. She washed the glass and placed it on a drying rack. "Vi . . . I don't know if this would interest you at all, but I'd love to have you come to Crozat B and B as our guest sometime."

"I believe I'd enjoy that very much," Vi said with a smile warmed by the women's connection . . . and her third bourbon. She checked a wall clock. "I've got a class coming in a few minutes. Let's put one last session on the books before my residency ends."

"Great." Maggie dug her phone out of her purse and opened the calendar app. "To be honest, it'll be the first session I don't dread."

Vi made a wry face. "You and me both, honey."

They set a time and hugged good-bye. Maggie practically danced back to her car, thrilled that if Bo asked how the session had gone, she could respond "Great!" and mean it for a change.

On the ride home, a rumbling stomach reminded her it was lunchtime. She had an idea. She'd stop at Abel's Home Cookin' and put in an order for catfish po' boys with a side of hush puppies and gossip.

Shortly after, she arrived in the café's parking lot to a symphony of oyster shells crunching under the weight of her vintage Falcon convertible. Abel's was housed in an old, tin-roofed Creole cottage. Aged tables and chairs filled the building's front porch and cozy interior, which was decorated with luscious shots of local seafood that were the culinary equivalent of boudoir photography. Abel's offered counter service only. Maggie got in line behind a group of men still dressed in their uniforms from a nearby chemical plant. The restaurant's menu was written on large chalkboards hanging on the wall above the kitchen pass-through, next to a poster proclaiming the four seasons of Louisiana were crab, shrimp, oysters, and crawfish. The men finished placing their orders, and Maggie stepped up to the register, which was being manned by Abel's son and Maggie's brief former flame, Ash. The old friends exchanged warm greetings. "It's good to have you back in town, Ash."

"Thanks. A little less fun for me to be back, now that you're taken," he teased. "Couldn't see yourself with a ginger, could you?"

"What? No," Maggie protested. "I mean, not no, I couldn't see myself with a ginger—no, you're wrong. If anything, this boring brunette was jealous of your gorgeous red hair." Ash pretended to whip his short hair back and forth, and Maggie laughed. "I heard you were living up north. Boston. Is this a permanent move back home?"

Ash grew serious. "I don't know yet. My dad's arthritis is getting bad and his blood pressure isn't much better. He needed help here, so I'm doing that right now. I'm an accountant by trade, which is a pretty reliable job. I can always go back to it full-time or even do it on the side if I have to run this place."

Maggie steered the conversation in the direction of Phillippe Chanson. "I saw your dad get hauled away after confronting that chef who got killed about stealing his recipe. Same thing happened to my mother."

Anger colored Ash's face. "I heard. The last thing Dad needs is that kind of stress. I'd be lying if I said I was sorry about what happened to that man. I mean, I wouldn't wish murder on anyone, but . . ."

"I hear you." Maggie lowered her voice. "Did Abel get interviewed by one of the law enforcement agencies? Mom did. Luckily, she has an alibi for the time period of the boat tampering."

"Yeah, they interviewed us." Ash looked over Maggie's shoulder. "Another ferry must've docked. I better get your order."

"Right, sorry. We can catch up another time."

Maggie placed her order, paid, and moved out of the way. She thought about Ash's response to her question. His answer had been vague and his change of topic cagey. And what was with "they interviewed *us*"? Abel *and* Ash? What had given law enforcement cause to consider Ash a suspect as well as his father?

"Maggie," someone called to her.

She glanced around the eating area and saw Delano Poche, Clinton and Brianna's father, sitting at a table with coworkers. All wore light-blue coveralls featuring the logo for Worldwide Chemical Corporation. Delano waved her over. "Hey, Delano. How's Clinton doing? I've been meaning to check in with him."

"Great, thanks to you," the man said. He rested his po' boy on its butcher paper and flashed two thumbs-ups. "He don't wanna talk about what happened in New Orleans, but whatever it was, he's all over his college apps now. He's gonna be the first Poche in our family to attend college. Even says he wants to go law school, if you can believe that." Delano beamed with pride. "Hey, take a seat with us while you're waiting on your order."

Maggie did so. She checked out Delano's order. "You got what I got. Catfish and hush puppies."

"Best of both in the parish, except for Junie's. But even Junie's can't match Abel's catfish. Can't blame the man for getting all up in the business of that chef who stole the recipe. It's Abel's signature dish, man."

"Heard you talkin' to Ash 'bout it," said a grizzled older man whose coveralls were embroidered with the name FRANK. "I eat here pretty regular, and the police been here a coupla times. Only makes sense, when you recall Garavant got arrested once for assault."

"He did?" This was news to Maggie. "I never heard that. Who did Abel assault?"

"Not Abel," Frank said. "Ash."

Chapter 16

This proved even bigger news to Maggie. "Ash?" she repeated. She glanced at her ex, who was busy retrieving orders from the pass-through and delivering them to customers. "I've known him since high school. I can't imagine him being violent."

"Frank, don't go bringing up old news," Delano reproached the other man. "It was a long time ago," he explained to Maggie. "Maybe ten, fifteen years or something."

"Oh, no wonder I don't know anything about this. I was living in New York. What happened?"

Frank, who apparently enjoyed gossiping as much as a tween, leaned forward. "Road rage. Some guy driving too close bumped his truck and then passed him over a double yellow line. Ash chased him down, they got into it, Ash clocked him, guy clocked him back. Both got arrested but the judge tossed the case, saying they canceled each other out."

Delano sat back and looked askance at Frank. "How you remember all this? Man, you got way too much time on your hands."

"I do," Frank said, sounding a little sad. "I need a hobby."

"Maggie, your order's up," Ash called.

Maggie stood up. "Nice seeing you, Delano, and meeting y'all. Delano, tell Clinton if he needs a recommendation for any of his college apps, I would love to provide one."

Delano mimed a salute. "Yes, ma'am. Thanks again for everything you've done for my boy."

Maggie picked up her order and thanked Ash. She mulled over what Frank had shared. Abel possessed a large, almost overwhelming personality, but Ash, despite his intimidating height, always struck Maggie as a passive introvert—a yin and yang not uncommon in relationships where one family member dominated the way Abel did. Knowing Ash possessed a dark side unsettled her. Past murders in Pelican had proved that when a soft-spoken person released their bottled-up rage, it could be lethal. She could see why law enforcement might view Ash as a suspect.

By the time Maggie reached home, the po' boys were lukewarm. That didn't stop Bo and Xander from devouring the delicious sandwiches as soon as she set them down on the table, where the two were working on a project. They'd hurried to hide red paper and doilies from her when she walked into the apartment. It was obvious they were making homemade valentines, but Maggie didn't reveal she was onto them.

The family followed their early dinner with a game of fetch. Lazy basset Gopher watched as Jolie gleefully chased a gator-shaped dog toy up and down the hallway. Jolie eventually traded chasing the toy for chewing on it, and Maggie took her laptop into the bedroom so Bo and Xander could complete their "secret" task. She returned emails and organized the files she'd need for future Doucet exhibits, which reminded her to finish the graphic for the gala invitation and program. Maggie sent the completed design to the committee members and received raves in return.

After a large chunk of time passed, she poked her head into the spacious living area. Noticing her, Bo swept detritus from the dining room table, making sure it was devoid of all telltale Valentine scraps. Xander had relocated to the room's club chair, where he was focused on drawing in a sketch pad Maggie had bought him, along with a slew of other art supplies, for his eighth birthday. "Okay if I see what you're working on, buddy?" she asked.

Xander nodded. He held up the sketch pad, revealing a beautifully yet uniquely rendered illustration of a cat. Maggie contemplated the irony that this preternaturally talented child had instinctually connected with his "it" while she still searched for hers. "For Esme," the boy said. "Her cat. It's a Valentine's Day present."

"She'll love it."

Xander yawned. "Bedtime, son," Bo said. "Tomorrow's a school day."

Once Bo and Maggie had tucked Xander in, they returned to the living area. Bo stretched out on the couch, his head in Maggie's lap. "Did you know Ash Garavant was once arrested for assault?" she asked.

"The sheriff's department interviewed the Garavants," Bo replied, "so I don't know much about them besides the fact they make the best catfish po' boy in town."

"I was just surprised to hear it," Maggie said. "Ash has always been the quiet sort. Thinking about it, I knew him more through the restaurant than anywhere else. He went to St. Francis High in Ville Platte, but it wasn't our brother school, so I didn't see him that much. We only dated a few times."

Bo raised an eyebrow. "You dated? I don't remember you mentioning that."

"It was, what? Sixteen years ago? A mere blip in my romantic life. Not that it was loaded with blips, but you get the idea. I think we both realized pretty quick that we didn't have much chemistry. The only reason I'm even talking about Ash is I'm worried for JJ."

"With good reason. To anyone who doesn't know him, he's the most likely suspect."

"Any leads on who tried to put him out of business?"

Bo, frustrated, shook his head. "This town really needs to step up its security game, if only to make my job easier. I do have some updates on the stalker investigation, which is taking a distant second to Chanson's murder for everyone except me."

"I appreciate that, husband."

"You're welcome, wife. I brought the doughnuts you got over to Daily Donuts in Ville Platte. The owner took a good look at them and is fairly sure they were fresh when they were delivered, but not straight from the oven. His guess is they were ordered the night before delivery. The amateur sleuth team of Crozat, Crozat, and Bertrand—"

"Mom, Dad, and Lee—"

"—did come up with some useful intel. They were able to determine that the last guest staying here returned at one AM. Tug found the doughnuts at five AM. I checked a database, and there's no doughnut shop in the state opened past nine, which gives our suspect an eight-hour window to purchase and deliver."

"So whoever did this could have bought the doughnuts eight hours from here and driven straight through to deliver them. That's a wide net from Dallas to Atlanta to Memphis."

"I'm drafting Rufus onto the team, and we're starting locally. Not that I can't see you generating the kind of obsession that would make someone drive to Dallas to buy doughnuts, then drive back here to deliver them, but it's a reach."

"I should be insulted, but I'm not. I don't see me generating that kind of obsession either. What's going on is bad enough as it is."

Bo furrowed his brow. "Hold on. Let's go back to this Ash guy. You said you two dated."

"Barely. It fizzled before it ignited."

"For you."

"No, it was mutual." What Bo was inferring dawned on Maggie. "Wait. You don't think *he's* my stalker, do you?"

"It's a possibility. Think about it. Guy you used to date comes back to town. Flowers and doughnuts suddenly arrive on your doorstep. Could be a coincidence. But my job is to be very suspicious of coincidences. You just saw him at Abel's. You've got the instincts of a seer. Did you pick up anything from your interaction with the guy?"

Maggie closed her eyes and relived the conversation with Ash. He had flirted with her, for sure. But try as she might, she couldn't mine anything from the moment except a harmless interaction between old friends. She was about to dismiss the whole thing when she flashed on something. "I did pick up a vibe. Not about me. It was when I mentioned the police interviewed Mom about her alibi and then asked if they interviewed Abel. Ash became uncomfortable and changed the subject."

"I'll tell Rufus to take a closer look at him. On both counts." Bo reached up and caressed Maggie's cheek. "Whatcha thinking?"

"The truth?" Maggie sounded sheepish. "That I really, *really* want a doughnut."

Bo laughed and sat up. "Then you shall have one, milady," he said with a grand flourish, to Maggie's amusement. "Is your mom still awake? Would she be up for a few hours of babysitting?"

"I'm sure. But you said all the shops close at nine."

"The shops do. But that's when the baking begins."

Maggie fake-swooned. "Doughnuts straight from the oven? Have I told you much I love you?"

"Not in the last five minutes," Bo said with a grin.

Ninette was happy to look after her beloved step-grandson and showed up within minutes of receiving Maggie's text. Maggie hopped into the passenger seat of Bo's SUV, excited about the impulsive errand, which offered welcome relief from the stress of Chanson's murder, Doucet's precarious financial situation, and her unidentified stalker. Bo thumbed through a screen on his phone. "Not to play into the cops-and-doughnuts stereotype, but Rufus created a spreadsheet of shop baking hours for when he works the night shift, complete with a rating system. Here's one that sounds great. Ru gave it his highest rating—five sprinkle doughnuts. It's right near LSU."

"Well placed on their part."

"Very."

"I have a feeling we won't be the only ones there scrounging for late-night treats. You might want to wear your badge so the college stoners know to hide their weed," Maggie advised.

Bo chuckled, and the couple took off for Baton Rouge. He called up his favorite Zachary Richard playlist, and he and Maggie sang along to the legendary Cajun musician's songs. Bo's phone pinged a text from Rufus, letting them know he'd called ahead to a baker friend at Voodoolicious Donuts and he was expecting them. They exited I-10, driving past storefronts and strip malls. "There." Maggie pointed to the left. A large sign read *Do-not Pass Us By!* The name VOODOOLICIOUS DONUTS was painted on the window of the storefront below the sign, along with the shop's logo of a voodoo doll whose body comprised a variety of colorfully decorated doughnuts.

"I'll go around the back," Bo said. "That's where the baking action is right now."

In the back of the mall, all was quiet except for the doughnut shop. Bo parked. He took Maggie's hand and led her to the shop's service entrance. A young Asian man with a shaved head opened the door. A butcher's apron covered his jeans and T-shirt. He greeted them with a wide smile. "Rufus's friends, right? Hi, I'm Tan. Come on in."

ELLEN BYRON

The work area was a hive of activity. Bakers pulled doughnuts out of ovens and off conveyor belts, passing them to
employees to decorate with frostings, jams, and other designer
doughnut accoutrements. Maggie inhaled a smell so delicious
it made her weak-kneed. "How can you work here? I'd never
stop eating the merchandise."

"After a few weeks, you get used to it," Tan said. "In fact,
it kind of becomes a turnoff. My girlfriend is like, uh, can
you come home one night *not* smelling like doughnuts?" He
handed each of them a round confection topped with crum-
bles. "I packed you a variety box to take home. These'll tide
you over until then. Baked Saigon Cinnamon Crumble."

Maggie bit into hers. It was as melt-in-our-mouth as a
baked doughnut could be, with the cinnamon adding an aro-
matic sweetness. "Oh, wow. If this were the last thing I ever
ate on earth, I would die happy."

"I may paint that quote under our logo," Tan joked.

She took another large bite. "I'm surprised you don't have
students lined up in back at night, begging to buy these for a
midnight study break."

"We don't sell at night, or we'd have nothing to sell in
the morning. Although I did get an offer last night I couldn't
pass up." He held a bakery box out to Bo, who reached for his
wallet. "Put the wallet away. It's on me."

Bo shook his head. "Very generous of you, but I can't
accept gifts. It's a departmental thing."

"Your captain doesn't have that problem," Tan said with
a grin.

Bo sighed. "My cousin and I are very different people."

174

"Then I'll give them to her."

Tan handed the box to Maggie. "Thank you," she said. "We'll leave the price of the doughnuts as a tip."

"That's super nice, but you don't have to. The tip the guy from last night left us filled the jar for the week."

Maggie, about to take another bite of her doughnut, stopped. She exchanged a look with Bo. "How much of a tip?" Bo kept his tone even, but Maggie knew they were thinking the same thing.

"A hundred bucks. For only four of our heart-shaped Valentine's doughnuts. He said he'd been to every shop in the city and we were the only ones who were offering that shape."

"Did he happen to say why he wanted them?" Bo asked in the same even tone, but now his jaw twitched.

"Yeah. He said he wanted to send a message to a girl."

Chapter 17

The minute Tan revealed that Maggie's stalker had visited the shop, Bo dropped the casual act and morphed into a detective. Discerning that the situation was serious, Tan moved them all into his office, out of earshot from his curious coworkers. Bo extricated the pad and pencil he was never without from the inside pocket of his windbreaker. "Tell me everything you remember about this guy. You're sure it *was* a guy?"

"Yes. I think." Tan squirmed in the utilitarian metal chair behind his desk. "I've never been questioned by the police before. It makes you second-guess a lot. Okay. Settle, Tan." The hip young shop owner drew in a breath. He closed his eyes, bowed his head, and placed his hands on his thighs as if meditating. "He—or she—" Maggie couldn't help muttering a small groan, triggered by her fear that Tan's second-guessing would render his memories useless. Bo shot her a warning glance. "I'll go with *they*. It's more politically correct anyway. They were definitely white, that I can say for sure. They wore a black hoodie. No markings, plain. They wore a mask, but that's not unusual these days. They also wore thick black glasses that made it hard to see their eyes, so I have no idea what color their eyes were. I guess that was intentional, huh?"

Insecure, Tan posed this as a question. Bo responded with a nod. Encouraged, the doughnut maven continued. "I'm not sure about their height, because they hunched, like this." Tan illustrated. "You know, seeing how desperate they were, I thought they might be an addict. Driving around to all the stores because you're jonesing that much for a doughnut? Who does that? Except they didn't want just any doughnut. They specifically wanted heart-shaped ones. Which takes more thought than what an addict would put into getting a sugar rush." Tan looked worried. "Am I in trouble for taking the money from them?"

"No, not at all," Bo assured him. "But if you still have the hundred dollars, I would like to borrow the bills to test for evidence."

"Sure. I was going to take the money to the bank to split into smaller denominations so I could share the tip with the crew, but I haven't had time to do it yet. Money's in the safe." Tan got up, then stopped. "I just thought of something I forgot to tell you. They were wearing gloves. Short, thin black ones like you get at the dollar store. I thought that was strange, because it wasn't too cold last night."

Maggie and Bo left with Tan's mysterious tip money and a second box of doughnuts. On the ride home, Maggie couldn't resist sampling a raised doughnut with a peanut butter–and–bacon glaze. "So, that was something. Doughnuts and dirt on the stalker. I just wish there were a positive gender ID so we could land on a pronoun."

"I'm with you on that," Bo said with a vigorous nod. "Let's review what we learned. Perp wore nondescript black hoodie and gloves, glasses to try and hide eye color, helped by the fact the exchange with Tan took place at night. Purposely neutral behavior. Tried other shops first, looking specifically for heart-shaped doughnuts. When we get home, I'm gonna call Baton Rouge PD and bring them into this. They can canvass the other doughnut shops. Maybe some of the old-timers will be less politically correct and more willing to commit to a gender."

"I appreciate that Tan cares. And he makes a *great* doughnut." She fed Bo a bite and he *mmm*ed agreement. Maggie deliberated as she finished the pastry. "Little Earlie wanted to do a story about my stalker, but I told him no. Now I wonder if it might be a good idea to publicize it. What do you think?"

"I need a bite of the German chocolate doughnut before I come to a decision." Maggie pulled out a chocolate-cake doughnut slathered with coconut-pecan frosting and fed it to Bo. "Much better," he said. "It's a good idea. Little E can interview me for the article, as a detective on the case. I'll share enough to make this creep know we're onto him but not enough to scare him off, because I wanna capture the SOB."

"I'll call Little E in the morning." Maggie noticed a piece of coconut on the side of Bo's lip. She took a napkin and gently wiped it away. "Thank you for tonight. For at least a couple of hours, all I had to think about were baked goods and my man."

Bo faked a frown. "Hmm, not sure I like the order you put those in."

"Sorry, but these are *really* exceptional doughnuts."

*   *   *

Bo left early in the morning to drop Xander off at school before heading in to work. Maggie shared her story with the *Pelican Penny Clipper* scion, who was beside himself at landing exclusive interviews with both Maggie and her detective husband. Reliving the unnerving incidents with the publisher/ reporter/editor left Maggie feeling apprehensive. She helped her parents check out a few guests, and then Tug and Ninette departed to run errands, leaving her alone in the capacious manor house.

She was cleaning out the B and B's inbox when she heard footsteps. Maggie froze. The footsteps stopped—and then resumed. They grew louder, indicating an insidious approach to the office. Maggie, heart in her mouth, grabbed a letter opener with a sharp tip. She could hear the steps stop at the office door. The knob turned, and the door began to open with a creaking whine. Deciding the best defense was a good offense, Maggie threw the door open with a warrior's scream and brandished the letter opener as a weapon. She was met with a louder scream. Grand-mère dropped an armful of carpet samples to the floor and staggered into the room, where she collapsed into a wingback chair, clutching her heart.

Maggie dropped the letter opener and ran to her grandmother. "Gran, I'm so, so sorry. I thought you were my stalker."

Gran gasped for air. "Water, please." Maggie ran to a carafe and poured a full glass. She brought it to Gran, who downed it. She fanned herself, trying to recover from the shock. "That was no help at all. Two fingers of bourbon. Neat." Maggie opened the doors of a Victorian curio cabinet and removed a tumbler and bottle of bourbon. She poured the drink and handed it to Gran, who took a few slugs. "Much better."

Maggie rubbed her forehead, hoping to forestall a headache that was beginning to take root. "I've been working from home because stalker-person was sending me flowers at work. But they sent the last 'gift' here, so maybe I'm better off going to Doucet today."

"I second that. At least you'd have distractions. You wouldn't consider every sound a harbinger of doom."

"It didn't sound like you. Your footsteps were heavier than usual."

"My arms were full of carpet samples. They're heavy and made it hard for me to walk. I was hoping for an opinion, not a heart attack." Gran finished her drink. "You can make up for that early push into my grave by picking out your favorite."

"Yes, sure. Again, sorry." Maggie picked up the samples and laid them out on the room's coffee table. She studied them. "I like this one best," she said, pointing to a square of beige carpet with a textured loop finish. "It's neutral, and the loop finish makes it sturdier and less likely to show stains."

"Good choice. It was on the top of my list. Vanessa was pushing the one at the end on the left."

Maggie checked out the sample in question, which had an impractical velvety pink plush pile. "It's perfect for Barbie's Dream House."

"Which appears to be the direction in which I'm being steered. It's time for a come-to-Jesus talk with my interior design consultant."

This gave Maggie a feeling of satisfaction that she immediately felt guilty for having. "The last decorating Van did was Charli's bedroom. She's probably still a little stuck in pretty, pretty princess mode."

"I've always thought of myself as more of a diva than a princess," Gran said, flicking stray carpet fibers off her navy wool slacks.

Maggie graced her grandmother with an affectionate smile. "To me, you'll always be the best grand-mère in the universe." She kissed her on both cheeks. "I'm off to Doucet. Hopefully, I won't have to wait long to catch the ferry."

Maggie lucked out on that score. She arrived at the ferry landing on an off hour, so there were only a few cars ahead of her waiting to board. Captain Antonio rested against the railing of the staircase that led to the pilot deck. He watched as the deckhands directed the cars onto the boat. Maggie waved to him. He waved back and gestured for her to join him. She parked and trekked past the cars behind her to Antonio. "*Ciao, mia amica,*" he greeted her amiably. "Haven't seen you in a couple of days. Thought you might have the cold that's going around."

"No, I'm healthy, thankfully. At least physically." The ferry captain gave her a quizzical look, and Maggie regretted the blurt. She noticed Antonio rubbing a rosary between his thumb and forefinger and took advantage of this to shift the conversation. "That's a beautiful rosary. I've never seen one like it before."

"*Grazie.*" Antonio held it up for closer inspection. Each bead featured a violet glass rose enclosed in a bright-green glass bead. "Belonged to my mama. It's Murano glass. She got it at Vatican City. The medal is St. Nicholas, patron saint of ships and sailors. Mama gave it to me when I started working the river. I've had it with me ever since."

"My father has a medal of St. Martin de Porres, the patron saint of innkeepers," Maggie said. "Dad always wears his. It's like his talisman."

Talismans. Maggie felt a frisson of excitement. She repeated the word to herself. *Talismans*—objects people kept close to them for spirituality. Support. Comfort. A saint medal. A wedding ring. Or, in a broader sense, whatever was dearest to a person . . . and even helped define them. "Antonio, would you mind if I sketched you on the ride over to the west bank?"

"Mind?" The elderly man's wide smile revealed a few missing teeth. "What, are you kidding? I feel like a movie star." He started up the stairs. "I gotta get this old gal moving. Come on up to the bridge with me."

Maggie followed Antonio up to the pilot's deck. She took her sketch pad out of her purse and worked quickly. As she drew, a painting formed in her mind. Antonio, black and white, in shadow; his talisman, the beautiful glass rosary, in vivid color. The ferry slowed as it approached the west bank landing. Maggie, spirits buoyed for the first time in days, pocketed the sketch pad. She had found her "it."

Once at Doucet, Maggie shared her talisman brainstorm with Ione, who loved it. "Mine is this charm." Ione fingered the tiny hula dancer that hung around her neck on a simple gold chain. "It was the last gift from Pascal before he died," she said, referencing her late husband, who had died from cancer twenty years prior. "He bought it for me on our bucket-list trip to Hawaii. I wear it to remember him. I almost never take it off."

"Ione, that's beautiful." Maggie imagined a black-and-white silhouette of her friend— the charm, gold and glistening, providing the portrait's color.

"What's your talisman?" Ione asked.

This brought Maggie back to reality. She considered the question. "I don't know," she had to admit. "Which is embarrassing. I have to think about it."

Planning the gala and mounting the wedding dress exhibit scheduled to open on Valentine's Day filled Maggie's schedule, and she reluctantly shelved her talisman project for the time being. She finished the day relaxed and with a sense of accomplishment. There had been no new deliveries from her stalker either at work or at home, according to her parents when she called to check in. Little Earlie's interview with Bo for the cover story in the *Pelican Penny Clipper* also helped ease her fears. Bo hyped the measures Pelican PD was taking to hunt down the stalker and asked for witnesses who might realize they'd seen something suspicious to come forward. On Maggie's ferry ride home, her detective husband called to share a new avenue of investigation. "Rufus and I were talking about motivation," Bo said, "and it occurred to both of us that there's a lack of sexuality to this modus operandi."

"Huh?" Maggie said, not following.

"Stalkers are usually motivated by an obsession, a passion even, for their victim. But this guy's approach—and I'm committing to a gender here—is methodical. He's getting his kicks from scaring you and throwing you off-balance. I'm not ruling out Ash or someone like him. You know, not a crazed admirer. More like a spurned lover."

"That's a very short list. Ash might be the only one on it, and I think if he heard himself called a 'spurned lover,' he'd laugh like a hyena."

"Stop selling yourself short. But Rufus also brought up people you helped incarcerate who could be counted on to hold a grudge."

Maggie recalled the half dozen or so murder suspects she'd assisted Pelican PD in IDing. "There are a lot more of them than jilted boyfriends in my past."

"Yup. We're looking into the whereabouts of everyone arrested and/or convicted of murder in a case that involved you over the last couple of years." Bo paused. "There's also news on the Chanson case. I hate saying this, but the law enforcement agencies that aren't the kinder, gentler Pelican PD are building their case against JJ. An arrest could come in the next couple of days."

"*No*," Maggie protested. "You can't let them do that."

"We're doing our best to pivot the investigation in other directions, but it's rough without a clear alternative suspect."

On this downer note, Bo signed off. Maggie got out of the car and walked to the side of the ferry. The wind, coming across the Mississippi from the east, whipped her chestnut hair away from her face. She shivered and zipped up her hoodie. The east bank landing loomed, so Maggie returned to her car. The ship docked. Maggie was the last car off. She was about to make a right on the River Road towards home when she had an idea. She made a left, heading into town instead. She parked and forged ahead toward Chanson's. It was only four PM, an hour before the restaurant opened for dinner. The staff would already be there, prepping for the evening crowd.

Maggie pulled open the restaurant door. To her surprise, the Chanson employees were milling around, champagne glasses in hand, as if at a party. Scooter, who had returned to work, held his glass with his unbandaged right hand. Trick handed Maggie a glass of champagne. "Hi, Maggie. We're celebrating. Come join us."

Maggie took the glass, noting with satisfaction that her brief waitressing stint had accomplished the goal of establishing her as a Chanson insider. The demanding job had precluded much investigation. But Maggie had come up with a new plan that would offer the observational opportunities she needed to ferret out clues pointing to any suspect besides JJ. "What are we celebrating?"

"Kate hired me an immigration lawyer," Luis said. "He's gonna find me a path to citizenship." The young chef's voice, though soft, radiated happiness. "Phillippe kept saying he would but never did."

"You know it wasn't personal, Luis," Becca said. "He was like that."

"Like making promises he never kept?" There was an edge to Luis's tone. "Promises that played with someone's life?"

"Hey." Kate held up a hand. "Let's stay in the moment, 'kay?"

"Yes, sorry." Luis held up his glass. "To Kate. I'll never forget this."

Kate waved him off. "I'm doing this for me, not you. I can't stand the thought of having to break in someone new if you got shipped back to Guatemala."

"*Back* sounds so strange to me," Luis said, "considering my mother brought me here when I was two."

Maggie polished off her champagne, then got down to the reason for her visit. "I didn't mean to crash your party, although I appreciate the champagne. I came by because I'm working on a new portrait series and would love to include all of you."

This got everyone's attention. *Nothing flatters like being told 'I want to paint you,'* Maggie thought. She explained the talisman concept, ending with, "All I need is a sketch of each of you with what you would consider your talisman. I could probably get it done in one night, two at the most. I promise to stay out of the way. I want you to forget I'm even here."

"Talisman." Scooter wiggled his eyebrows. "Can it be a body part?" This elicited groans and hoots. Scooter held up his hands, his injured hand still encased in a bandage. "I was talking about these."

"No you weren't," Becca scoffed. She pondered the concept. "I'm trying to decide what my talisman would be."

"Mine would be my chef knife," Luis said.

"Yeah," Becca said. "Mine would be too."

"First, you gotta learn how to use it," Luis teased.

Becca gaped at him. "This from someone who almost chopped off a finger."

"Only because you bumped into me." The teasing tone was gone from Luis's voice. Tension permeated the air.

"Speaking of chopping, party's over," Kate said. The tension dissipated. "Maggie, do what you need to do. If I like the series, I might buy it from you for the restaurant."

"That would be great," Maggie said, genuinely delighted. The thought that she might produce something she could actually sell hadn't occurred to her.

Since Kate and Trick drew blanks trying to land on their personal talismans, Maggie spent the evening focusing on Luis, Becca, and Scooter. Luis was a machine, repeating each cold dish with a precision that made him easy to sketch. Becca worked well with executive chef Jerome, but Maggie could see where Luis's jab about her knife skills might sting. Considering Maggie's only knife skill was spreading peanut butter on white bread, she wasn't one to judge. Still, she sensed Becca lacked Luis's fluidity with the vital tool of their trade.

While her hours of observation produced some great sketches, nothing sparked as a clue to who killed Phillippe. Maggie's hand ached from drawing. In need of a break, she transitioned from the kitchen to the dining room, where Scooter performed a modified version of his oyster-shucking act for a rapt audience of diners. He tossed and juggled oysters with brio but made sure to open each bivalve with more care than he had in the past. Maggie resumed sketching and continued until the restaurant emptied out. She paged through her drawings, looking for expressions or interactions she'd captured that hadn't seemed significant at the time but would pop as clues upon further examination. Nothing did, although she gave herself credit for a particularly good rendering of Scooter juggling four oysters.

Discouraged, Maggie threaded her fingers together and stretched her arms over her head. She got up and was about to leave when she heard yelling coming from outside the restaurant. She glanced out the window and saw Kate screaming at Dyer Gossmer. Kate lunged for him, but Trick pulled her back.

"What's going on?"

The question came from Luis. Maggie turned to see him and Becca standing behind her, taking in the argument outside.

"I think," Maggie said, "Dyer just broke some very unwelcome news to Kate."

Chapter 18

Trick dragged a steaming-mad Kate back into the dining room, where the entire staff had gathered. They peppered her with a chorus of questions until the businesswoman threw her hands in the air and yelled, "Shut up!" She paced the room, slamming her fist into her palm as she marched back and forth. "That—" She unleashed a stream of invectives to describe Dyer that even gave Scooter, a foul-mouth himself, pause. "I swear, I'll kill that idiot. Instead of the simple, basic autobiography of Phillippe the SOB was hired to write, he returned the advance and signed with a publisher to do a tell-all."

The staff exchanged nervous looks. "Uh, what exactly is he gonna tell?" Luis asked.

"Nothing good." Kate took a whiskey Trick had poured her and downed it. "He's been shadowing us for months. Who knows what he has in his notes and recordings?"

"But . . . but . . ." Becca stammered. "He can't do that. Can he?"

"We'll have lawyers look into it, of course," Trick said, his voice calm, "and stop whatever we can. Kate was smart enough to insist he record every interview and give her copies of the transcripts. But 'unauthorized biographies' get published all the time. You may have to bring a libel suit to get any action. And truth is a defense."

Given Dyer's past as a respected journalist, Maggie was sure he knew better than to leave himself open to a libel lawsuit. She said nothing. Instead, she observed. Kate ranted; Trick calmed. Scooter glowered; Becca panicked. Luis worked at a neutral expression, but the nervous twitching of his left leg crossed over his right betrayed him.

"It's too late in the evening to do anything about this now," Trick said. "I'll deal with it first thing tomorrow."

The staff took the hint and dispersed. A night that had begun with a celebration ended on a glum note.

On the ride home, Maggie reflected on everyone's reactions to the news that Dyer's puff piece was segueing into a more threatening opus. It was obvious all the Chanson employees had concerns about what the journalist might reveal. But did one person's concerns top the others because it involved murder? That, Maggie couldn't tell, which frustrated her.

Her cell rang as she drove into the Crozat parking lot. She pressed the button on her Bluetooth earbud. "Hey, Vanessa. Everything okay? It's almost midnight."

"Everything is A-okay," Vanessa chirped. "I just decided we're going shopping for dresses to wear to the gala. Meet at ten AM tomorrow in front of Bon Bon."

She hung up before Maggie could say no.

*   *   *

Maggie did as ordered, showing up to Bon Bon at ten on the dot. "I'll keep you company, but I'm not planning on buying anything new," she told Van. "It feels hypocritical to spend money that could be going to Doucet on a dress."

Vanessa gave her bleached-blond mane a toss. "Quentin made a very generous donation to the Save Doucet fund, so I have no problem spending more of his money. Besides, with this baby growing every day, these'll be my last days fitting into anything besides a muumuu. Hey, y'all!"

Maggie turned in the direction of Vanessa's wave and saw Gaynell and Ione approaching. "She corralled us too," Gaynell said with a grin.

"Ione, you're spending your day off with me?" Maggie placed a hand on her heart. "I'm deeply moved."

Ione responded with an eye roll. "Only half the day. We have to finish hanging the wedding exhibit later, remember?"

"No worries, that's my plan. Are we waiting on Sandy?"

"She can't make it," Vanessa said. "She's got rehearsal with the senior dance group. They're choreographing a new number. All righty, ladies, let's pile into the Lexus."

Van drove the group to a Baton Rouge bridal shop that also sold cocktail and evening attire, a smart business move in a state with a months-long carnival season and more festivals than days of the year. The women browsed through racks of sequined, beaded gowns. Maggie, realizing she had reduced her wardrobe to jeans, leggings, and T-shirts, joined the search, but she stuck to the sales rack. Vanessa kept a saleswoman busy pulling so many gowns that they filled an entire dressing room, forcing her to try on the merchandise in a second dressing room. She came out clad in a tight bejeweled blue-green gown. "What'd y'all think?"

"You look like a pregnant, aging mermaid," Ione, ever blunt, said. The saleswoman coughed to hide a laugh. Vanessa harrumphed and flounced back to the fitting rooms.

"I'm not finding anything that feels right," Gaynell said. "But since I'm performing, I can get away with wearing my onstage outfit, lucky me." She pulled an elegant tomato-red jersey cocktail dress from a rack. "Maggie, this would look wonderful on you."

She held the dress up to her friend. Ione nodded her approval. "Not too fancy, not too plain. And a gorgeous color. You can wear it on Valentine's Day, too. I'm sure Bo has great plans in mind for your first one as marrieds."

Maggie tamped down an unexpected well of emotion. "We're going to New Orleans. Dinner at Broussard's, and then we're spending the night at the Reveille New Orleans Hotel, where my friend Lulu works."

"Lucky girl," Ione said.

"He's getting me out of town to save me," Maggie blurted. "He's afraid of what my stalker might do." Tears bubbled up and then flooded down her cheeks. "I'm sorry," she wept. "I don't know why I'm so emotional. It must be my cycle."

Her friends guided her to the large tufted gray ottoman that served as the store's seating area. "Chère, you got nothing to apologize for," Ione said. Gaynell's vigorous nods backed her up. "Some loon is messing with your life. If anyone's got reason for tears, it's you."

"True dat," Gaynell seconded.

Ione extracted tissues from a box labeled *Mother of the Bride* and handed them to Maggie, who wiped her cheeks. "I should be excited about my first Valentine's Day as a married woman. Instead I'm dreading it."

Ione crouched down in front of Maggie. "Nuh-uh. No dreading. Like the saying goes, worry is paying interest on a debt you may not owe." She took Maggie's hands in hers and squeezed them. "You are one of the strongest women it's my gift to know, way stronger than some bully who's too cowardly to face a person and has to play tricks on them instead. You go to New Orleans with that handsome husband of yours and y'all pass a good time. Pass a *real* good time, if you know what I mean."

Gaynell gave a hoot and Maggie had to laugh. "Ha. The way you said that, there's no way I could miss what you mean." She hugged Ione, then stood up and hugged Gaynell. "I'm so blessed to have y'all as friends. You're my *gal*entines."

"Awww," Gaynell said. "Group hug."

The three hugged. "Y'all, prepare to be wowed," Vanessa called from the dressing room. She burst into the shop area clad in a flattering Empire-style tangerine chiffon gown with a beaded bodice and struck a model pose. She noticed the group hug and dropped the stance. "What'd I miss?"

* * *

After lunch in Baton Rouge, Maggie returned to Crozat with the red dress. Her friends were right. The dress looked stunning on her and would work for both Valentine's Day and the Doucet gala. She stopped by the party tent to check out Rosé the Riveters' new song and witnessed chaos. The Riveters struggled with the choreography for "Beat Me Dad Eight to the Bar," resulting in collisions and eventually a pileup when senior Mariella Fleur lost her balance and fell, taking several riveters down with her. Sandy, watching from the audience, caught Maggie's eye and mouthed, "Help me." Then she announced, "Take a break, gals," adding with a mutter, "Lord knows I need one."

Gran, out of breath, came off the dance floor and dropped onto a folding chair. Her granddaughter handed her a cup of water. "*Merci.* We could use some more work on this number."

"A little," Maggie said, amused.

Gran adjusted her bandanna headkerchief, which had come askew during the disastrous dancing. "It doesn't look like Sandy choreographed anything more difficult than she did for the other song," Maggie said. "What's the problem here?"

Gran eyeballed the area to make sure no one was in listening distance, then whispered, "There was a bit of a kerfuffle about who got the front row, so Sandy had the marvelous idea of rotating rows, giving everyone a chance to shine up front. But it's been a bit tricky getting the timing right."

"I can see that."

Gran stood up. "Time to get back on the—" She stopped and stared. "What the what?"

Maggie followed Gran's gaze to see Quentin MacIlhoney leading a dozen men, some close to his own sixty-plus years in age, some older, into the tent. All wore bomber jackets and baseball caps, many sporting the insignia of the military branch in which the wearer presumably once served. "Greetings, all," Quentin said.

Gran put a hand on her hip and eyed him. "What exactly are you up to, Quentin?"

"My friends and I thought it'd be fun to entertain the gala 'troops' with the male equivalent of what y'all are doing." He made a show of his outfit. "In keeping with the theme, we're dressed as fly-boys."

"Except," Abel Garavant, one of Quentin's compatriots, said, "We're *fry*-boys." He illustrated this by holding up a fry basket from his restaurant.

Gran gleefully clapped her hands together. "What a fantabulous idea! I *love* it! I'm sure Sandy can come up with a wonderful number for the *Fry*boys. Can't you, Sandy?"

Sandy, who was unscrewing the cap to her flask, whimpered. Maggie gave her friend a comforting pat on the shoulder. "Remember, it's for a good cause. And I promise to make a vat of whatever it is you're drinking available to you at every rehearsal."

The Riveters and Fryboys busied themselves chattering and flirting with each other. Maggie started for home to change into work clothes before crossing the river to Doucet. She passed Abel on her way out. "I have to say, that fry basket is a great touch, Abel."

"Thanks. I was hoping we could all have them and do some kind of routine. I read about a drill team that does a synchronized act with briefcases. Something like that."

"Sounds fun."

Abel fiddled with the fry basket. "Ash told me you stopped by and asked about my police interview. It wasn't fun. I'm sure your mama's wasn't either." He hesitated. "I know you and Ash didn't date for long . . ."

"Hardly at all," Maggie said.

"I was sorry about that. I would've loved to see my boy settle down here with a nice girl. Like you."

The conversation was beginning to make Maggie uncomfortable. "Ash is a catch. He'll find the right girl."

"Maybe he did. And maybe she got away." Abel backtracked. "I don't mean just you. Could be someone else. He doesn't tell me much. I blame that big-deal college education of his." Abel forced a laugh. "I'm kidding."

No you're not. Maggie felt for the man, a laborer and widower who'd done everything in his power to give his son the opportunities he'd never had, only to feel the unexpected distance they'd put between them. "I'm proud of him," Abel continued. "I know his mama would be too."

"You've got a lot to be proud of," Maggie said. "And I know he's proud of you too." Her cell alerted her to a text. She retrieved the phone from her jeans back pocket and checked it. "My mother's asking for me."

"Go." Abel shooed her off, fry basket still in hand. "Tell her I say hey and that after this whole dang thing is over, we gotta compare notes on our arrests. I had no idea handcuffs hurt your wrists so much."

Per Ninette's instructions, Maggie met her parents in the manor house kitchen. The minute she walked in, the expressions on their faces told her something was wrong. "Dyer never showed up for breakfast or lunch," Tug said. "But his car is in the parking lot."

"I thought maybe he wasn't feeling well, so I brought breakfast to his room," Ninette added, her brow creased with worry. "I knocked, but there was no answer. Same with lunch. Given what all's been going on around here, we asked Pelican PD for a welfare check. Artie and Cal are on their way over."

Maggie's nerves vibrated with alarm. She and her parents waited in silence. They heard a car pull into the parking area, arriving with the rattles, snorts, and rumbles usually associated with a cartoon vehicle. Moments later, Officers Cal Vichet and Artie Belloise came in through the back door. "What smells so good?" was Artie's first question, which came as no surprise. The portly officer was a fan of Ninette's cooking to the point of regretting a lull in criminal activity at Crozat, where an investigation always came with treats, if not a full meal.

"I got a pan of Gooey Pineapple Pecan Cake I just took out of the oven," Ninette said. "While it's cooling, we'll take you to our guest's room."

Artie nodded his approval. "Glad the timing worked out. Our patrol junker is leaking oil. I had to stop and feed the beast."

The group left the manor house for the garconniere. Cal gave Tug the nod to unlock the door, and he complied. The five stepped inside the room. The instant they saw it, Maggie and her parents let out a collective gasp. The room had been trashed. Furniture lay upended. Several broken lamps littered the floor, which was covered with a mess of papers and what looked to be pieces of a computer. Ninette covered her mouth with a shaking hand. "I . . . I . . . Oh . . ."

Tug surveyed the scene, his face grim. "Somebody wanted to send Gossmer a message."

"I'm guessing he got it," Artie said. "And then some."

The others followed Artie's gaze to a large, deep-red puddle on the floor. The Crozats didn't need the officers to tell them the liquid was blood.

Chapter 19

Police tape marking off a deadly location was an all-too-familiar sight at Crozat B and B. But new to the B and B were (a) the lack of an actual body and (b) a glut of law enforcement officers from at least four different agencies, the assumption being that Dyer Gossmer's disappearance was tied to Phillippe Chanson's murder.

Bo kept the Crozats updated on developments. "The parish sheriff's Criminal Investigation Division is taking the lead on this one," he shared. "One of the broken items in the room was a clock—"

"Not the antique inlaid French mantel clock, I hope," Gran said, concerned. "It was in perfect working condition. I can't imagine what it might cost to repair that. Sorry," she added, seeing the reproachful looks from her family, "insensitive First World problems. Continue."

"The clock gave us a tentative time to work with of three-fifteen AM."

"I didn't hear a thing," Tug said. He turned to the others. "Did any of you?"

They all shook their heads. "Between the garconniere's thick walls and isolation from the rest of the B and B, you'll probably have a hard time finding anyone who heard anything," Maggie said to her husband.

"I figured as much. But we still need to interview everyone who was here during that time period."

"Do you mind starting with me, cher—I mean, Detective—I mean—" Hearing her mother giggle, Maggie flushed. "I have to finish hanging the wedding dress exhibit at Doucet."

Bo tried to hide a smile. "A great example of why I won't be interviewing my wife. He will."

Bo indicated a St. Pierre Parish officer hovering nearby. He motioned to the woman, who acknowledged this and came to them. "I'm Detective Shawn Holahan of the St. Pierre Parish Sheriff's Office. I just need to run a few questions by y'all, one at a time."

"We know the drill," Tug said with a sigh. "Maggie, take Detective Holahan to the office."

Maggie led the detective toward the manor house. They passed Becca, who was crossing from the parking area to the carriage house. She wore her chef jacket and carried her toque under her arm. "Hey, Maggie. I'm taking a break between lunch and dinner. What's going on with all these cops?" Her eyes widened in fear. "There hasn't been another murder, has there?"

Not sure what to say, Maggie gave the detective a questioning look. Holahan responded with a slight nod, then trained her eyes on Becca. Maggie had been through enough investigations to know she was gauging the *sous-chef*'s response to the news Maggie was about to deliver. "Dyer is missing. His room was trashed. There's evidence of blood."

Becca gasped, clapped a hand over her mouth, and then dropped it. "She said she'd kill him."

Not surprisingly, the detective sparked to this. "Who did?"

"Kate Chanson."

Maggie saw the gleam in Holahan's eyes. "Phillippe Chanson's widow? She said she'd kill the missing individual?"

"Yes," Kate said. "You heard her, right, Maggie?"

Holahan's gleam pivoted toward her. "Yes, I forgot about that," Maggie admitted. "I did hear Kate say she'd kill him, but it really felt like a throwaway. A figure of speech. She'd found out Dyer had done a number on her by switching Phillippe Chanson's 'autobiography' to a tell-all. She was justifiably angry."

"Maggie's right," Becca said. "She was mad at him. We all were. But I can't see Kate killing someone. No way."

But would someone kill for her? Maggie thought of Trick, whom she'd come to see as the epitome of the old saying *Still waters run deep.*

Maggie's interview with Holahan was mercifully brief. After establishing that she'd heard nothing of a struggle, the detective asked for her impression of the writer. "I got that he was humiliated by his fall from Pulitzer heights," she said. "And struggling financially. He seemed miserable working on the Chanson autobiography and excited about the new direction. Excited to the point of arrogant. It represented a bigger payday, more career heat, and also . . .

kind of a middle finger to Kate, who kept him on a tight writer leash."

Holahan jotted notes, thanked Maggie, and released her. She held the door open for a nervous Becca. "I've never been interviewed by the police before in my life, and now twice in, like, weeks," Becca said tearfully. "I hate this."

Maggie, veteran of too many police interviews, sympathized with the young woman. "Stay calm, stay focused, stick to stating facts as simply as possible. You'll be fine."

She texted Ione to say she was on her way. Her explanation of what caused the delay precipitated a string of horror and scream emojis. Next, Maggie made a pit stop in the kitchen to grab a piece of Ninette's Gooey Pineapple Pecan Cake. She found Artie Belloise already there, along with Quentin. "This guy's not half bad once you get to know him." Artie spoke of his defense attorney adversary through a mouthful of dessert.

"Remember that the next time you wanna throttle me for demolishing your testimony against one of my clients." Quentin took a dainty bite of his own piece of cake. "While we're on the subject of clients, I figured I'd dawdle and see if my services might be needed here."

"Doesn't look like it," Maggie said. "But the police will probably be interviewing the Chanson staff at the restaurant. You might want to do your dawdling there."

"Au revoir, my friends." Quentin helped himself to a piece of cake for the road and took off.

* * *

There was a damp chill in the air, so Maggie stayed in her car during the ferry ride across the river. She shivered when the ferry passed a phalanx of police boats—not from the cold but from the assumption that the search was on for Dyer Gossmer's body. Maggie's cell sang out a few notes of Trombone Shorty's "Buckjump." The caller was JJ. *Please don't be bad news*, Maggie prayed. "Hey," she said in the cheeriest voice she could muster. "I'm so glad to hear from you."

"I'm calling with good news for a change. The health inspector signed off on Junie's repairs, so I figure, long as I'm not in jail yet, I might as well reopen tomorrow. If you got nothing better going on tonight, I thought maybe you could stop by for some moral support. Maybe wipe down a table or two. I know you been real busy with all that's going on at Doucet—"

"Don't worry about that one bit. I'd love to come by, and I'll see about rounding up a couple of others. Junie's is back. Yay!"

Maggie felt upbeat after JJ's news, choosing to see it as a sign that life in Pelican would eventually return to normal. After the ferry docked, Maggie made the short drive to Doucet and hurried inside. The interview with Detective Holahan had set her back an hour. She found tour guide and Little Earlie inamorata Ginny Parvenue lounging in the break room with a couple of interns. To Maggie's annoyance, her entry into the space set off a spate of whispers and giggles. "All right, what's the deal?" Her nerves frayed by the day's events, the question came out clipped. Maggie didn't have the patience for office intrigue.

"Somebody got a present," Ginny said, her tone knowing. "A big one."

Maggie noticed a large, heart-shaped box of chocolates on the break room table and her stomach lurched. "Where did this come from?"

"I don't know. It was here when we opened this morning."

Aileen, one of the interns, scrunched her face. "I forgot to lock the door last night," she said. "Oops."

Maggie made a mental note to let Ione know she needed to keep an eye on slacker Aileen. "Have any of you touched the box?"

The three girls, faces now solemn, shook their heads. Maggie opened a cabinet and hunted for a box of disposable gloves. It took a search through all the old room's worn cabinets, but she finally located a half-empty box. She pulled on a pair, then slowly and carefully lifted the chocolate-box lid. The girls peered over her shoulder. A single chocolate rested inside the box. "That," Ginny said, "is a really crummy present."

"I need you to tell me the truth." Maggie knew the answer to the question she was about to ask but put it to the girls anyway. "Did any of you sneak a chocolate from this box? I promise you won't get in trouble, but I have to know." She received a vociferous chorus of *no*s in response. "What about the rest of the staff?"

"We're it today, thanks to the whole Doucet having-no-money thing," Ginny said. Her cell phone buzzed. "That's Ione. We got customers. *Allons-y.*"

The interns decamped, but Ginny lingered. "I'm kinda dating Little Earlie . . ." she began.

"Yes, he told me," Maggie said with a smile. "He likes you a lot."

"He said that?" Ginny's sweet face lit up. "Well, I like him back. Anyways, he told me about your stalker, and then I read the piece in the *Penny Clipper*. You think this is from them?"

"I do."

A troubled expression replaced Ginny's glow. "I'm so sorry. If I can do anything, lemme know. I took karate when I was a kid. I don't remember much, but if this person shows up— yah!" Ginny showed off a few karate moves. She grimaced. "Ouch. That's hard to do in a hoop skirt."

"I'm impressed," Maggie said. "And appreciate the offer. But hopefully you won't have to go jujitsu on anyone."

Ginny left to lead a tour group. Maggie shot a few photos of the chocolate box and sent them to Bo, who texted back that he'd send a Pelican PD officer to retrieve the evidence. Having done everything she could about the latest disturbing dispatch from her stalker, Maggie made her way to the exhibit space next to the gift shop. She found Ione waiting for her. "I heard about the chocolate box," her friend and boss said. "We can talk about it or focus on the show."

"Column B," Maggie replied.

"Noted," Ione said. "I'm gonna put on some cheerful music to work by. I downloaded Gaynell and the Gator Girls' new album."

She pressed play on her phone, and the room filled with one of Gaynell's up-tempo tunes. The women hummed along as they mounted and posted descriptions under each painting of a Doucet antecedent posing in the resplendent wedding gown. Maggie placed protective velvet rope stanchions around the gown itself, which sparkled and glimmered under a soft light. Finally, she positioned a retractable banner with the exhibit's title at the entrance: *Say Yes to This Dress: The History of an Iconic Wedding Gown.* Maggie wiped perspiration from her brow with the back of her hand. "Could we actually be done?"

Ione did a walk-through of the space. She used a rag to dust the tops of a few frames and said, "I believe we are." The two women high-fived. "All that's left to do is set up the souvenir display, but I can do that with the interns. You, my friend, have had a *day*. Why don't you go home?"

"I'll take you up on the early release. JJ got the all-clear to open up Junie's tomorrow. If you're free after work, we'll be getting the place back on its feet tonight."

Ione clasped her hands together and gazed upward. "Lord, thank you for some good news. If I'm not worn out from making sure Aileen doesn't break anything or spend all her time sexting her boyfriend, I'll be there."

Anticipating a fun evening helping a close friend, Maggie went to her car in good spirits. *Maybe JJ will reward my good deed with some popcorn crawfish,* she thought as she headed down the road leading from Doucet to the West River Road. She drove past a dirt road that wove through the sugarcane field next to the old plantation. A nondescript sedan pulled out behind her. Maggie glanced in her rearview mirror. The car was on her tail. *I'm not going slow*, she thought, annoyed, *but fine, I'll speed up*. She accelerated. The sedan followed suit. Maggie's heart began to thump. She slowed down and waved for the sedan to pass. Instead, it slowed down. She sped up again. The sedan matched her speed. Fear coursed through Maggie. This wasn't a case of a car being piloted by an aggressive driver.

She was being followed.

Chapter 20

Maggie inhaled and exhaled to calm herself. She kept her eyes on the road and maintained a steady speed. She pressed a button on her phone to call Bo. It went straight to voice mail. Rather than leaving a message, she hung up and called back several times, knowing the frequency of calls would sound an alarm for her husband. She was about to try for a fifth time when he called her. "What's wrong?" he said as soon as she took the call.

"I'm being followed."

Bo cursed. "Where are you?"

"Almost at the ferry landing." Maggie glanced at the river, and her heart sank. She saw the ferry idling on the other side of the Mississippi. "It's on the east bank and doesn't look like it's coming west any time soon."

"Pull a U-turn," Bo instructed. "I'm gonna get you to the nearest police station."

Maggie checked for oncoming traffic. Seeing none, she swung the wheel. Her tires screeched as she did a one-eighty and drove north. She heard a screech behind her as the sedan followed her move.

The next fifteen minutes felt like fifteen hours. There were street closures in the nearest town due to a funeral second line, so Bo directed her to Beausoleil, a historic town upriver from Doucet. She and her pursuer fell into a bizarre, almost hypnotic ballet of speeding up and slowing down. Finally, a painted wooden sign welcomed her to Beausoleil. Maggie released the breath she'd been holding, then cried out when the sedan suddenly bumped her rear fender. She clutched the wheel so hard her knuckles whitened. The sedan bumped her again with more force. Maggie gritted her teeth and concentrated on maintaining control of the Falcon. A road sign indicating a drop in the speed limit filled her with relief. It meant they were about to enter a populated area. The sedan bumped her one more time, then made a sharp turn to the west and roared off, the sound of its engine fading with distance.

Maggie pulled over to the side of the road. She closed her eyes and rested her head against the steering wheel. Her body buzzed with an adrenaline rush of fear. She opened her eyes and raised her head. Then, hands shaking, she drove to the Beausoleil police station.

The most welcome sight in the world waited for her on the steps of the century-old red-brick building housing Beausoleil PD. Maggie fell into her husband's arms. "Thank you for being here."

Bo held her tight. "Like I wouldn't be."

Maggie rested her head against the crisp white cotton button-down shirt Bo wore under his sport jacket. "I have to admit, it was terrifying. Which was the goal. Not to kill me. To scare me."

"Let's go inside and file a report."

Bo put a protective arm around Maggie's waist and led her inside the station, where the couple was met by Beausoleil PD captain Kevin McCaffrey. He was a trim fiftysomething with a taciturn demeanor, but his pale-blue eyes radiated warmth. McCaffrey ushered the couple into his office, motioning for a patrol officer to join them. "Luneville, take notes," he instructed the officer. "Okay, Mrs. Durand, walk me through what happened."

Maggie's lower lip quivered. She pressed her palms against her eyelids to hold back tears. "I'm sorry. I get like that whenever anyone calls me Mrs. Durand." She composed herself and managed an apologetic smile. "I've been a ball of emotions lately."

"Sounds like you got good reason for that. So . . ."

Prompted by the captain, Maggie recounted her frightening experience in detail while Officer Luneville took notes. "I got everything I need," Luneville said when she was done. "There's gotta be a security camera along the route that caught this SOB's license plate number. I'll take a patrol car and hunt them down."

Captain McCaffrey stood up. The others followed suit. "Someone using local roadways as a bullying demolition derby ticks me off. We're all over this. I'll be in touch, Durand." He shook hands with Bo and then showed them out of the building.

Maggie and Bo were far enough north to take the bridge over the river. Once home, Maggie fixed an early-bird dinner. While they ate, the couple debated who might have given chase to her, maybe the stalker or a killer who'd picked up on the fact that Maggie was nosing around Chanson's murder. "I'd bet money on the stalker," she said. "I haven't sensed any of the Chansonniers—"

"Chansonniers. I like that."

"Thanks. I haven't sensed any of them being suspicious of me. Between the waitressing and sketching, I've wormed my way into the inner circle."

Bo frowned. "Sounding a skosh cocky, chère. Don't go there. It's a breeding ground for mistakes."

"You're right," Maggie said, chastised. "The goal is to save Junie's. We're taking a big step toward that tonight." She explained the evening's plan. "I'd love for you to come with me."

"I'm picking Xander up from soccer practice, but I'll try and stop by after if he doesn't need help with his homework."

Bo left to get Xander. Maggie trudged over to the manor house with the goal of recruiting family members for the Junie's cleanup project. Her parents were out, but she found Gran in the front parlor mixing a drink for Kate. The restaurateur wore a stylish navy jumpsuit and expensive-looking black suede pumps. She'd pulled her sleek brown hair into a low ponytail that showed off trendy large silver hoop earrings. Gran handed her the cocktail. "A Sazerac. The recipe's been in our family for generations. I hope you enjoy it. And don't steal it."

Kate released an exasperated grunt. "Like I've said over and over again, stealing recipes was on Phillippe, not me, and it's not illegal. But it pushes buttons, especially for guy chefs, who can be a lethal combo of egotistical and insecure. I told Phillippe his recipe kleptomania would get him into trouble. I never thought it would get him killed." She tasted the drink and expelled a breath. "Yikes. This is strong."

"You're welcome," Gran said. She held up a bottle of rye whiskey. "Maggie?"

Maggie shook her head. "Pass. I'm due at Junie's. We're setting it up to reopen tomorrow. Are you up for lending a hand?"

"Absolutely," Gran said. She gestured to her peach-patterned silk top and ivory slacks. "I'd best change into something a little more worker bee. I'll meet you back here."

Gran went off to change. Maggie parked herself on a barstool. "Do you really think Phillippe was killed over a recipe?"

Kate shrugged. Maggie noticed shadows under her dark-brown eyes. She'd also dropped weight, her slim frame now bony. "It's as good a reason as any in this psycho situation. I know your mom's off the hook. But there's that Abel guy. And probably a bunch of other angry chefs I don't even know about." She took a sip of the Sazerac. "But now *I'm* somehow the number-one suspect in Dyer's disappearance. My lovely staff, who apparently never heard of the word *loyalty*, told the police they heard me say I wanted to kill Dyer." Maggie, feeling guilty, chose not to mention she'd also ratted out Kate.

"I'd fire everyone, but we'd have to shut down. It's bad enough that idiot Scooter's almost useless. He's like an exposed nerve lately. I swear, I sometimes wonder if he's back on meth."

This got Maggie's full attention. "Back on? Huh." She recalled Scooter's edgy behavior. Her instinct that drugs were involved had been right.

"He was up front with us about it. You know, the whole twelve-step thing about being in recovery. He did time for robbery and trained for the kitchen through a prison antire-cidivism program. We'd never have hired him if we thought he'd gone back to selling, but being a recovering addict isn't a job killer in our business. You can't swing a roast duck without hitting someone in a restaurant kitchen who either has or had a drug problem."

"I wonder where he went to high school."

Kate shook her head, amused. "That's such a funny tradition in Louisiana, asking where people went to high school. Like, that's what defines them for their entire life."

"It's because so many of us go to Catholic school," Maggie said. "And the schools all have different atmospheres and reputations. So yes, at least in this parish, you do get a sense of someone from knowing where they went to high school."

"Well, I'm from Darien, Connecticut, and went to Darien High School, which is like a hundred other upscale Connecticut high schools that breed high-strung overachievers like me," Kate said. "Okay, that was an overshare. I blame the drink."

Maggie chuckled. "Maybe I should have told you our nickname for Gran's Sazeracs—Truth Serum."

Kate put down the glass. "I better not drink any more of this or I'll tell you my real age."

She got off the stool and patted the wrinkles from her jumpsuit. "Great outfit," Maggie said.

"Trick and I are going to New Orleans to meet with potential investors." Kate ran her hands up and down the jumpsuit with a wry smile. "Dress for the job you want. And the job I want is CEO of the most successful restaurant group in the country."

Kate left, and Maggie brought her almost-empty glass into the kitchen, placing it in the dishwasher. She returned to the front parlor and pondered Scooter's behavior. Was it drug induced, or the by-product of keeping a deadly secret? He was a talented bad boy who had done time in prison. But was he a murderer? She tried to recall any conversations about Phillippe they'd had and any interaction she'd witnessed between the two men. The shucker hadn't seemed particularly fond of the chef, but he hadn't seemed to hate him or carry some kind of grudge either. Maggie's cell alerted her to a text from Gran: *On my way. Junie's, here we come!*

Sabotaging Junie's, Maggie thought. *That I can see Scooter doing. But . . . why?* She sighed, discouraged by the lack of motives for the recent spate of crimes, from Phillippe's murder to Junie's to her stalker.

Gran appeared in the doorway dressed in overalls, her hair hidden under a bandanna. Maggie did a double take. "Are you wearing your Rosé the Riveter costume?"

"You betcha. It's perfect for the task at hand." Gran made a muscle, copying the iconic Rosie the Riveter poster. "'We can do it,'" she said, quoting from the poster. She flashed an impish grin and added the town motto. "Yes, we Peli-can!"

*   *   *

Maggie and her friends lived up to the Pelican motto at Junie's. By the time they finished scrubbing, dusting, and polishing, the charming but shabby old place looked like it had received an extreme makeover. Every surface gleamed, even the embossed tin ceiling. JJ rewarded the volunteer work crew with pots of gumbo and crawfish fricassee, and Lia and Kyle Bruner donated an array of desserts from Fais Dough Dough and Bon Bon. Gaynell jumped up on the restaurant's small stage, where she and her bandmates had stashed their instruments. "Time to make sure the sound system's working. Who's up for some music?"

The question proved rhetorical as she and the Gator Gals launched into a Cajun two-step, and people traded their forks for the dance floor. Despite the mid-February date, the night was hot and humid, and the body heat emitted by the exuberant celebrants ratcheted up the temperature in the restaurant to uncomfortably stuffy. When perspiration dripped into Maggie's eyes, making them burn, she decided to take a break. She exited into the alley next to the restaurant. Ash Garavant was already there, having a smoke. The two exchanged a casual greeting. "It's nice of you to help the competition," Maggie said.

"There's always been room for two places to eat in Pelican." Ash glanced toward Chanson's Cajun Kitchen. "Whether there's room for three . . ."

"Chanson's does attract newcomers, which is a good thing. I hope."

"If the newcomers decide to try other restaurants in town. If not, somebody's going out of business. And it better not be my dad." Ash dropped his butt to the ground and extinguished it with his foot. He picked up the butt, made sure it was out, and placed it in the garbage.

"Ash, I've got a question for you."

"Shoot."

"You grew up in Ville Platte. Did you know Scooter Pitot?"

Maggie didn't expect Ash's reaction to what she assumed was a simple question. He flushed, clearly taken aback. He began to stammer a response and stopped. Then he recovered. "A little, but not much. We knew some of the same people. Why do you ask?" Ash tried to sound casual but failed.

It was Maggie's turn to force a casual response. She had no idea why she'd triggered such an emotional response from Ash, but instinct told her to diffuse the situation. "No reason, really. I'm just kind of fascinated by what an odd guy he is. Ignore me. I'm being a gossip."

Her tactic worked. Ash relaxed. "He's definitely that. Odd." He checked his watch. "I better go. I told my dad I'd balance the register tonight."

Maggie thanked him again for helping, and Ash strode off at a fast clip. *Someone's gonna be doing a whole lotta of digging on the internet tonight*, Maggie thought, watching him hurry away, *and that someone is me.*

She went back inside. JJ waved her over to where he'd set up the trays of food. He dished out a bowl of fricassee and handed it to her. "Eat up," he said. "I got plenty. More than I need by far. I was stress cooking."

Maggie inhaled the aroma of vegetables, seasonings, and crustaceans. She took a bite—heaven. "JJ, I never thought you could improve on your cooking, but stress may be your new secret ingredient. Kidding! Still, whatever you did here, keep doing it. This fricassee is beyond great."

"Thanks, chère. But . . ." The large man's face creased with anxiety. He clenched and unclenched the edge of the canvas apron he wore, decorated with the image of a grinning crawfish and the sentence *Who's your crawdaddy?* "What if people don't come back? I been closed a while. Locals could find other eats in the parish. And visitors may rather go to Chanson's place."

"We won't let that happen." She motioned to the volunteers taking a spin on the dance floor or relaxing at tables, eating and chatting. "The locals will come—if not on their own, then every one of us here will call in the favors we need to fill the place the first week. After that, the food'll bring them back. Trust me on this. And we can put together a campaign to attract the tourists. I'll design an ad and you can run a coupon in the *Penny Clipper*. I'll tell you one person who owes me plenty of favors—Little Earlie—so I'll make sure that coupon's a freebie. And—"

Junie's front door opened. A hipster in his early thirties stepped into the restaurant. "Hey," he greeted them. He glanced around. "Are y'all serving?"

"Yes," Maggie quickly said, before JJ could respond otherwise. He shot her a quizzical glance. "We're having a small reopening party. Come on in."

"Awesome." The man turned and called behind him, "They're serving."

A half dozen fellow hipsters of assorted sexes followed him inside. "You said you had made too much food," Maggie muttered to JJ under her breath. "Here's a chance to impress some newcomers."

JJ gave a slight nod, then slapped on his sunniest smile. He held up his hands in a welcoming gesture. "Welcome to Junie's Oyster Bar and Dance Hall. We may be sans oysters thanks to the shortage, but we are never sans fun and fabulous food. Magnolia, will you help my new friends while I change into something more festive?"

"It'd be my pleasure." Maggie watched with fondness as JJ sashayed into his office to don one of the showy caftans he always kept on hand. She led the visitors to the buffet table. They took plates and filled them with hefty servings of JJ's dishes. "This is great," a young woman with a nose ring and hair dyed half pink and half black said. "We're starving. We came up from New Orleans to try Chanson's, but they had to close the place."

Maggie stopped in the middle of spooning shrimp étouffée onto the woman's plate. "Really? That's strange. Why?"

"Whole staff got food poisoning or something." The woman took a bite of shrimp. "Oh, this rocks."

"Uh-huh," said Maggie, distracted, with a perfunctory smile and nod.

She continued to serve the guests, but her mind was elsewhere. An entire kitchen staff incapacitated? Maggie found it hard to believe this could be written off as an accidental case of food poisoning. Someone wanted to cripple the restaurant. But who? And why?

Chapter 21

Maggie had assumed Bo never showed to the Junie's let's-put-on-a-restaurant show because he was helping Xander with homework. Now she assumed otherwise.

She checked Find My Friend on her cell and saw her husband was at St. Pierre Parish Medical Center. Rather than disturb him with a call, Maggie texted what she'd learned from the customer about the Chanson staff being laid out by food poisoning. Bo responded with a phone call. She stepped into the alley for privacy. "You heard right," he said. "I'm at the hospital now, seeing if anyone's well enough to talk to me. A couple of employees didn't get hit with throwing up and a case of the Fais Do Gotta Go's, but they're looking after their sick coworkers. I'm waiting on them."

"You don't think it was an accident."

"Nope. The staff ate a different meal from what they served to the guests. The kitchen cooked up a big batch of chicken and seafood pastalaya for the employees." Despite her full stomach, Maggie's mouth watered at the mere mention of her favorite Cajun meal, a twist on jambalaya with pasta substituting for rice. "Officers from the State Police Toxicology Unit commandeered the pot of leftovers and trashed pastayala to run tests on. I gotta go. I see the guys who didn't get nailed by this."

"Who?" Maggie couldn't resist asking.

"Trick Costello and Luis Alvaro. Costello wasn't around for dinner. He was in the city."

"Right," Maggie said, recalling her conversation with Kate. "What about Luis?"

"He says he didn't eat the dish because he's gluten-free. He had a sandwich. With gluten-free bread."

Maggie heard the skepticism in her husband's voice but wasn't sure if it was inspired by Luis's purported alibi or Bo's general disdain, as a man with an iron stomach, for people claiming food sensitivities. "I'll see you at home," she said. "Eventually."

Bo snorted. "Don't wait up."

The call over, Maggie went back inside Junie's, where she found a festive atmosphere. More Chanson's patrons had found their way there, some enjoying a meal, others twirling and two-stepping on the dance floor. JJ, who had changed into a black silk caftan decorated with red sequined hearts, was in his element. He stood behind the bar shaking a cocktail shaker in time with Gaynell's upbeat tune. Maggie approached. "Here you go, chère," he said to a woman in her forties with a high blond ponytail, clad in purple leggings and purple sheepskin knee-high boots. "One Ragin' Cajun

Martini, heavy on the Ragin'." The woman walked away with her drink. JJ, beaming, clapped his hands together. "Thoughts and prayers to the Chanson staff, but dang, this is a great sign for my li'l eatery."

Another customer approached the bar, earning JJ's attention. Maggie watched her friend joke and entertain him. She'd realized something that deeply pained her, something she doubted had occurred to JJ yet. Unless he had an alibi, the ebullient restauranter had just painted himself as a prime suspect in the Chanson poisoning debacle.

*   *   *

Once home, Maggie fixed herself a cup of tea, sat down at her antique secretary desk, and opened her laptop. She shot off emails to her cousin Lia and a few friends to jog their memories about Ash and ask if anyone knew Scooter. Then she searched the *Pelican Penny Clipper*'s archives for a story about Ash's arrest for assault. Knowing the publication's bend toward the salacious, she was sure they'd covered it. The search quickly proved her right. She opened the article, housed between coupons for the local Laundromat and car wash, and read it. Her eyes widened when she hit one particular sentence. She reread the sentence, then began a new search, hunting for confirmation from another source. She found what she was looking for in a short report of the incident buried deep inside an issue of the *Advocate*, Baton Rouge's leading newspaper.

Maggie heard the downstairs door open, then the sound of Bo tromping up the stairs. She met him on the landing. "I found something interesting."

"Hello to you too. Gimme a minute. It's pouring outside."

Bo shed his jacket. He shook the water off, hung it to dry on the landing's coatrack, and came inside the apartment. Maggie gave him a towel to dry his hair, then took his hand and led him to her laptop. He pulled up a dining room chair and gazed at the laptop screen. "Here." Maggie highlighted a line in the *Advocate* article. "This is about Ash's arrest for assault. Guess who he assaulted? And who assaulted him back?"

Bo squinted as he read the line. His face registered surprise. "Scooter Pitot. Huh. I don't remember seeing any of this in the notes from the sheriff's interview with Ash Garavant. But they were focused on recent events, and he's not high up on the list of suspects."

"I emailed some friends to see if anyone remembers anything about Ash or Scooter from the past. Let me check my inbox and see if anyone got back to me." Maggie tabbed to her email and scanned the messages. "Ah, here's something from my friend Annette. She was the token popular girl and knew everyone. Especially the boys." She read Annette's response to Bo. " 'OMG, I haven't heard either of those names in a bazillion years! Scooter went to St. Francis with Ash, the superquiet guy you dated. Total bad boy. And totally hot! They hung together until Scooter got expelled for selling pot. Not sure where he ended up. Why?' "

Bo leaned back in his chair and considered Annette's email. "So, Ash has a history with Scooter, who has a history with prison."

"Scooter must have been expelled before I dated Ash; otherwise I'd have recognized him."

Bo leaned forward. "I need to access a database."

"Let me write back to Annette first. She's a big gossip. She'll be all over me until I respond." Maggie typed a reply: *No reason. Ash back working with his dad. Met Scooter in town. We need to get together!*

Bo nodded his approval. "Good boring answer." Maggie traded seats with Bo so he could use her laptop. "The fact these two lunks have a history tells me they didn't get into a fight over road rage. That was a cover story." He tapped on the keys. "I'm accessing a confidential law enforcement database. Cover your eyes." Maggie covered her eyes. "I'm in. You can open them."

Maggie blinked her eyes open. "What are you looking up?"

"Deets on Scooter's rap sheet. I want to compare dates to the dustup with Ash." Bo perused the document on the screen. "Hmmm . . ."

"*Hmmm* what?"

"The arrest that sent Scooter to prison happened a few weeks after the 'road rage' incident. He tried holding up the Ville Platte Park 'n Shop. The cashier was able to trigger a silent alarm, and VPD nabbed Pitot. He was convicted of armed robbery. Only got out a few years ago." Pensive, Bo rested an elbow on the desk and his chin on his fist. "Your friend painted Scooter as a bad boy and Ash as his sidekick. Maybe Ash was supposed to be his accomplice in the robbery and got cold feet. Let me look something else up." Bo's fingers flew over the keyboard. "Here we go. The arrest record for the road rage incident. Let's see . . . Route 22. Pickup truck chasing older-model sedan . . . assault. A couple of eyewitnesses to the fight."

"Scooter drives a pickup," Maggie said. "A beat-up one that looks pretty old. What if Ash told him he wanted out? They get into an argument, Ash jumps in his car and takes off, Scooter follows. They get into a fight but then lie to the police about what caused it." Maggie sat up straight as something occurred to her. "You know what, I remember stopping off at Abel's place during a visit home from college and asking about Ash and being surprised when Abel said he'd gone up north for college and planned to stay there. Ash didn't seem the kind of kid who would do that. He was a huge LSU fan. You know, the kind who spells the word *go* in *Go Tigers*, g-e-a-u-x."

"Sounds like someone who wanted to put a lot of distance between himself and Pelican."

Bo pushed back from the desk. He stifled a yawn and rubbed his eyes. Maggie felt a pang for not giving him a moment to unwind from the Chanson calamity. "I'm sorry, cher. I haven't even asked about your night."

He quirked the corner of his mouth in a tired half smile. "The good news is everyone will be fine, some faster than others. The restaurant will be open for lunch tomorrow, which is a big relief to Kate Chanson, who was way more hysterical about that than the condition of her employees. Luis, the guy in charge of cold stuff—"

"The garde-manger," Maggie said, a little impressed with herself for knowing this.

"Whatever. He's moving up to executive chef while the others recover. They're bringing in waitstaff from the city."

"Phew. I was afraid I'd be asked to waitress again."

"Which your husband would have had a big old problem with. Tomorrow is Valentine's Day, and I have plans for us." Bo favored his wife with a sexy smile. He checked the time in the right-hand corner of the laptop screen. "And it's almost midnight, so they start . . . right . . ." The number dissolved into twelve AM. "Now." He placed an index finger under Maggie's chin and gently lifted her lips to his.

*   *   *

Maggie and Bo agreed to put recent events aside and focus on celebrating their first Valentine's Day as a couple. Maggie tried but couldn't get past her fear that her stalker might be planning an unpleasant surprise. First thing in the morning, Bo scoured the B and B grounds for any sign of the interloper. "All clear," he told his wife, who breathed a sigh of relief.

Maggie challenged herself to up her breakfast game and succeeded by creating a meal featuring cane syrup–drenched heart-shaped pancakes she made using a mold borrowed from the Crozat kitchen, where the romantic dish was de rigueur for honeymooning guests.

"Time for gifts," she told her husband. They moved into the living room. She handed him a flat rectangular package wrapped in red tissue paper. Bo ripped off the paper and opened the box. He extracted a canvas. "Wow," was all he could say as he admired it. Maggie had found a new way to artistically express the relationship between Bo and Xander. She'd painted Bo in black and white, half in silhouette, a hand on his son's shoulder as he gazed down at the boy, who was curled up in the living room chair reading a book. Maggie had rendered Xander in vivid, bright colors. "He's your talisman," she said.

"It's . . . wow. Chère, I don't what to say." He admired the painting again. Then he rose and exchanged a heartfelt kiss with Maggie. "My gift isn't anywhere near as good," he said, embarrassed. "It's, um, a couples massage at the spa."

Maggie laughed and wrapped her arms around Bo's waist. "First art lessons with Vi, now that? Husband o' mine, you are the best gift giver ever. I can't think of anything I'd like better than a long, relaxing massage."

Relaxing proved the word of the day. Both Maggie and Bo were lulled to sleep by the nimble ministrations of the talented masseuse and masseur tending to them. After completing their massages, they ran into Gran and Lee in the spa lobby, emerging from their own couple's massage. "My first massage ever," Lee announced. "All I gotta say is, where's the time machine that'd take me back eighty years so I could book one of these every Valentine's Day?"

"I told you so," Gran said, who'd dressed for the holiday in black slacks and a purposely kitschy sweater decorated with embroidered hearts and chubby cupids.

Lee checked his watch. "I gotta go. I need all of you to be at the ferry landing in half an hour." He wagged a finger at Gran. "Especially you, Mrs. Bertrand."

"My goodness, listen to you ordering me around like that." Gran said it with a hint of delight.

Lee gave his wife a wink and headed off. "We're going to Junie's for JJ's special grand-reopening Valentine's Day luncheon," Gran said. "Would you like to join us?"

"Normally, we'd jump at it," Bo said, "but I'm taking Maggie down to New Orleans. We're gonna spend the night there."

"What a wonderful idea." Gran threw Maggie a sympathetic look. She'd immediately understood the impetus behind Bo's plan: remove his wife from anywhere her stalker might be.

"But we'll make sure to stop at the ferry landing on our way out of town," Maggie said, summoning a smile to counteract the conversation's somber undercurrent. "It sounds like Lee has something special planned."

"It does indeed," Gran said. "He's been dropping hints that alternately excite and terrify me."

"I bet," Maggie said, amused.

The three walked out of the spa, chatting with each other. They were greeted by a sight that stopped them in their tracks. The path leading from the building to the B and B manor house was strewn with red rose petals. Bile rose in Maggie's throat. She clutched Bo's arm. "No," she said in a whisper.

A vein in Bo's forehead pulsed. He was about to respond when Tug approached them from the parking lot, carrying an armful of roses. "Happy Valentine's Day, y'all," he said in a cheerful voice. "You like my surprise for Ninette? We're the one old married couple at Crozat this year, so I wanted to do something special for her to compete with all the newlywed energy going around. The path leads from the house to the spa. Guess what we're gonna do?"

"Get a couple's massage?" Gran asked.

"Yeah," Tug said, a bit deflated.

"It's a great gift, Dad," Maggie, relieved, assured her father. "So, the rose petals. That's from you? For Mom?"

Tug, cheery again, nodded. He held up his armful of flowers. "I ran out of petals, so I had to go buy more roses."

"I'll help you distribute them," Gran said. "I have a little time before I need to be at the ferry landing."

"I'll get our overnight bags," Bo said to Maggie. "See? Nothing to worry about."

"Yup, nothing to worry about," Maggie responded with a confidence she didn't feel.

While waiting for Bo to return with their luggage, Maggie helped her father and grandmother build a soft path of petals for Ninette, who gasped with delight when Tug summoned her from the house. Maggie watched fondly as her parents embraced. She saw a vision of herself and Bo years hence, still filled with the kind of love and respect for each other that had sustained Tug and Ninette's thirty-five-year marriage.

Bo showed up a few minutes later, and everyone trooped off in their various modes of transportation to the ferry landing. A crowd had gathered. As the ferry crossed from the east to its landing on the river's west bank, they could see it was festooned with red hearts, some as large as a man, and could hear Lee's band of seniors performing a jazzed-up version of the song "My Funny Valentine." Quentin and his fellow

Fryboys, decked out in red flannel shirts and red bandannas, marched to the front of the ship. The band stopped midsong and switched to their version of the classic Elvis Presley tune "All Shook Up," to which the Fryboys performed a synchronized dance routine. When they were done, their delighted audience reacted with hoots and hollers. The Fryboys then formed the lines of a singing chorus and performed an a capella version of "Love Me Tender" so sweet and lovely that Maggie found herself tearing up. Bo clutched her hand. She glanced at her husband and was touched to see his eyes glistening as well.

The ferry docked. Wives and girlfriends rushed onboard to commingle with their loved ones. "Ready to pass a good time in N'Awlins?" Bo asked Maggie with a grin.

Maggie pumped a fist. "*Laissez les bon temps rouler!*"

Bo had made the couple a reservation at their favorite New Orleans eatery, Gumbo Ya Ya. Housed in what was once a nineteenth-century stable, the restaurant had the building's original slate floor. Every wall featured faded murals of life two centuries ago. Maggie loved to inhale the muggy cloud of herbs, meats, seafood, and spices that hung low over the patrons. Bo was disappointed to learn that Gulf oysters still weren't available, but a shared bowl of chicken and andouille sausage gumbo, followed by a Creole combination platter featuring generous servings of jambalaya, red beans and rice, and blackened catfish helped ease the pain. He and Maggie topped off their meal with café brûlot and a pecan sundae.

Stomachs full, the couple agreed they needed a walk, so they wandered the French Quarter for half an hour, reveling in the unseasonably warm and dry evening. Eventually they made their way to the Reveille Orleans hotel, where Maggie's high school friend Lulu Colombe worked as the general manager. Lulu greeted them with warm hugs and her usual bubbly energy. "I put y'all in our best suite for the price of our cheapest room," Lulu said. She held a finger to her lips. "Don't tell my boss."

Maggie mimed zipping her lips. "Thanks so much, Lulu."

"Consider it part of my wedding present. Let me get you a couple of key cards." She went behind the desk and set up the cards. "Oh, I never got back to you on that email you sent about Scooter Pitot and Ash Garavant."

"I figured you didn't know them," Maggie said.

Lulu's preternaturally cheery face darkened. "Oh, I knew them. Scooter was trouble. Ash was real sweet but had problems. That's all I'm gonna say." Her chipper demeanor returned as she handed Bo the key cards. "There you go. Have fun, you two." Her blatantly suggestive tone made Maggie blush.

The suite proved stunning, a perfect blend of traditional French provincial furniture and modern touches, like a black marble floor and a sleek bathroom featuring a two-person Jacuzzi tub. As the suite was situated on the top floor, the windows provided a picturesque view of the Quarter's centuries-old garrets and slate roofs. "Nice to have friends in high places," Bo said, referencing a bottle of champagne that sat chilling in a brass bucket on top of a round, silver-gilded table in the center of the suite's sitting room. He pulled his phone out of his jeans back pocket and tapped it a couple of times. Marvin Gaye's sexy classic "Let's Get It On" began playing. "Settin' the mood," Bo said, mimicking a Rico Suave type of character, much to Maggie's amusement. He removed the champagne bottle from the bucket. "A bit of bubbly for madame," he said, switching his imitation to a French accent. He was about to pop the cork when a phone call interrupted Gaye's sultry crooning. Bo checked his phone. "It's Rufus. I gotta take it."

"I'll go change."

Maggie took her carry-on bag into the bedroom. She extracted a wedding shower present she'd received from Vanessa, a barely-there lacy beige negligee meant to be removed as quickly as possible. Maggie held it up to herself in front of the bedroom's full-length mirror. *Props to Vanessa for some spot-on boudoir shopping*, she thought, admiring the image.

Maggie was about to disrobe when Bo appeared in the doorway. The look on his face caused her to drop the negligee back into her suitcase. "Chère, breaks my heart to tell you this, especially after seeing that nightie. But we have to get back to Pelican."

"What's wrong?"

When Bo spoke, there was no hint of Rico Suave. He was all grim detective. "They found Dyer Gossmer. Or what's left of him."

Chapter 22

Maggie plopped down on the edge of the bed. Bo sat next to her. "Well, that is all kinds of bad. How did they . . . find him?" she asked.

"A guy took his girlfriend out for a romantic pirogue ride on the bayou. He was gonna propose. The boat got stuck on a log. Only it wasn't a log." Bo paused. "It was Gossmer's leg."

Maggie winced. "Ouch. Talk about a mood killer. I assume the leg was attached to enough of Dyer to identify him?"

"There was a gator—"

Maggie held up a hand to stop Bo from talking. "No need to give me the gory details. Just nod."

Bo nodded. "So, we need to get home. I'm sorry."

"Nothing to be sorry about." Maggie kissed Bo. She stroked his cheek. "You gave me a wonderful Valentine's Day. We'll finish celebrating when everything settles down."

Lulu understood the situation and banked their reservation. They made it back to Pelican in less than an hour. Still, it was close to midnight by the time they got home. Bo dropped Maggie off and went to inspect the crime scene, which was located on a stretch of Bayou Beurre halfway between Crozat B and B and the Pelican village center.

Maggie tried to sleep but found it impossible with her nerves buzzing from this new development. She checked the nightstand clock. It read 12:15 AM. She felt a weight lifted from her. Valentine's Day had come and gone without a memento or visit from her stalker. Maggie had to assume he—or she—had finally been scared off. She wriggled out from under the colorful heirloom quilt from Bo's side of the family that decorated their king-size bed and stuck her feet into a pair of low-rise sheepskin boots. She slipped each arm into a sleeve of her purple terry cloth bathrobe and belted it, then strode into the living room.

Gopher and Jolie lay fast asleep on their fluffy dog beds, the basset hound snoring like a hockey player with a deviated septum. Maggie went to her desk and picked up her sketch pad, which lay on top of a pile of papers. *If I can't sleep, I might as well be productive.* She thumbed through the sketches, searching for one that might inspire a painting. She reached a sketch of Scooter Pitot juggling oysters. Maggie wasn't one to admire her own work, but she had to give herself credit for capturing the oyster shucker's showboating style. She gave her artwork another onceover and did a double take. *Am I imagining this?* Maggie peered at the sketch more closely, then tore it out of the sketchbook. She flipped through the pages to find another sketch she'd done of Scooter in action and held the first sketch next to the second. Holding the drawings side by side confirmed her instinct, but to be absolutely sure, she put down the sketches and hurried to her laptop. An internet search yielded the additional confirmation she needed.

When Bo finally made it home an hour later, he found his wife pacing the room, wired with excitement. "Scooter's serving two kinds of oysters."

"Oh-kay," Bo said, confused.

"There's only one type on the menu. Gulf oysters. But he's serving another type too."

"You're sure?"

"Yes. Look." Maggie held up the first sketch. "This was the first time I sketched Scooter. See how I drew all the oysters exactly the same size?" She held up the second one. "But here's the second one I did two days ago. Some of the oysters are large, others small, and they're not shaped the same way. I looked up oysters on the computer." She dragged her weary husband to her secretary desk. She held the second sketch next to the screen. "The smaller ones are West Coast oysters. Kumamotos from Washington."

"Locals would instantly know the difference."

"But a lot of visitors wouldn't. Except foodies. I think Scooter eyeballs the clientele and makes sure the wrong oysters go to the right customers. He's taking a chance, but if someone complains, he probably has a couple of apologies and explanations ready for them."

Bo scratched his chin, where stubble had sprouted. Almost forty, his beard was starting to lean more gray than black. "I'm not sure what the fine is for false advertising, but right now the expression *bigger fish* comes to mind."

"I think there's a *bigger fish* issue here," Maggie said. "Scooter had plenty of Gulf oysters on day one, which is highly suspicious when you think about how hard they are to come by these days. And Phillippe was selling them for only fifty cents each, an insanely low price. But on the second day I drew him . . ." She waved both sketches in the air. "Something happened between these sketches that led Scooter to try and stretch out his supply of Gulf oysters. And somewhere in that time frame, Dyer Gossmer switched from ghostwriting a suck-up 'autobiography' to a Chanson exposé. He told me he'd uncovered criminal activity. Then he disappeared."

"You think there's a link between oysters and Gossmer's murder?"

Bo's tone was so filled with skepticism that Maggie wavered. "Yes." She said this loudly, half to reinforce her own conviction. "It's not the worst idea in the world," she added, much less emphatically.

"It's an idea."

Bo's acknowledgment was weak, but Maggie clung to it as affirmation that she might have dropped a few bread crumbs on the trail to the writer's killer.

* * *

On the way to her car in the morning, Maggie passed Trick Costello sitting on the wrought-iron bench outside the carriage house, finishing a phone call.

"Kate has family pictures of him," he was saying. "Some from when he was a kid. I'll have her email them to you . . . Sounds good . . . You too." He ended the call and noticed

Maggie. "The Food Channel is doing a memorial segment on Phillippe. Death hasn't dimmed his star. At least not yet."

"That's an interesting way to put it."

Trick shrugged. "It's realistic. The memories of everyone fade, except for the most famous. The single-namers like Marilyn. Elvis. Kobe. That's what we want for Phillippe. To be iconic. If his fame goes, it'll take the restaurant group with it, unless we find a successful way to rebrand."

"How's everyone at Chanson's feeling? Any better?"

"Some yes, some no. Jerome and Becca are still down for the count. But Luis is taking over until they're back. And maybe after. It's a great opportunity for him."

"He seems like a good guy. I hope it works out for him." She adopted a gossipy tone. "Did you hear they found Dyer? Or what's left of him," she added, borrowing the line from Bo to see if the shock value might elicit a reaction.

Trick's body tensed. "I'd heard they found him, but not how. What exactly does 'what's left of him' mean?" Maggie told him, and the mixologist reacted with horror. "Dear God." He was speechless for a moment. Then he recovered his composure. "I'll have Luis take the alligator po' boy off the menu tonight. It might push buttons for anyone who heard how Dyer died."

"Smart move."

Maggie left Trick putting in a call to the restaurant. She drove toward town. The *Say Yes to This Dress* exhibit had opened the day before without her, per Ione, who'd insisted Maggie celebrate her newlyweds Valentine's Day. Maggie had given in but decided to thank her coworkers with an assortment of baked goods from Fais Dough Dough. As she drove, she replayed Trick's reaction to the news of Dyer's grisly death. His investment in keeping the Chanson brand alive gave him a motive to get rid of a nosy writer determined to profit from a tell-all that might destroy Phillippe's reputation. But the mixologist's horrified reaction at the thought of Dyer being alligator chum seemed sincere, although he'd made a quick transition to the business of adjusting the menu accordingly.

She parked in the small lot behind the bakery and its sister candy shop. A bell tinkled when she opened the back door, alerting employees to a customer entering via the parking lot. She walked through the bakery's kitchen into the storefront. "Hey, Kyle," she greeted her cousin Lia's husband, who was behind the glass counter filling a large brown paper bag with the football-shaped loaves used for local po' boy sandwiches.

"Hey. Be with you in a minute. I'm filling a standing order."

"No rush. How was your Valentine's Day?"

"Perfect. We went out to dinner at a new place in LaPlace with a view of Lake Pontchartrain. Kind of a drive, but we hired the Poche kids to babysit and wanted to take advantage of the break. Don't get too many of those with triplet infants."

"I bet. When you're done there, I'll take a dozen assorted croissants and Danishes."

"You got it."

The bell over the shop's front door tinkled, indicating the arrival of a customer. The newcomer was Ash Garavant.

Maggie's contemporary appeared to have aged overnight. His red hair was flecked with gray. Wrinkles had taken root in his cheeks and forehead. His normally bright blue eyes were cloudy and dulled; the pockets beneath them sagged. "Ash, hi," Maggie said. She felt a rush of concern for him. "Are you okay?"

"I'm fine, totally fine," he said. The nervous tapping of his foot betrayed him. "Got our rolls, Kyle?"

"Here you go. I'll put it on your account." Kyle handed Ash the brown paper bag.

"Thanks." Ash started for the door and then stopped. He approached Maggie. "Is it true?" he asked in a low voice. "About the guy who was writing the book? They found him? His body?"

"Yes," Maggie said. Ash grimaced and released a choked whimper. "Did you know him?"

Ash gave his head a vigorous shake. "But he came into our place and I heard him on the phone, talking about how he was onto a big case tied to Chanson's. Oh man. Oh man, oh man, oh man."

Maggie placed a hand on Ash's arm, hoping to calm him. "Ash, if you know anything, you have to go to the police."

Ash brushed her off. "I can't. I gotta get outta here."

He bolted out the door. Maggie chased after him. "Ash, don't run," she yelled. "Please."

He ignored her. They reached his car. Ash yanked open his car door and jumped in. Maggie dove out of the way as he rapidly accelerated in reverse, hitting a puddle and splattering

Maggie with mud. Then he screeched off, disappearing down the road at high speed. Maggie removed her phone from the back pocket of her jeans and placed a call that went to voice mail. She left a message.

"Bo, it's me. I just had a strange convo with Ash Garavant. He knows something. And whatever it is scares him."

Chapter 23

Maggie washed herself off in the Fais Dough Dough restroom. She collected her pastries from Kyle and set off for Doucet. Rather than backtracking to the ferry, she drove up the River Road to the nearest bridge. Either way, it was a longer-than-usual ride. She arrived at Doucet forty-five minutes later, where she and her pastries were beset upon by Ginny and intern Aileen in the break room. "Thanks for stuffing her mouth," Aileen said, indicating Ginny. "It gives me a break from listening to"—she switched from her own voice to mimicking Ginny's—"how *awesome* her Valentine's Day was."

"Well, it was." Ginny chomped down on her pecan bear claw. "Little Earlie brought me flowers and took me out to dinner in Baton Rouge. And he gave me this." She pushed back her curly brown hair to reveal a delicate hoop earring in her cartilage piercing. "He's the best boyfriend ever."

Maggie grinned, pleased the pugnacious journalist had taken her advice. "I'm glad it's working out with y'all." She placed the remaining pastries on a platter. "I'm gonna see which of these Ione wants. I'll bring back what's left."

She left for the gift shop, where Ione was finishing the sale of a needlepoint kit featuring an image of the Doucet wedding gown. "The craft souvenirs were a great idea," she told Maggie after the customer departed. "It's only our second day and I've already sold two needlepoint and three counted-cross-stitch kits. Oooh, croissants. Thanks." Ione removed one from the platter.

"Thanks for giving me the day off yesterday. Bo and I had a great time. Until Dyer Gossmer's remains popped up."

"I can see how that might take the romance out of a night." Ione wiped a crumb from her face. "No word from . . . ?"

Ione hesitated, but Maggie knew what she wanted to ask. "Nothing from the stalker."

"Good."

"How was the exhibit opening?" asked Maggie, eager to change the subject. She crossed her fingers on both hands and held them up. "A success, I hope, I hope."

"A big success. It drew twice the number of our usual visitors, and not one person squawked at being charged separately for a 'special exhibit.' "

"I'm so glad," Maggie said, relieved. Her nerves were on edge with every exhibit she curated, but given Doucet's dire financials at the moment, there was extra pressure on this one.

"Still, it doesn't replace the money that sorry piece of work Steve Collins stole." Ione spoke in a grim tone.

"Which reminds me," Maggie said, "now that Valentine's Day is over, it's time for another gala committee meeting. We can hold it at Junie's. Give JJ the business. I'll call and tell him to hold us a table for tonight."

She tapped the number for Junie's into her cell. JJ replied in a singsongy voice, "How-do, Miss Magnolia, or should I say Mrs. Magnolia now?"

She reacted with amusement to her friend's chipper tone. "Somebody's in a good mood."

"Speak up, chère. It's hard to hear you over the crowd in here."

"You're crowded? JJ, that's terrific."

"You know it. The locals are back and, hoo mama, they are *hungry*. Plus, Chanson's is closed again, so I'm drawing their crowd."

Maggie's brow creased. "Chanson's closed, huh? I wonder why."

"*What?*"

"Never mind," she yelled. "I was gonna ask you to save a table for a Doucet gala committee meeting, but I think it's gonna be too loud over there."

"*What?*"

"*Never mind!*" Maggie practically screamed. Ione recoiled, covering her ears. "*Have fun!*" She ended the call. "New plan," she said to Ione. "We'll meet at Crozat, seven PM for anyone who can make it."

"*What?*" Ione yelled.

She broke into a grin, and Maggie rolled her eyes. "Funny stuff. I hear the Ha Ha Comedy Club in Baton Rouge has an open-mic night."

Maggie brought the rest of the pastries back to the break room, then went to her office. After texting the gala committee to set up the evening's meeting, she donned cotton museum-curator gloves and climbed to the attic up a set of stairs restricted to employees. Combing through Doucet's treasure trove of antiques was one of her favorite tasks, particularly since the planation had belonged to her mother's family until they donated it to be used as a historical site. She threaded her way through a sea of centuries-old furniture, trunks, knickknacks, and ephemera, finally landing on a collection of paintings that were the work of Carrie Jones, a once-enslaved woman who'd found fame and fortune as a folk artist in the early twentieth century. Doucet's next exhibit would be a tribute to Jones's work. Maggie checked her phone to make sure she hadn't missed a response from Bo, then began searching through generations of arts and crafts.

She emerged from the attic hours later carrying paintings, drawings, and a couple of Carrie's small, rudimentary clay sculptures. She parked the items in her office and shook the attic dust out of her hair. Hungry, she trooped over to the break room, hoping to find a leftover pastry. She was semi in luck. Someone had split a Creole Cream Cheese Danish in two and left half on the plate. Maggie inhaled the pastry, finishing just as Bo returned her call. She detailed her exchange with Ash. "Something's spooking him. And I'm sure it has to do with Dyer's death."

"I'll hunt him down and bring him in for questioning."

"I hope he hasn't taken off. I got the feeling he might."

"Great, just what I need. Wait, Ru's trying to get my attention. Hey, Ru . . ." Maggie heard an angry Rufus yelling in the background but couldn't make out what he was saying. "*What?* Son of a—" Bo released a stream of epithets. "I gotta go, chère. Parish police are interviewing Luis Alvaro about the doctored eats at Chanson's and we're only learning about it now. This is what happens when you got a bunch of agencies working at cross-purposes."

"Did forensics figure out what made the staff sick?"

"They found a trace of monkshood. The stuff is deadly but less so if used in a very minute amount. It was also diluted by being added to a dish meant to serve a crowd. Still, whoever did it is lucky no one died. I'll see you at home. Whenever I get there."

"Love you. Be safe."

Maggie pocketed her phone. She wrapped her arms around herself for emotional as well as physical warmth. She'd noticed that Luis kept to himself. Maggie figured this had more to do with his immigration status than a nefarious plot to move up the culinary ladder at Chanson's from *sous-chef* to executive chef, which she assumed would be the motivation for rendering coworkers out of commission.

The day passed quickly, with Maggie immersed in Carrie Jones's simple, powerful creations. Eventually the bells from a nearby church tolled five PM. She covered the folk artist's drawings, sculptures, and paintings in acid-free tissue paper to protect them, then set off for home, using the short ride to the ferry landing to organize her thoughts. With Junie's back in business, Maggie sensed JJ had shelved his fears about being a person of interest in Phillippe's murder. Once word got out about Luis, that would cement her friend's relief. If law enforcement—whichever department of the too many that were involved—found a link between the poisonings and

Phillippe's murder, the young chef would become the primary suspect.

She was happy to see the ferry, engine humming, unloading westbound cars. Maggie got in line behind a half dozen other cars waiting to board for the boat ride east. She brooded while idling. Something about the Luis twist felt off to her. He'd seemed nothing but grateful for the opportunities Phillippe had given him. She wondered if it had all been an act.

Maggie realized she possessed a way to prove or disprove this. She pulled her sketchbook from her tote bag. A drawing had exposed Scooter; maybe one would do the same with Luis. She skipped through the pages until she reached her renderings of him. There was Luis teasing Becca; another drawing showed him chopping onions with a skill that Maggie, who hated chopping the tear-inducing veggie, coveted; in a third sketch, Luis admired the results of his work after adding a decorative garnish to an avocado stuffed with shrimp remoulade. Maggie analyzed every drawing in the book, but nothing stood out for her. She gave a frustrated grunt and was about to toss the sketchbook aside when one particular sketch flashed in her mind. She zipped through the book until she found the drawing in question. *I wonder*, she thought. She took out her phone and typed in a word. An image came up. She matched it to the odd detail in her sketch.

The car behind her honked. Maggie looked up to see a deckhand ushering eastbound vehicles onto the ferry. Captain DiVirgilio, who was strolling among the cars, waved to her. Maggie tore a page from her sketchbook and exited the car.

"*Ciao, mia amica.*" The genial man doffed his captain's hat to her.

"*Ciao.*" Maggie handed him the sketch. "I thought you might like this."

DiVirgilio examined her drawing of him. "*Eccellente.* Thank you." He placed the gift inside his jacket and studied Maggie. "If you don't mind a little honesty from an old man, you look weary. Like something's bothering you."

Maggie quirked the corner of her mouth. "You're pretty observant."

The captain gestured to the Mississippi. "Chalk it up to a life spent on the river. Gotta have all your senses on alert." He tapped his eyelids. "Especially these."

"That's like me. People joke that being an artist makes me see things other people miss because my visual sense is so acute."

"What do you see now?"

"I'm not sure," Maggie admitted. "It may be important. Or it may be me wishing it were important because I don't want to see someone who may be innocent accused of murder. Like my friend JJ." She gazed down at the muddy waters of the Mississippi slapping rhythmically against the side of the boat. "My husband once told me that the primary motivation for killing someone isn't greed or even rage. It's humiliation. I wonder if that's the case here."

DiVirgilio pushed back his cap and scratched a spot on his forehead with a crepey, liver-spotted hand. "There's an old Italian saying: *Chi offende scrive sulla carta. Chi è offeso scrive sulla pietra.* He who offends writes on paper. He who is offended writes on stone." A deckhand shouted to the captain and gave him a thumbs-up. "Thank you for the drawing. It's time for me to ferry you across the river."

Maggie shuddered. "No offense, but I just thought of the River Styx and souls being ferried across it to their doom in Greek myths."

DiVirgilio let out a roar of laughter. "I've been called a lotta things but not a god. I can't wait to tell Mrs. DiVirgilio she's married to Hercules."

"I'm pretty sure Charon was the ferryman and more of a spirit or demon. But you don't have to mention that to your wife."

DiVirgilio headed up to the pilot's deck. Moments later he sounded the ferry's horn, and the boat crept away from the landing. A cold wind came with the ferry's chug across the Mississippi, and Maggie decamped for the warmth of her car. She turned up the heat and reflected on the Italian saying the ferry captain had shared. "He who is offended writes on stone," she said aloud.

In the case of Phillippe Chanson, Maggie had an idea who might have carved his death warrant onto stone. But what she needed was proof.

Chapter 24

When she reached Crozat, Maggie stopped at the manor house to meet with her mother and grandmother to coordinate snacks and drinks for the gala committee meeting. "I'll put out the china and flatware," Gran said.

"I can do it, Charlotte," Ninette responded.

"Please, you have to let me do something," Gran pleaded, clasping her hands together to mime praying. "Lee's at work, and Vanessa banished me from the cottage so she can surprise me with the design results, which quite frankly terrifies me. She's a dear, but signing on for her design advice was a drunken impulse I fear I'll live to regret."

Maggie exchanged a clandestine amused smile with her mother. "I'm sure we can make adjustments to Van's choices that will make you happy and not hurt her feelings," Ninette said.

"Or we stage a 'burglary,' " Maggie said, throwing air quotes around the word, "and hope Van doesn't notice that the only stuff stolen is the stuff she picked out."

Maggie left the manor house for her apartment. On the way, she saw Kate striding toward her lodgings. She noticed Maggie. "Oh, hey. Would it be possible to buy a bottle of wine from the B and B? Any bottle. I'm not picky. I'll take a belt of anything to wash down today."

"I'll have my father bring over a bottle of Chardonnay and a bottle of Merlot. On the house."

"Thanks."

"I heard about Luis being interviewed by the parish police."

Kate slapped her hands against her forehead in a gesture of incredulity. "Can you believe it? I can't. Phillippe was Luis's biggest supporter. He thought he had a ton of promise." This should have come as a revelation to Maggie, given what she'd once been told. Instead, it helped confirm what she suspected. "I don't know," Kate continued. "Maybe I'm too *kumbaya*, love your fellow man. Trick's way more skeptical. He said there was a dark side to Luis. I thought he was jealous because Luis had a crush on me." She took a tin of mints from her designer purse and popped one into her mouth. "I'm pretending these are Xanax, which I could really use right now, except my doctor wouldn't refill the prescription. I need to have someone sneak me in a bottle of antianxiety meds from Canada."

"What's your plan for the restaurant? Are people in shape to work?"

"Yes, thank God. Jerome is back on his feet. Becca is better too. She'll train under him and hopefully eventually take over. And Scooter is still Scooter, for better or worse.

So, oysters will be shucked, and meals will be served." She pointed to her smartwatch. "Ticktock on that wine."

Kate continued into the carriage house. Maggie made her way to the spa and traipsed upstairs. She texted Kate's wine order to Tug, who replied with a thumbs-up and a string of wine bottle emojis. Rather than phone Bo, she decided to wait until he got home from work to run her theory by him. Overcome by an intense wave of exhaustion, she collapsed into bed for an hourlong nap. When she awoke, she showered and changed before returning to the manor house. The warm water was rejuvenating, and Maggie could have lingered under it forever. Instead, she switched off the hot water and endured a blast of cold that she hoped would give her the energy she'd need for the gala committee meeting.

Maggie tried but found it impossible to focus on the meeting. Her mind kept straying to the events at Chanson. She fidgeted with a pencil, finally breaking it, which earned her a quizzical glance from Ninette. Finally, much to her relief, Ione snapped her laptop shut. "We're in great shape, ladies. Meeting adjourned. Now, let's adjourn to the bar."

"That will have to wait a few minutes." Gran held up her phone. "Vanessa's done with my cottage. She wants us to come over and see the results."

The women left the manor and trod the path to the Crozat-Bertrand home. Gran's front door flew open and Vanessa stepped out to welcome them. She wore a bright-pink satin cocktail dress that hugged her baby bump. "Come on in, y'all. Take a look-see at Charlotte and Lee Bertrand's abode,

ELLEN BYRON

updates brought to you by Vanessa MacIlhoney's Fine Interior Design."

Gran gripped Maggie's hand. "Pray for me," she said under her breath.

Maggie followed her inside. She and the others gasped at what they saw. The living room walls were painted pale taupe. An elegant mix of antique and contemporary furniture upholstered in neutral shades filled the room, with tomato-red throw pillows adding a pop of color. A stunning bayou landscape painted by a beloved local artist—the one and only Maggie Crozat—hung over the couch. "Vanessa, I . . . I . . ." Gran stammered. "I don't know what to say."

"I got the hint when you asked me to paint over the yellow in your bedroom," Vanessa said. "And took it from there."

The women toured the now-lovely home, heaping compliments on the newly minted interior decorator. They finished in the sparkling, remodeled kitchen where Van poured each of them a glass of chilled champagne. Gran raised her glass. "To my brilliant designer and beautiful new home." The women toasted Vanessa, who blushed. "Let's take this party into the living room," Gran said. "Very, very carefully. If a single drop spills anywhere on this gloriousness, I might sue."

"I know a lawyer," Vanessa joked.

The women moved en masse, but Vanessa held Maggie back. "Thanks for sharing your gran with me." Emotional, her voice quavered. "It made me a little less sad about losing my mama."

"Of course." Maggie, with newfound insight into Vanessa's attachment to Grand-mère, hugged her. There was a

252

crunch of gravel from the parking area outside. "I think Bo's home. I'm gonna sneak out of here. The place is gorgeous, Van. I wish it looked this nice when I lived here."

Maggie hurried home. Bo was already in the apartment nursing a beer by the time she arrived. They shared a kiss. "It's been a day," he said, taking a seat in the living room club chair and hefting his long legs onto the chair's matching ottoman.

He pulled Maggie onto his lap, and she curled up in his arms. "What happened with Luis?" she asked.

"He's released for now, due to a lack of evidence, but he's still in the parish police cross hairs."

"I have a theory about the poisoning, and it ties into Phillippe's murder."

"You have a theory, huh? Why am I not surprised?" Bo didn't bother to hide his amusement. "You've got a dang good track record with your theories, so lay it on me."

Bo listened as Maggie mapped out a possible scenario. "Does that make any sense?" she asked when she was done, suddenly insecure.

"Yes. But I need a whole lot more than a supposition to sell it."

Maggie, now animated and determined, jumped off her husband's lap. "No worries. I don't just have a theory. I have a plan."

Bo raised his eyebrows. "Uh-oh."

Chapter 25

There was an excellent turnout at Chanson's Cajun Kitchen that evening. Maggie's offer to sketch patrons for free was eagerly welcomed and attracted a steady stream of diners. But the energy of the staff hummed with tension. Since no charges had been brought against Luis and he was vociferous in declaring his innocence, he was back working in the kitchen. Distracted, his ill-at-ease coworkers made more mistakes than usual filling orders, but customers were placated with a round of complimentary drinks.

As the night wore on and the time to put her plan in place drew near, Maggie grew increasingly anxious. Perspiration, a by-product of nerves and the unseasonably muggy weather, dripped down her forehead, stinging her eyes. She felt the Chanson employees eyeing her suspiciously, then wondered if it was her imagination, made overactive by the circumstances. Her hand cramped up from drawing, but she soldiered on. Finally, around eleven PM, the restaurant emptied out. One lone patron remained at the bar, back to the dining room, hunched over his drink. Kate had instructed the staff to stick around for drinks after the restaurant closed, explaining that she had important news to share. But she herself was MIA. The waitstaff lined up at the bar. The kitchen staff sauntered out of the kitchen and joined them, with only executive chef Jerome begging off, citing his long drive home to Algiers, a historic enclave across the river from New Orleans proper. Maggie, heart pounding, began to fear her plan was going to fall through. Then Kate strode through the door.

The restaurateur didn't bother with niceties. "You're all here? Good. Sit."

The others exchanged curious looks but followed her order. She pulled a file from her black leather tote bag. "It took a while, but I finally wrangled a copy of Phillippe's will from his lawyer." She held up the file to illustrate. "Nothing was more important to Phillippe than his restaurants. Not our relationship. Not yours." She said this to Becca, who acknowledged it with a sigh. "Because the restaurants were the true loves of his life, he provided for them in his will. For example, I know Jerome left already, but Phillippe willed him twenty percent ownership of Chanson's in the Quarter."

"Phillippe was always a generous guy," Trick said, with a tone Maggie couldn't quite place.

"He also had a plan for this place that he thought would guarantee its success," Kate continued. She extracted a pair of reading glasses from her tote, put them on, and read from the will. " 'To ensure the future of the newest addition to our restaurant family, Chanson's Cajun Country, I bequeath twenty percent ownership to a protégé who constantly impresses me with their commitment, devotion and talent . . .' " The room waited, holding a collective breath. Kate looked up. " 'Luis Alvaro.' "

There was a sharp intake of breaths. "A share of the restaurant?" Becca said. Her stunned reaction turned to anger. "Not just a job but a *share*? To Luis?" She closed her eyes as she processed this, then snapped them open. "Oh my God. That's why Luis killed him. He wanted him out of the way so he could take over the restaurant."

Luis jumped up with such force he knocked over his chair. "Liar," he yelled, lunging for Becca.

Scooter pulled the young chef back. "Dude, chill." He spoke in a calm voice but kept hold of Luis's arm.

"I didn't know, I swear," the young immigrant said, on the verge of tears.

"Who's lying now?" Becca shot back at him.

"Shut up, both of you." Kate's dark tone caught everyone's attention. "Do you remember how I made Dyer record all his interviews? He was old-timey that way. He insisted on using the microcassette recorder he used to use as a journalist. I had to send the tapes to a transcription service in New York. The police requested the transcripts for the investigation into Dyer's death and discovered something interesting."

Maggie watched for reactions from the staff members as Kate reached into her purse and brought out a small, worn cassette recorder. She placed play, and Phillippe's energetic voice filled the room. Becca whimpered at the sound of her ex-boyfriend's voice. ". . . The thing about running a successful restaurant is sometimes you have to be brutal. Even when you care about someone, you gotta be honest with them. They may be a great person and all that crap, but if they ain't got what it takes, they ain't got it. But breaking the news can get ugly."

Dyer's voice came on the tape. "How'd it go in this case?"

There was a mirthless laugh from the chef. "Oh man, it put the *ugh* in ugly. I tried to frame it in a nice way. 'You could be an executive chef somewhere else. A chain. A hotel even. But not for the Chanson Group. I'm sorry, Becca.' "

The room was dead silent, so quiet that Maggie could hear the faint strains of music coming from Junie's, where Gaynell and the Gator Girls were playing a late-night set. Becca opened and shut her mouth a couple of times, but nothing came out. She finally found her voice. "He never told me. He says he did, but you don't have proof. And I'm not the one who poisoned the staff to try and get ahead. I've never been so sick in my life."

Maggie finally spoke. "Which was kind of brilliant on your part—making yourself sick too. You knew Luis wouldn't eat the pastalaya because of his gluten intolerance and that not eating it would make him look like the prime suspect. Except you're the one who had the monkshood."

"That's a crock," Becca scoffed.

Maggie held up a detailed, colorful charcoal pencil sketch of Becca in the Chanson kitchen. She pointed to a small spot of a bluish-purple color. "See the flower peeking out of your pocket? You can only see the smallest bit of it, but I'm really proud of how I captured the color. It's so unique. Very few flowers are the color of monkshood—if any."

Becca flushed. She stood up and began backing out of the room—right into the arms of Bo, Rufus, and other law enforcement officials, who had quietly positioned themselves in the doorway, unseen by the presumed murderess. She cried out as Detective Shawn Holahan cuffed her. "Becca Wittenberg, you're under arrest for the murder of Phillippe Remy Chanson."

"I want a lawyer," she spit out, furious.

The lone patron at the bar turned around, revealing himself to be Quentin MacIlhoney. "And you shall have one," he said with a flourish. He hopped off his barstool and trailed the captured woman out of the restaurant, stopping to say to Maggie, "I should really have you on a retainer, my friend."

The room devolved into a wall of sound as employees expressed their shocked reactions to what they'd just witnessed. Rufus put two fingers in his mouth and emitted an ear-piercing whistle. People winced and covered their ears, but he got their attention. "The artistic stylings of our talented friend Magnolia here clued us in to some additional criminal activity."

Maggie noticed Trick and Kate exchange a nervous look. Rufus ceded the floor to Bo and stepped aside. Bo held up Maggie's sketch of Scooter juggling oysters. "As an artist, Maggie has an eye for detail that a lot of people don't, and she noticed something was off about this drawing."

Scooter grew rigid. Kate examined the sketch. "I don't see anything—wait. The oysters aren't the same."

"Yup," Bo said. "Because they're two different varieties. We now know why Chanson's was able to get Gulf oysters so cheap. A Baton Rouge gang's been stealing them from productive oyster reefs and selling them to the restaurant."

"An oyster gang?" Maggie said in disbelief. Even she hadn't been expecting this development.

"Just one branch of their criminal enterprises. People make the mistake of thinking gang members are dumbbells. A lot of the bottom feeders are, but some of the leaders could run corporations. Seems this crew tried to sell their wares to Ash Garavant, with a few threats attached. He was able to avoid doing business with them by hooking the gang up with Scooter here instead. His sketchy friend from high school."

"This is total BS." Scooter crossed his arms in front of his chest. He glowered at Bo. Maggie saw he was clutching his oyster-shucking knife and telegraphed this with her eyes to Bo, who turned to face him.

"You forced Ash into being the middleman on the oyster scheme with threats to share that he helped plan the Park 'n Shop robbery that landed you in jail," Bo said. "He chickened out when it came to going through with the robbery, though. That's what your fight was about. The one that got you both arrested."

The oyster shucker cocked his head. "Y'all planning to turn this into a book? Cuz it sounds like fiction to me."

"We have a witness. Your former friend, Ash." Bo picked up Dyer's tape recorder, which Kate had placed on a table.

"We also have a detailed trail that Dyer Gossmer was following. I can see why he won so many awards for his reporting. His research was meticulous. And vetted. But he couldn't resist dropping a few braggy hints that he was onto your scheme. The gang pulled back on deliveries, which is what forced you to fill in with West Coast oysters that you only served to tourists, figuring they wouldn't notice the difference like locals would. You confronted Gossmer, and it didn't go well for him. As the stab wound shaped just like that"—Bo gestured to the knife in Scooter's hand—"in what's left of Gossmer's body indicates."

"Huh." Scooter assumed a thoughtful expression. Then he released a guttural yell and lunged at Bo with the knife. But Bo was ready for him, as were Pelican PD officers Artie and Cal. The three tackled the man and took him down. He fought back, but the officers subdued him.

"Nobody messes with my Gulf oysters, you SOB," Artie hissed into the criminal's ear. He and Artie dragged Scooter out of the restaurant.

Bo snapped on latex gloves. He picked up the oyster knife and dropped it in an evidence bag. He kissed his wife on the cheek. "Nice work, chère. See you at home." Bo followed his fellow officers out the door.

There was a pause. Then the room dissolved into a cacophony of conversation as the employees attempted to process the whipsaw of events. Trick positioned himself behind the bar, where Maggie and Kate joined him. "For a minute, I was afraid your husband was gonna bust me for watering down drinks," the mixologist said.

Maggie gave the bourbon he'd poured her a suspicious glance. "Are you?"

"No. Well," Trick admitted with a sheepish expression, "sometimes. But only when someone orders a third round. We don't want anyone driving drunk from here. Which is a poor segue to me offering you a drink. I know I could use a belt of something right now."

"Thanks," Maggie said, "but I'll pass. My stomach's a mess of nerves after what all went down tonight. You did a great job, Kate."

"It helped knowing the police were right outside, on alert." Kate cast an apologetic glance at her boyfriend. "The setup was Maggie's idea. I'm sorry I couldn't clue you in to what we were doing, hon. We thought the less people who knew the truth, the better."

"I get it," Trick said.

"We hoped the will might break Becca, and then we'd seal the deal with the recording," Kate said.

"It almost did break her," Maggie said. "She recovered better than I expected. But hearing you had important news worked for motivating people to stick around after closing, Kate. And it sure ratcheted up the tension."

"Did it ever," Trick said. "I'd bet good money my blood pressure was off the charts—and I was only watching." He hesitated, then said to Kate, "If it's okay with you, I'd like to see Phil's will."

"Here."

Kate handed Trick the folder. He opened it. There was nothing inside. "There's no will?"

"Oh, there's a will. I got it the day after Phillippe died. And he did share his faith in Jerome and Luis in it. Aside from that . . ." Kate stopped, overcome with emotion. Maggie, sympathetic, put a reassuring arm around her. "Phillippe left everything to you and me. A fifty-fifty split."

Trick worked his jaw. When he spoke, his voice was husky. "Like I said . . . he was a generous guy."

Chapter 26

Stomach issues, which Maggie attributed to the stress of the last couple of weeks, laid her out for the next few days. She awoke after a late-afternoon nap that wound up lasting ten hours to find Bo by her bedside. Shafts of sunlight striped the wooden bedroom floor. The bright gold rays made Maggie blink.

Bo gently stroked her hair. "How do you feel?"

"Much better." Maggie released a loud yawn, then sat up and stretched. "Any updates?"

"Why am I not surprised that's your first question?" Bo said with an affectionate grin. "Yes, a variety of them. But the one you'll be most happy to hear about is what's going on with Ash. I know that at the end of the day you still think of him as a friend."

"I do. I feel for him. And Abel. He's so proud of his son. This has to be breaking his heart."

"There's some good news. Since Ash is willing to testify against Scooter Pitot, the DA is dropping the charges against him for aiding a criminal enterprise, especially given that he was threatened into it. Ash also revealed that Phillippe Chanson knew Scooter was coming by the Gulf oysters illegally and didn't care. If anything, he encouraged it. I'm guessing that was a combination of wanting to see Chanson's Cajun Kitchen succeed at all costs and getting off on the hotdogging thrill of a little illicit activity."

"I can see that with Chanson. It was obvious he liked to think of himself as a rebel. But really, he was mostly just cocky and arrogant."

"I gotta say, that ex-boyfriend of yours is making himself useful."

"Agh," Maggie said, peeved. "Will you stop with that? I wish I'd never told you about Ash."

Bo shot her a devilish grin, then continued. "We finally know who trolled JJ on that website Tasteful and vandalized his trash and bathroom."

"Scooter?"

"Affirmative. He bragged to Ash that Chanson paid him good money to torpedo the competition."

"Dyer did tell me that for all Chanson's grandstanding, he was worried about his business."

"Enough to break the law."

Maggie thought about what poor JJ had endured thanks to his ruthless competitor. While she'd never condone murder, it was hard to summon sympathy for Phillippe Chanson. "What's going on with Becca?"

"Based on Gossmer's recordings, we were able to establish a timeline between when Chanson broke the bad news to her that she didn't cut it in his kitchen and when she messed with the boat's thermostat. Somewhere between breakfast and the dinner shift on the restaurant's opening day."

Maggie thought back to that day. "I remember I saw Becca crying and Phillippe chasing after her. I bet that's when he broke the news. She seemed fine when I saw her a little later. She must have formulated her plan to remove him as an obstacle to her career. But how did she know what to do with the boat?"

"As with everything, from building a bomb to a mass poisoning, you can find directions on how to install a thermostat on the internet—correctly or incorrectly. Incorrectly can lead to a fire. The combination of that plus the crash into the barge triggered the explosion. We got a warrant for Becca's laptop and found a bunch of searches for what might cause a powerboat to explode. Her family had a summer place on a lake in New Hampshire and she was big into water-skiing as a kid, so she was already familiar with them."

"Representing Becca will be a challenge. Which, knowing Quentin, will thrill him."

"His defense will probably be that she never intended to kill Chanson, only scare him. She swears she thought the boat would simply catch fire and he'd jump out and be rescued."

"Do you think she's telling the truth?"

"I do. She completely collapsed and it feels real, not like she's acting." Bo shrugged. "Bottom line, though, a man is dead and she's responsible."

"True dat." Maggie tossed off the covers and planted her feet on the floor. "Now I need to be a functional human being. We have our final gala committee meeting at Doucet."

Bo's cell phone suddenly erupted with a blizzard of alarms. "What the—" He checked and let out a profanity.

"What?" Maggie asked, her stomach knotted with worry.

Bo held up a hand as he continued to read the flurry of messages. Fury colored his face. "Scooter Pitot escaped."

"When?" Maggie said, stunned. "How?"

"Just now. Cal and Artie were transporting him from Pelican to Plaquemines Parish to face charges for stealing from their oyster beds. They were driving one of the patrol cars that the dang insurance refused to total, and it died en route. Artie couldn't figure out the problem, so Cal called for backup but then stepped out of the car, which was a mistake on his part, because it left Pitot alone in the car. The partition between the front and back seats is loose, thanks to the car's damage. Pitot's such a bag of bones he was able to wiggle the partition open and get out through the front side door. Artie and Cal had the hood up, which blocked their view of him making a run for it."

"Oh no." Once again, Maggie's stomach roiled. "What happens now?"

"The good news is that Cal and Artie had crossed into Ville Blanc when it happened, so Ville Blanc PD is all over it. They need a win after coming off like fools during the Halloween murders."

Maggie shared a knowing grin with her husband. "I bet." The larger and way more arrogant VPD had embarrassed themselves by considering Maggie the prime suspect in a murder in the fall, completely ignoring clues that led to the real killer.

Bo favored his wife with a gentle smile and caressed her cheek. "My job is to rearrest the suspect. Yours is to feel better."

He kissed Maggie, his lips lingering on hers. "Well, that sure helped," she said with a wink when they finally pulled apart.

Maggie opted for an intestinal-soothing cup of chamomile tea, then showered and dressed for work. On the ferry ride across the river, she accepted Captain DiVirgilio's invitation to join him on the bridge. She was happy to see her sketch of him standing in a frame on a small worktable. "The *Baroness Pontalba* and I are going back into retirement soon," he told her. "The bridge'll be up and running again in a day or so."

"I should say 'Good,' but I'll miss you."

A smile lit up the old man's craggy face. "Right back at ya, my young friend."

The two gazed at the river before them in companionable silence. "I owe you much thanks," Maggie said after a short while. "That saying you shared about people who are offended writing on stone clued me in to who might have been offended enough to kill."

DiVirgilio, keeping his eyes on the watery road, acknowledged this with a slight nod. "We Italians have a lot of good sayings. I'll see if I can come up with a couple more for you before I go."

Maggie looked at him askance. "You're teasing me, aren't you?"

"Yes. And no."

The ferry ride ended too quickly for Maggie, who'd come to view the relaxing trip as meditative. At Doucet, the gala committee convened in the gift shop. Ione led the group through the manor house and grounds, explaining where party events would be set up. The party tent used for wedding bookings would house most of the activities: buffet stations, entertainment, dancing. The silent auction would be held in the special exhibit gallery, giving attendees a chance to admire the *Say Yes to This Dress* display. "We've also added a VIP feature," Ione said. "For an extra fifty dollars a person, I'll lead small groups on a personal tour of Doucet where I'll share any insider info I can come up with to make them feel like they're getting their money's worth." As Maggie listened to Ione, it occurred to her that when Doucet treasurer Steve Collins's secret second wife spent every stolen dime he'd given her in a failed attempt to buy her silence, the infuriated woman had also written on stone.

Ione steered the women back to the gift shop. "Before we break up, are there any problems we haven't addressed?"

There was a chorus of *nos* and one *yes* from Sandy. "Now that the Fryboys have added themselves to the entertainment lineup along with the Rosé the Riveters troop, I'm short on time. Especially since the Riveters are begging for a *third* number."

The dance instructor glared at Grand-mère, who flashed an impish grin. "I can't help it if my fellow dancers are so inspired by your marvelous choreography that they begged for more of it," she said, all innocence.

"Nice try, Charlotte," Sandy said, not buying the flattery. "It ain't happening."

"The Gator Girls can cut a number from our set," Gaynell said, which drew a vociferous response from the others. Even Gran chimed in with an objection. "Okay, okay." Gaynell threw her hands up in mock surrender. "We'll just make the entertainment portion of the evening a little longer to get in everything."

"See?" Gran said. "Problem solved. And remember, the Riveters and Fryboys will be bidding on auction items, as will all their friends and relatives who've bought gala tickets to see them perform. I've solicited several items that will go over big with the Medicare crowd. I hope people don't come to blows over the medic alert necklace with a year of free monitoring."

The group adjourned, and Maggie made her way to her office, where she worked on curating Carrie Jones's artwork. After a few hours, her stomach began bothering her again, so she decided to head home. The day was warm and sunny despite it still being winter. As soon as she parked the Falcon on the ferry, Maggie left the car and stood by the ship's railing, enjoying the light breeze as they began chugging toward the river's opposite shore.

"Hey there, Maggie."

Maggie turned. The instant she saw who was speaking, she was overwhelmed by fear. Scooter Pitot stood in front of her. His lank, unwashed dirty-blond hair sat plastered to his head. His eyes, their pupils dilated, twitched back and forth. He sniffed and rubbed his nose, repeating the gesture with tic-like frequency. He was on something for sure, Maggie thought. Most likely meth.

"Surprise, surprise." Scooter delivered this with a sick smile. "Did you like my gifts? I hope you ate the doughnuts. They weren't poisoned, I swear."

Maggie forced her response to sound calm even while her heart hammered in her chest. "Those were from you? Why, Scooter? We barely know each other."

He threw back his head and cackled, the sound chilling, then abruptly stopped—which was even more chilling. "Bingo. That's exactly why. You think we 'barely know each other.' " He accompanied the statement with exaggerated air quotes. "But we know each other way better than that. Remember after you broke up with Ash and came to a football game at St. Francis? I'd been kicked out of school, but I still hung around because I didn't have much better to do. You remember that game? Huh? You remember it?"

Desperate, Maggie searched her bank of memories from high school. A foggy image came up. Hanging out in the woods by the football field after the game. Bottles of booze and beer lifted from parents' liquor cabinets. "I do. But not well. I'm sorry."

"You were hot. I flirted. You were nice but not into it. I made a move and you slapped me. The guys made fun of me for that, I'll tell you." Scooter leaned into her. She took a step away and backed up against the ship's railing, leaving her with no place to go. "And then when I showed up at Crozat for the Chanson meetings, all bright and shiny with my new job at the restaurant—you didn't even recognize me. It's like I'd never existed. *Ouch.* I'll be honest, that really undermined my self-confidence. It hurt, Maggie. Hurt a lot."

Maggie again recalled how Bo once told her the main underlying motive for murder wasn't revenge or anger or even financial gain—it was humiliation. The drugged-up addict in front of her was proving Bo right in the most frightening way possible.

"Yup, you really ticked me off," Scooter said. "But . . ." He rubbed his hands together, a smug smile on his face "I had a lot of fun planning how to get back at you. I even borrowed a friend's car to follow you from Doucet that one time. Told him I needed to run an errand. The errand? Scaring you."

Maggie subtly scanned Scooter for a weapon but saw nothing. He was no longer the cocky restaurant employee she knew from Chanson's. The drugs had dragged Scooter down, turning him into the worst version of himself. "It's been a long time since high school, Scooter," she said, keeping her tone even. "We've both changed a lot since then. I'm sorry if I hurt your feelings. I never meant to. But if you kill me, you'll spend the rest of your life in prison. Or face the death penalty. I'm not worth that."

Scooter cackled again. He waved away her fear. "You don't have to worry about being offed. Really. That's not my plan at all. It's too boring. Nope." The twisted smile returned.

"Peoples in Louisiana is always bragging about how we're the most haunted state in America, right? So, I'm gonna haunt you. You'll never know when or where me or my 'gifts' will show up. Who is or isn't me." He facetiously wagged a finger at her. "I know what you're thinking. You're thinking, 'That nutjob Scooter'll be off in jail, so I'll be okay. I got nothing to worry about.' Sorry, but I done time before. I know how to work the system. I got connections. And friends. Even better, people who owe me favors. You'll be living in a waking hell for the rest of your life. At least that's my goal. It's good to have goals, isn't it? Gives you a reason to get up in the morning."

"Oh, I'm big believer in goals," Maggie said. "Like, right now mine is to end the nightmare you've inflicted on me. Which is why the minute I saw you, I pressed 911 on my phone, which is in my pocket."

This didn't remotely faze Scooter. He hooted and mock-applauded. "Nice try." He sniffed and rubbed his nose. "Except you know what else friends who owe you favors do? Pilot a boat to help you escape."

Maggie looked down at the river and saw a speedboat idling by the side of the ferry. She heard a siren. A police boat sped down the river toward them. Her 911 call had gone through. Scooter climbed the side of the ship and positioned himself to jump. Suddenly the ferry made an unexpected sharp turn starboard. Scooter lost his balance and tumbled into the Mississippi. He tried to swim toward the speedboat, but the speedboat took off, the police in pursuit. "Help!" Scooter screamed. A deckhand raced to throw him a life preserver. But Scooter failed in his battle against the river's mighty current. Maggie, horrified, watched as he disappeared. She looked up to the captain's bridge and caught Antonio DiVirgilio's eye. As he steered the ship to the eastern landing, the expression on his face told her that the ferry's unexpected veer off course had been no accident.

*   *   *

Scooter's body was recovered the next day, down the river almost to New Orleans. Bo insisted on being there. "I know I sound paranoid, but I wanna make sure that psycho didn't pull off another escape act," he told his wife, who didn't think he sounded remotely paranoid. Traumatized by witnessing Scooter's death, Maggie took it easy the few days prior to the gala. Her friends and family periodically dropped by with gossip and sustenance. Trick and Kate gave up trying to make a go of Chanson's Cajun Kitchen, deeming it cursed. They turned over the lease to new proprietors: JJ and Abel Garavant in a joint venture, helmed by executive chef Luis Alvaro. Luis planned to marry Cajun and Central American cuisine, giving the restaurant a unique twist that could make it a culinary destination. And the Department of Transportation finally announced the Sunshine Bridge's reopening date. Ferry service would be suspended the day after the Doucet gala.

Maggie, who now understood her friend Lulu Colombe's negative attitude toward Scooter, made a point of calling her friend to recount his criminal activity and demise. "No surprise there," Lulu said. "Although I'm disappointed in Ash."

"He was an unwilling participant trying to save his father's business. He's staying in town to help Abel and is going to testify against the criminals who stole the oysters."

"That's brave." Lulu paused. "I always thought Ash was basically a good guy. It'd be great to see him again. Show some support."

"Long story, but we're having a gala to raise funds for Doucet. He and his dad donated to the silent auction, so they'll be there. Why don't you come as my guest?"

"I'd love that, thanks. Send me the deets."

The night of the gala finally arrived. Maggie donned the red dress she'd bought in Baton Rouge. Bo, who was seated in the living room, let out an admiring whistle when Maggie emerged from the bedroom. "*Whoa.* My hottie valentine. If you're ready, gorgeous, let's book."

Bo stood up, and Maggie responded with a whistle of her own. He was clad in a charcoal suit and red tie that complemented his dark, winter coloring. "*Oooh, baby.* Too bad we have to go out tonight."

Bo shot her a sexy grin. "I'm gonna wear a suit more often around here."

The couple joined Ninette and Tug to carpool on the ferry across the river. Gran and Lee had gone to Doucet earlier for a dress rehearsal of the talent show. Maggie was thrilled to see throngs of guests streaming into the historical site, which glowed like an architectural jewel. The evening's entertainment was a huge hit. Gran had the satisfaction of being proven right on two points: the performers and supporters alike bid a bundle on the silent-auction items, and two seventy-year-old men almost came to blows over the medic alert necklace and year of free monitoring. Ash Garavant stepped in to avert a case of geriatric fisticuffs—the only break he took from Lulu Colombe's company.

As the evening drew to a close, Ione took the mic from Gaynell and got everyone's attention. "I'm very pleased to announce that not only have we reached our fund-raising goal for tonight, we've exceeded it." The partygoers roared their approval. Ione held up a glass of champagne. "A toast to the committee that put together this amazing evening. Judging by its success, I think we're gonna make the gala an annual event."

There were more roars and many toasts. Vanessa, who happened to be standing next to the Crozat-Durands, eyed Maggie. "You don't have champagne."

"My stomach's still a little off."

"Mm-hmm," Vanessa said, skeptical. "Now that I think about it, I ain't seen you with a drink for a while now." Her jaw dropped as it dawned on her. "Oh. My. Goodness. Magnolia Maria Crozat—you're pregnant!"

Caught, Maggie exchanged a look with Bo. "No point hiding it now that Van's sniffed it out," Bo said with a proud grin, pulling her close to him.

"Then yes, Vanessa," Maggie said. "We're going to have a baby."

Vanessa let out a scream, startling nearby guests. "OMG, OMG, OMG!" she exclaimed, jumping up and down.

"Careful," Maggie warned with a laugh. "You've got your own little one to worry about."

Van waved her off. "Oh, he's a fighter. I'm so excited!" She threw her arms around Maggie, released her, and threw her arms around Bo. She let go of him and embraced Maggie again. "Our kids are gonna be the same age! We're gonna do everything together. Play groups, PTA, room parents, extra-curriculars. You and me are gonna be together twenty-four/seven, three-sixty-five."

Maggie, getting a glimpse into a future filled with the human steamroller that was Vanessa Fleer MacIlhoney, blanched. She wriggled out of Vanessa's grasp and clutched her stomach. "Excuse me." Maggie made a run for the bathroom, dodging scads of well-wishers who'd heard that Maggie and Bo were expecting their first child together. Pelican didn't need a 5G network for news to travel fast.

"It's never too early to open a savings account for your little one," bank president Bob Monnin called after her as his wife Mary rolled her eyes.

When the party wound down around one AM, Maggie, Bo, and a phalanx of family and guests crowded onto the ferry for its last run across the river. It was a clear night. The deckhands had strung fairy lights all over the *Baroness Pontalba*, creating a festive atmosphere. Maggie eyed the group with great affection. Tug had wrapped his suit jacket around Ninette's shoulders, the couple standing together as one at the ship's railing. Step-grandfather Lee was showing off his wife of six weeks to some friends he hadn't seen in a while.

Maggie, amused, could tell Gran reveled in being the center of attention.

Maggie looked to the port side of the ship, where friends had congregated. Quentin, surrounded by a small coterie of pals and probably former clients, entertained them with one of his droll anecdotes, engendering peals of laughter while his wife beamed with pride at being the spouse of the indefatigable attorney. Kyle Bruner had claimed the deck's sole bench. He and wife Lia rested against each other, the parents of triplets both sound asleep. Rufus teased his giggling bride Sandy by sneaking unexpected kisses while Gaynell and boyfriend Chret kissed for real. Maggie sensed a new engagement would soon provide local gossip with fresh material. She noticed another couple romantically entangled in the shadows: Ginny and Little Earlie. *Might have to make that two engagements*, she thought.

Bo wrapped his arms around his wife, and they snuggled together, watching the river reflect the sky full of stars blinking above them. As the ferry approached the eastern levee, Maggie could see the widow's walk that sat atop her family's manor house. Crozat Plantation Bed and Breakfast. Her home. Her talisman.

Grand-mère and Lee wandered over to the couple. "Our mighty Mississippi," Gran said, gazing with fondness at the dark waters. "It really does keep rolling along, doesn't it?"

"Just like with life," her husband concurred.

"Cher, how profound," Gran said, impressed.

Maggie cast an affectionate glance at her grandmother. "My friend Captain Antonio has a saying. He has a lot of them, actually, but this may be my favorite. *Mangia bene, ridi spesso, e ama molto.*"

"Translation, please." The request came from Bo.

"Eat well, laugh often . . ." Maggie took Bo's hand. She placed it on her stomach. "And love much."

Epilogue

Twenty-ish years later . . .

It was once said by a local wag that the little village of Pelican, Louisiana, was so fond of parties it should change its name to "Partycan." But there was true cause for celebration this particular evening. The Art Institute of Manhattan was mounting an exhibit of *Talismans*, an iconic series of paintings by renowned Louisiana artist Magnolia Marie Crozat. Maggie and her husband Bo were flying to New York on a late flight that evening. Joining them would be their twenty-year-old daughter, Nola. She'd celebrate the opening with her parents, then leave for Paris the next day for a semester abroad from her college, New Orleans's Tulane University, her grandfather Tug's alma mater.

While friends and family two-stepped into the B and B party tent to a tune by the internationally popular Cajun band Gaynell and the Gator Girls, Nola left the festivities to finish packing, which basically amounted to throwing leggings and T-shirts into a suitcase. Like her mother Maggie, Nola was all about simple, convenient outfits. And like her mother, she was an artist, although she also shared her father's fascination with law enforcement. She'd soon have to make the final call on which direction to pursue as a major.

Nola heard a light rap on the bedroom door. She smiled when she saw it was her boyfriend QJ, short for Quentin Junior. She and QJ, only a few months apart in age, had grown up together. QJ's mother Vanessa had claimed Nola at birth for her son, to much skepticism from Maggie. But Van had proved prescient. After Nola and QJ fought their attraction to each other, they finally gave in as lonely freshman at adjoining colleges. Like Nola, Q J was now a junior, but at *his* father's alma mater, the Crescent City's Loyola University, separated from Tulane by only a wall.

"Hey. You went missing on us." QJ came into the room, followed by the couples' friends. He kissed his girlfriend.

"We're leaving soon," Nola said. "I had to finish packing." Nola pulled out a drawer filled with underwear and dumped it in her suitcase. "Finished." She zipped the suitcase shut and yanked it onto the floor, then collapsed onto the bed. QJ fell back next to her, and then their friends piled on. "We're gonna break the bed," Nola said, laughing.

"Sorry," chorused Lia and Kyle's triplets, Kika, Asha, and Jabari.

"It's hi-larious when y'all do that," said Charli, QJ's twenty-three-year-old half sister, the self-proclaimed den mom of the group. "You're like three fleas on the same dog." Rather than crowding on the bed with the others, Charli swayed back and forth in the room's antique rocking chair, where infant Nola had been rocked to sleep by her mother like so many Crozats before her. "So, did you hear the latest about Vanessa?" Charli enjoyed the slightly rebellious tack of referring to her mother by her given name. Still not used to her new tongue piercing, she spoke with a slight lisp.

"It's a good one." QJ exchanged an amused look with his half sister. "Mom's outdone herself."

Charli and Vanessa's relationship had been contentious over the years. Vanessa wanted nothing more than a daughter she could dress up and enter in beauty pageants. All Charli wanted was to be accepted for who she was: a proud young gay woman. They both prayed: one for change, the other for acceptance. It took time, but acceptance finally won. In a small town like Pelican, generally Catholic and conservative, this took courage on both their parts. But luckily for its citizens, at the end of the day, Pelican was a town that fiercely loved its own.

"Mom joined this group, Free Mom Hugs," Charli said. "They give out hugs to queer people and act as stand-in moms at weddings for people who've been disowned by their families."

Nola popped up to sitting. "Your mom signed on for that? *Your* mom?"

Charli nodded. "She wants me to go shopping with her for the grooms' mother's dress. I gotta say, when Mom commits, she is all in."

"What does your dad think?"

"Birth or step?" Charli shared a mother with QJ, but retired police chief Rufus Durand was her birth father. "Step loves everything she does. Birth is so busy with his other kiddles that he's just relieved I'm out of the house and freeing up a bedroom."

Rufus and wife Sandy's marriage had proved fruitful—extremely so. They now had five children ranging in age from nineteen to nine. Their journey hadn't been without bumps, even the occasional separation. But Sandy had somehow convinced her old-fashioned, macho husband to try couples counseling. To the surprise of all—especially Rufus—he reveled in pouring out his soul, particularly to someone who was paid to listen and not argue with him. He even took up journaling and writing the occasional poem, to the consternation of those he foisted his musings upon. Wife Sandy was happy to attend local poetry slams with "the new Ru."

Nola's phone pinged a text. "It's my dad. We're doing a video chat with Xander in a few minutes. He wants to say good-bye."

She stood up, and the others followed suit. QJ grabbed her largest suitcase. "I'll bring this one down for you." He went to pull it and almost fell backward. "Man, this is heavy. What do you have in here?"

"All my art supplies and art books."

QJ, who intended on following in his father's footsteps and take over the family law practice, released a dramatic sigh. "I had to fall in love with an artist."

The friends trooped down the stairs, past the B and B's parterre garden into the manor house. Immediate family and friends were huddled in front of a large computer screen. Tug and Ninette, Nola's grandparents, in their eighties, claimed a front-row seat, next to great-grand-mère Charlotte, wheelchair bound at age 104 but as amazingly sharp as ever. Next to her sat her roommate, Helene Brevelle, the town voodoo priestess. Helene had moved in with Gran when Gran's second husband Lee Bertrand shuffled off his mortal coil ten years prior, collapsing on the dance floor of a local lounge. "He died with his dancing shoes on," Gran said. "A respectable Cajun passing."

"Chère, over here." Maggie motioned for Nola to join her and Bo. The years had been generous to the couple. Faces might be lined and hair flecked with gray, but they maintained their health, energy, and passion for each other and for life.

The screen fluttered, and then Xander appeared before them. At twenty-eight, he didn't look much different than he had at eight. He still wore wire-rim glasses and a serious expression on his boyish face. "Hey, y'all. Can you see me?"

"Yes," the viewers answered in one voice.

"How are things in Silicon Valley, son?" Bo asked. Xander, also a gifted artist, had combined his talents with computer science and become a hugely successful web designer in the Bay Area.

"Good. In another ten years, Ess and I may have enough money to buy a house," said Xander with a wry smile.

A beautiful, flaxen-haired young woman appeared onscreen. Xander had fallen in love with Esme when the two were seven years old and never considered dating anyone else. He'd waited while Esme went through a string of boyfriends before accepting that yes, it was possible that the love of your life was the shy boy once seated next to you in a second-grade classroom. They'd married two years earlier.

Esme waved to everyone. "Hey there! Miss y'all."

"Miss you too, chère." Maggie bit her lip to keep from tearing up. Nola put an arm around her mother's waist and hugged her.

"I'm so sorry we can't fly out for your show," Esme said. "Or see you off to Paris, Nola honey. Just come back ready to be an aunt." She repositioned herself, exposing a pregnancy in its eighth month.

"Will do," Nola said. "I can't wait to go shopping for baby presents in France. I bet they're *très joli.*"

"Please tell me you know more French than that," her stepbrother Xander teased.

"*Tais-toi,*" she joked back. "Which means, shut up."

"We've got a surprise guest for you," Esme said.

She leaned to the side and another young woman peered over her shoulder—Bella, Xander's adopted sister. The delighted viewers gasped. The UCLA student waved and laughed as their greetings overlapped each other. "Hey, everyone. Made the trip up from SoCal for a dose of fam and NorCal." Grinning, she pointed a finger. "I see that blank look on your face, Tug, sir. Let me translate. I drove up from Southern California for some quality time with my big brother and sister-in-law in Northern California."

The blank look that had been coloring Tug's face cleared. "Ah. Thank you."

"The older gen here doesn't speak West Coast," Nola said, casting an affectionate glance at her grandparents.

Bo tapped his watch, a self-winding relic from the 2020s. "It's time. We need to get going." Bo waved to his son. "Stay well, you two."

"Love you," Maggie said, blowing a kiss to the screen. Can't wait to meet Baby Durand."

The California-based couple signed off amid a hail of good-byes and kisses being blown their way. The screen faded to black. The room devolved into a sea of hugs, happy tears, and emotional send-offs for Maggie, Bo, and Nola. QJ and Bo then packed the back of the family's SUV with luggage. QJ kissed his girlfriend. *"Je t'aime,"* he whispered to her.

"Je t'aime aussi," she whispered back.

Maggie, Bo, and Nola loaded themselves into the car and pulled out of the family parking area. They followed the side road to the River Road, where Bo made a left. Nola twisted in her seat and craned her neck to look back at the family homestead. Tears welled up and she choked them back. "I wish you could hug a house."

Maggie, equally emotional, reached back and patted her daughter's leg. "It will be there when you get back, chère. Crozat's not going anywhere."

Nola caught a final glimpse of the majestic home's iconic thirty-two white columns before the car turned left, heading southeast to the Louis Armstrong International Airport and the next adventures in her family's lives.

"Yes," she said. "Crozat will always be there . . . for however long forever lasts."

Recipes

Maggie's Beer Bread

I love this recipe—it's so easy and delicious! When my friends and I used to make it, we called it One-Two-Three Bread because it basically requires only three ingredients . . . plus a little butter.

Ingredients

3 cups self-rising flour (or regular flour plus 3 teaspoons baking powder and 1 teaspoon salt)

¼ cup white sugar

12-ounce bottle or can of beer

¼ cup melted butter

Instructions

Preheat the oven to 375 degrees.

Grease a loaf pan and set aside.

Mix the dry ingredients together well to combine them. Pour the beer into the dry ingredients and mix well to combine.

Transfer the batter to the loaf pan. Pour the melted butter over the top of the batter to cover it as much as possible. (You can always add a little more melted butter if you need it.)

Bake for approximately one hour.

Serves about eight—or one, if you eat the whole loaf yourself!

Cajun Country Mystery Cocktail
Created by mixologist
D. Max Maxey

I'm lucky to have a friend who's a renowned mixologist: D. Max Maxey. I asked him if he would create a cocktail inspired by my Cajun Country Mystery series, and he was more than happy to oblige. Here's the delicious drink he invented.

Ingredients

1 ounce Bacardi 8 rum
1 ounce Smith & Cross rum
½ ounce Dolin sweet vermouth
½ ounce Pierre Ferrand dry curaçao
½ ounce Suze aperitif
1 light bar spoon absinthe
Luxardo cherries

Instructions

Build the drink by adding each ingredient to an old-fashioned glass.

Add block ice if you have it. Otherwise, use regular ice.

Stir to mix flavors and control the dilution.

Garnish with a Luxardo cherry.

Serves one.

Baked Catfish Po' boy With Quick Remoulade Sauce

Po' boys are a staple of Louisiana cuisine, as is catfish. You can make the remoulade sauce first or make it while the fish is cooking. You can even make it the night before and refrigerate it. This is a quick version of the unique Louisiana condiment. You'll find a made-from-scratch recipe for remoulade sauce in *A Cajun Christmas Killing*.

Ingredients

3 teaspoons oil
1½ pounds catfish filets
1 cup cornmeal
1 teaspoon dried thyme
1 teaspoon Creole seasoning
½ teaspoon garlic powder
½ teaspoon onion
1 teaspoon paprika
¼ to ½ teaspoon black pepper
½ teaspoon salt
1 egg
½ cup milk
Hot sauce (optional)
1 large baguette or 4 hero rolls
Lettuce, pieces or shredded

Sliced tomatoes
Quick Remoulade Sauce (see recipe below)

Instructions

Preheat oven to 425 degrees. Use the oil to grease a 13 × 9–inch glass baking dish.

Rinse and dry the catfish filets. Cut into serving-size pieces (approximately 4 × 2 inches).

Combine the dry ingredients in a shallow bowl.

Mix the egg and milk together. If you want to add hot sauce to the liquid, add a teaspoon to a tablespoon, depending on how spicy you like your catfish.

Dip the catfish into the liquid, then dredge in the cornmeal mixture. (If you find you're running low on the breading, you can always mix up a second batch and save what you don't use for another day.)

Bake for approximately fifteen minutes or until cooked through and golden brown, turning once during cooking. Turn off the oven, remove the fish, and set aside.

Either split the rolls down the middle or cut the baguette into four pieces and split each quarter down the middle. (Eating a po' boy can be a messy business. You can always pull out some of the bread dough to make more room for the other ingredients.)

Place two slabs of catfish in each roll or baguette section, then add the tomatoes and lettuce. Top the sandwich ingredients with as much Quick Remoulade Sauce as you'd like.

Serves four.

Quick Remoulade Sauce

Ingredients

1 cup mayonnaise, regular or low-fat
3 tablespoons Creole or brown mustard
1 tablespoon lemon juice
1 teaspoon Tabasco or your favorite hot sauce (you can add
    more if you like your sauce spicy)
½ teaspoon minced garlic
¼ teaspoon black pepper
¼ cup pickle relish, dill or sweet
1 teaspoon paprika
½ teaspoon Creole seasoning

Instructions

Mix together all ingredients until well combined.

Makes approximately one-plus cups.

Gooey Pineapple Pecan Cake

This cake is super sweet—and super tasty! If you prefer a less sweet version, simply skip the topping and just make the cake. Since it requires only three ingredients, it's very easy. You can always add a scoop of vanilla ice cream or dollop of whipped cream.

Ingredients

Cake

1 box yellow cake mix
1 can crushed pineapple (don't drain; use with juice)
1 cup chopped pecans

Topping

2 large eggs
8-ounce package regular or low-fat cream cheese, softened
1 tablespoon rum or rum flavor
1 pound (16 ounces) powdered sugar

Instructions

Preheat oven to 325 degrees.

Combine the cake mix and pineapple in a large bowl, stirring until well blended. Add the cup of pecans and mix well to incorporate.

Transfer the batter into a 13 × 9–inch baking pan, spreading so it covers the whole pan.

Beat the eggs with the cream cheese until well blended. Add the rum flavoring, then the powdered sugar one cup at a time, making sure to mix the ingredients together at medium speed before adding the next cup.

Pour the mixture over the cake layer, making the sure the cake layer is entirely covered.

Bake at 325 degrees for forty minutes or until set. Cool and cut into squares. *Note:* If you're skipping the topping and making only the cake, bake at 350 degrees for approximately twenty-five to thirty-five minutes until firm to the touch.

Serves sixteen to twenty-four, depending on serving size.

Calas
(Rice Balls or Fritters)

Calas, usually a breakfast dish, are like beignets made with rice. They have an interesting history. In the nineteenth century, Creole street vendors known as "Calas women" sold them hot from baskets or bowls they carried on their heads. Calas fell out of favor in the twentieth century, almost disappearing entirely until chefs and food preservationists rediscovered the treat and restored it to menus.

Ninette's secret ingredient? Substituting brown sugar for white. It is her opinion—and mine—that brown sugar adds a special extra something to a recipe.

Ingredients

Vegetable oil for frying
2 cups white rice, medium or long grain, cooked and cooled
6 tablespoons flour
¼ cup brown sugar
2 teaspoons baking powder
¼ teaspoon salt
¼ teaspoon nutmeg
2 large eggs
¼ teaspoon vanilla extract
Confectioner's sugar

Instructions

In a fryer or deep pot (I use a deep, round Dutch oven), pour oil to at least 3 inches in depth. Heat to 360 degrees.

In a large bowl, combine the rice, flour, sugar, baking powder, salt, and nutmeg. Stir well, breaking up any brown sugar clumps to make sure it's well incorporated.

In a small bowl, beat the eggs together with the vanilla.

Pour the liquid egg mixture into the rice mixture and mix together well. (It's best to keep the mixture cool so that it doesn't separate when dropped into the oil. I cool my rice in the refrigerator before making the recipe.)

Drop into the hot oil in heaping tablespoonfuls or serving spoonfuls. When the calas have reached a nice, rich brown on one side, use a metal slotted spoon to flip them over if they haven't flipped on their own. When a calas is completely brown (approximately five minutes), remove it from the oil and drain on paper towels.

Sprinkle the calas with powdered sugar and serve hot. You can also serve with a side of cane syrup for dunking.

Makes approximately twelve calas.

Butter Beans and River Shrimp
By Mrs. J. F. Guglielmo

My friend David J. Hubbell has deep Louisiana roots. He can trace his ancestors back to the 1720s and the settling of the "German Coast," now known as the River Parishes. Here he shares a "lost" recipe for a delicious dish unique to the River Parishes. You can find a video explaining the history of the recipe on David's "David J. Hubbell" YouTube channel, under the title "Butter Beans and Shrimp—River Parish Recipes—Lost & Found—Season 1 Episode 2." David's YouTube channel is a treasure trove of Cajun and Creole recipes. I can't recommend it highly enough.

David tells me that this recipe, courtesy of Mrs. J. F. Guglielmo, was published in Ms. Tommy C. Simmons's series of articles titled *In Baton Rouge Kitchens* in *The State Times Advocate* (now known as *The Advocate*) on Thursday, February 8, 1979.

Ingredients

3 tablespoons shortening
2 tablespoons flour
2 cups butter beans (also known as baby lima beans)
1 medium onion, chopped
1 small tomato, chopped

1 stalk of celery, chopped
1 small pod of garlic
3 tablespoons green onions
3 tablespoons parsley
2 cups shrimp (substitute regular saltwater shrimp, since river shrimp are hard to find)
Water
Parsley
Salt and red pepper (cayenne)

Instructions

In a small saucepan, brown the shortening and flour to make a roux.

Add butter beans and onion. Simmer.

Add tomato, celery, and garlic, simmering between each addition. Add shrimp and cook a little until grease starts to separate a little. Add green onions and enough water to cover by about 1½ inches.

Stir frequently to make sure it doesn't burn. Simmer for about 1½ hours.

At the end, add parsley and season with salt and red pepper.

Serve over rice with any meat entrée.

Serves four to six as a main dish, six to eight as a side dish.

The recipe for Jambalaya appears in *Body on the Bayou*.

The recipe for Étouffée appears in *Fatal Cajun Festival*.

The recipes for Muffuletta Frittata and Shrimp Remoulade appear in *A Cajun Christmas Killing*.

The recipe for Sugar High Pie appears in *Murder in the Bayou Boneyard*.

Lagniappe

For many years, the only way to cross the Mississippi River in Louisiana north of New Orleans was by ferry. During my college years at Tulane University, I have a vivid memory of making the crossing on the Luling-Destrehan ferry with my parents during one of their visits. The river's current is fierce and the river busy with commerce. I recall being nervous during the entire brief trip. Sadly, that fear was not unfounded. The Luling-Destrehan ferry route is responsible for the deadliest ferry disaster in our nation's history. On October 20, 1976, the George Prince Ferry was struck by a Norwegian tanker headed upriver. Seventy-eight people perished.

The ferry route was discontinued in 1983, after the opening of the Hale Boggs Memorial Bridge (aka the Luling-Destrehan Bridge), about a mile north of the original ferry landings. A memorial to those lost in the disaster is on display at the East Bank Bridge Park in Destrehan.

If the donation of a vasectomy to a silent auction strikes you as strange, it's based on reality. A local urologist donated one to our elementary school gala silent auction every year and you'll be amused to know the donations engendered many a bidding war.

Toward the end of this book, Maggie starts work on an exhibition honoring the folk art of a formerly enslaved woman, Carrie Jones. The fictional Carrie Jones was inspired by the real-life legendary folk artist Clementine Hunter. Clementine, born in the 1880s, was not enslaved. She was an illiterate farm laborer who took up painting in her fifties, using paint and brushes left behind by an artist visiting her workplace, Melrose Plantation. Her paintings portray Black life in Louisiana's Cane River Valley, where she lived and worked. Her most famous paintings are a set of murals installed at Melrose Plantation's African House, a unique enigma of a building on the plantation's grounds. I love Clementine's bold, bright creations. They paint a moving portrait of twentieth-century Black laborers.

Sometimes the internet brings you wonderful new friends. Cases in point for me: Mark Bologna, host of the fantastic podcast *Beyond Bourbon Street*, and David J. Hubbell.

Mark's podcast is an aural treat, filled with priceless insider insight into New Orleans's unique culture. You can find him on Apple Podcasts, Spotify, or your favorite podcast app. Links to episodes are also available through his website, Beyond Bourbon Street. And you can support Beyond Bourbon Street through his Patreon account.

David J. Hubbell is a font of knowledge about Cajun culture and cooking. David's Cajun genealogy dates back to the 1720s and the founding of Louisiana's "German Coast," now known as the River Parishes. He describes himself as a happily married chemical engineer with two kids who also happens to be a traditional Cajun/Creole cook, genealogist, and

Louisiana-centric gardener. (Even though he lives in Mobile, Alabama, which he likes to point out was the original capital of French Louisiana before New Orleans.) David's YouTube channel, under "David J. Hubbell: Exploring and Preserving River Parish Food, Culture, and History," features an array of Cajun/Creole cooking videos, including a subgroup titled "River Road Recipes: Lost and Found." His sideline as a culinary detective has enabled him to track down and share rare recipes that have been "lost" for generations.

David's commitment to honoring Louisiana's legendary cuisine extends to his work with the nonprofit organization Mirliton.org, which is dedicated to preserving and propagating the rare Louisiana heirloom strains of this unique squash. David, known as "The Mirliton Man of Mobile" (the original Mirliton Man is Dr. Lance Hill, who founded the nonprofit), even participated in a video where he and famed Cajun chef John Folse demonstrate how to cook this rare and wonderful vegetable. David also sells some of his delicious wares through his Facebook page, Hubbell's Hearth.

I don't think anyone likes good-byes. So I won't say good-bye to my beloved Cajun Country Mystery series. Instead I'll say *à bientôt*—"See you soon." Who knows? Perhaps the plot of a future book or short story will hinge on the battle over an heirloom strain of mirlitons.

Acknowledgments

A shout-out and immense gratitude to my indefatigable agent, Doug Grad, and the team at Crooked Lane Books, including Matt Martz, Madeline Rathle, Melissa Rechter, brilliant cover artist Stephen Gardner, and everyone who's helped edit, design, and sell my books since *Plantation Shudders* debuted in 2015. A special—and eternally grateful thank-you—to my amazing mystery editor. I know who you are but won't reveal your secret. But any honor I've received is shared with you.

Thanks to my fab fellow chicks Lisa Q. Mathews, Kellye Garrett, Mariella Krause, Vickie Fee, Cynthia Kuhn, Kathy Valenti, Leslie Karst, Becky Clark, and Jennifer J. Chow. Ladies, I am nothing without your priceless feedback. Especially you on this one, Leslie! I couldn't have written *Cajun Kiss of Death* without your help.

Nancy Cole Silverman, our weekly walks have been lifesavers. West Donas Walkers Kelly Goode, Lisa Libatique, Kathy Wood, and Nancy McIlvaney, same goes for our power walks! Jan Gilbert and Kevin McCaffrey, I couldn't write this—or any of my books—without your support. Same goes for you, my dear friends Charlotte Allen and Gaynell Bourgeois Moore. I love and value you both more than I can say. Additional thanks to more of my New Orleans "krewe": Laurie Becker, Shawn Holahan, Madeline Feldman, and Frank Moon. David J. Hubbell, the world owes you for your passion to preserve Cajun food heritage. Mark Bologna, New Orleans is blessed to have you as its champion. And D. Max Maxey, I owe you for that awesome cocktail recipe. Wendy Allen-Belleville, I cannot thank you enough for your sensitivity read. Thanks to *all* the friends who've supported me throughout this fabulous journey—I'm talking to you, June Stoddard (Mystery Guild—talk about support!), Nancy Adler, Denise and Stacy Smithers, Karen Fried, Von Rae Wood, and Kim Rose! Laurie Graff, your friendship means the world to me—as does your promo savvy! If I've missed anyone, I'm deeply sorry.

I'm blessed to belong to Sisters in Crime and Mystery Writers of America, specifically the chapters SinCLA and SoCalMWA. Without the Guppies, a SinC subgroup, I never would have gotten anywhere in the mystery world. A million fin flaps to all of you! Same goes for my fabulous groupmates at the Facebook page Cozy Mystery Crew. Malice Domestic, you gave me my start and I will be forever grateful. Left Coast Crime, I love you! And a super special heaping of love goes out to all the bloggers and reviewers who've supported me over the years, some of whom have become dear friends in the process. Without you, I think the only people who'd buy and read my books would be my immediate family, lol. I'm talking to you, Dru Ann Love, Mark Baker, Lesa Holstine, Lisa Kelly, Sandra Murphy, Lorie Hamm, Carol Papp, Jerri Cachero, Christine Gentes, Marie McNary, Danna, and

ACKNOWLEDGMENTS

Debra Jo Burnette. Apologies to anyone I missed. I could go on forever naming your wonderful names. I must also thank my intrepid readers group, the Cajun Country Mysteries Dirty (Rice) Dozen, affectionately known as the Gator Gals. Jane, Kimberley, Dianna, Jackie, Carol, Marci, Sheila, Mary, Kory, Nicole, Alisha, Melissa, Jerri, Kris, Staci, Cheryl, Cherie, Virginia, Jean, Ginger, Tillie, and Donnell—I am so grateful to each and every one of you. A special shout-out to reader-turned-pal and needlepoint guru, Ruth B. (Thanks for sharing Jennifer with me, Ruth!)

And finally, infinite thanks to my mom, my bros, and especially my husband Jerry and daughter Eliza. Words can't express how much I love you.

What an amazing ride this has been.